IZZY

SPIN IT: BOOK THREE

love you gu'll

Angera Allen

Printed in the United States of America

Angera Allen
www.authorangeraallen.com

Publisher's Note: This is a work of fiction. Names, characters, places, and incidents are a product of the author's imagination. Locales and public names are sometimes used for atmospheric purposes. Any resemblance to actual people, living or dead, or to businesses, companies, events, institutions, or locales is completely coincidental.

Editor Ellie McLove at My Brother's Editor
Formatted by My Brother's Editor
Cover Design by Clarise Tan at CT Cover Creations
Cover Photo Credit: Shutterstock
Proofreaders:
Petra with Love N Books , Jennifer Guibor, Kim Holtz, Michelle Kopp, Kari Jones, Tanya Farrell

Izzy / Angera Allen. -- 1st ed.
Paperback ISBN 978-0-9986829-7-6
Ebook ISBN 978-0-9986829-6-9

DEDICATION

I dedicate this book to my cousin 'T,' who lost her only son this past year. She's one of the strongest women I know, and I'm truly blessed to call her my family.

'T' just know you're forever in my heart, thoughts, and prayers. I'll always be here for you. Life might try to beat us down, but we always get back up, ready for another round. What doesn't kill us, only makes us stronger. Nothing will keep us down. I love you cousin!

We love you, Bubba, may you rest in peace
Love, your cousin

IZZY PLAYLIST

"Firestarter" by Prodigy
"Ghetto Kraviz" by Nina Kraviz
"The One" by Kodaline
"I Fall Apart" by Post Malone
"Say Something" by Justin Timberlake - Chris Stapleton
"Mr. Saxobeat" by Alexandra Stan
"Boss" by Mercer
"Your Love" by Mercer
"Satisfy" by Mercer feat. Ron Carroll
"One Kiss" by Calvin Harris - Dua Lipa
"Marry Me" by Train
"Like A Wrecking Ball" by Eric Church
"Tennessee Whiskey" by Chris Stapleton
"In Case You Didn't Know" by Brett Young
"We Speak No Americano" by Yolanda Be Cook & DCup

To Follow Izzy playlist on Spotify, click here

CHAPTER ONE | IZZY

"Relax," I breathe to myself as I wait for my luggage at the airport. I need to quit freaking out. My heart's racing, I can't stand still, and my hands are starting to sweat. I'm nervous to see him. I don't know why, he's the same ol' Gus.

He's finally going to be mine and no more questioning our relationship.

I smile at the thought. I've been in Los Angeles with my best friend, Ruby, for five days. It's the longest Gus and I have been apart since Dominic was arrested in Los Angeles.

We've been inseparable, but beating around the bush about us for months. Now there's flirting, little touches here and there. I've done everything he has asked, and I'm ready. I'm nervous but ready, especially after last weekend. We're finally going to sit down and have the 'talk' regarding us becoming a couple, officially.

Shit, we've been sleeping together. Well, not sexually, but we came close last weekend when he finally touched me, making me come for him. He stopped us from going any further, and I got upset. I left feeling unsure, but over the week he explained to me how he wants it to be between us.

When I close my eyes, I can still feel his breath against my skin. With everything that happened last weekend and his words this week of what's to come, I've been able to think of nothing else. Everything that I've wanted is waiting for me outside these airport doors. We'll finally become a couple. He won't be my bodyguard - he'll be my man, who I can touch and do whatever I want with in public. He promised we would sit down tonight and talk.

Butterflies erupt inside my stomach as I think about our last night together.

"Doll, I don't want ya to go," Gus whispers against my ear as we lay in bed. We've been fighting over me going back to LA with Ruby.

"Gus, I have to protect her and help her be strong. I'll be back in a couple of days," I rant, frustrated with him being so close to me.

Gus moves up leaning on his forearm turning his body into mine. We're inches apart. I can feel the heat of his body next to mine as he lays a hand over my stomach, "I want to be with ya. Let me come?" Gus asks.

Irritated, I blurt out, "You want to be with me, or you want to guard me? There is a difference."

His eyes are filled with lust and need, I know he wants me, but he's always holding back. I reach to touch him but am denied as he growls, "No, put your hands above your head."

I gasp. He's never demanded that of me. Goosebumps erupt across my body with anticipation of more as I lift my arms above my head. Please let it be tonight. Please.

Gus' stare is so intense I start breathing heavy, making my chest rise and fall. Gus slips his hand under my tank top, I gasp just from his touch, arching my back with a moan. I feel his breath on my neck as he moves his hand up my torso inch by inch.

"Isabella, I don't want ya to be without me." Gus breathes heavily against my chest as he moves slowly up toward my ear. "I need to be around ya," Gus pleads softly into my ear.

I don't say a word. I'm completely silent except for my labored breathing. I will not move or speak until he says I can. I've been waiting for this moment for so long.

Gus rotates slightly, moving one of his enormous thighs over mine, sliding it between my legs. I stop breathing. My body is aching with need. "Ya drive me insane," he drawls out before he rubs his thigh up thrusting it against my center. I let out a long breathy moan that sends tingles up my body. I'm so wet that my night shorts dampen against his bare knee that is pressed up against my mound.

Gus chuckles against my neck, "Hmm, very good, Doll. Don't move." He pauses. I have my eyes closed trying to calm my breathing. He continues slipping my tank top up over my bare chest, exposing my breasts. He doesn't remove it but leaves it secure around my armpits and shoulders.

My breathing is erratic as my chest heaves. Gus leans slightly over me as he blows a soft breath across my chest, barely inches away from my nipples, instantly hardening them. I whimper, biting my lip.

Oh, God, yes!

"Do you want me to touch you, Isabella?" He draws out my name inches from my ear.

I purr, "Yes, Aengus. Please." Knowing when I call him by his given name it fuels him with excitement. He likes me to call him that, but only when we're alone — so many things to remember.

"Last warnin' - Do not move," Gus says before slowly slipping a hand down my side caressing the side of my breast with this thumb. His warm wet mouth sucks my other breast into his mouth as his tongue swirls around my nipple sucking and pulling.

"Aengus," I moan, breathless.

Releasing that breast, he reaches up pinching it between his thumb and forefinger before engulfing my other breast.

Oh, God. Stay still. Fuck, I want him - I need him. *I arch my back wanting more.*

Gus' groans against my breast as he continues torturing each one of them back and forth.

Releasing my tit with a pop, Gus pants, "Christ, I want ya so fuckin' much." Sliding his hand down my stomach gripping my night shorts, he tugs them down just enough to slip his hand between my legs. "Jaysus… Mother of Christ," he says into my neck, inhaling my scent as he nibbles up and down the crevice of my neck. "You're so fuckin' wet." Gliding his middle finger through my wet folds.

"Fuck yes," I cry out, almost climaxing from his touch. My body goes completely ramrod straight, with so much tension that I'm about ready to explode.

He leans up facing me while he slides another finger through my wetness joining the other one at my entrance. "Look at me," Gus croaks out, his own emotions heighten with desire. I can feel his enormous hard cock pressed against my leg with only boxers between us. I open my eyes to see his beautiful sparkling emerald eyes staring wildly back at me. "I've wanted ya for so long. I don't want to lose control, so we need to take it slow," Gus says before kissing me gently.

His lips are soft and warm against mine. I lift my head wanting more, and he doesn't disappoint me as he deepens the kiss with his tongue swirling wildly with mine. Gus pulls back sucking my lower lip. "Isabella, ya been my undoing for years. I've almost lost my control with ya several times," Gus explains, taking my lips again but this time more demanding and forceful.

I want to move my hips against his fingers plunging into me, but I need to stay still. Breaking the kiss, I beg, "Please, Aengus."

Gus smiles down. "Yes, Isabella." He slips two fingers slowly inside me, as he licks his lower lip.

I throw my head back in ecstasy, crying out, "Uh-ah, yes."

Gus engulfs my lips, forcing his tongue between them while pumping his fingers in and out of me.

My body ignites with pressure building between my legs. It's not going to take much for me to come for him. I move my hips trying to increase the motion of his fingers. Gus thrusts his cock against my leg simultaneously with his fingers entering me.

We break the kiss moaning breathlessly. Gus tilts his forehead against mine as we stare into each other's eyes, trying to catch our breaths.

"Ah," I moan over and over again, chasing my climax.

"Fuck," Gus grunts through clench teeth.

I grip the bed above my head, throwing my head back, and grind out, "Oh, God," but Gus withdraws his fingers, and I scream, "No." He moves like lightening ripping my shorts off, shoving my legs apart. I beg, "Please."

"Have to taste ya, Doll." Gus lowers his face to my center, licking my clit he slides it straight down into my pussy, sucking in all my arousal. "So fuckin' good," he grunts right before he sucks and fucks my pussy with his tongue.

"Oh..." I mewl. He slides his thumb over my nub, circling my clit. "Yes... Yes... Yes..." I chant thrusting my hips.

"Ma'am?... Ma'am?" I snap my head. Embarrassed and mad at whoever interrupted me from my lustful memory.

An airport worker again asks, "Ma'am, do you need any help finding your luggage?"

My face heats, I clench my jacket feeling my body tingling with excitement. I look around, noticing almost everyone's gone.

"Shit!" I look at the man flustered, and say, "I mean, no that's my luggage right there. Thank you, though."

I hurry to the carousel grabbing my luggage and proceed toward the exit. My body's humming with so many emotions and my mind is at war between the lingering thoughts of that night and my self-doubt about us.

What if he tells me no again? Stop it, Izzy. I push all of the negative thoughts out of my head. He has told me several times how much he wants me.

As I walk out the doors of the airport my heart rate doubles. I follow his instructions on where to go for him to pick me up. I stand to wait for him when finally, I see his SUV. My adrenaline spikes and I smile from ear to ear.

You got this girl.

Gus leans over opening my door with a smile.

"Hey, good-looking?" I call out sliding my suitcase into the back seat before jumping into the passenger seat.

Gus chuckles, "*Howaya*, Doll?"

My belly does a flip hearing him call me Doll. It's new, and I absofuckinglutely love it.

I buckle up as he pulls away from the curb. I turn in my seat, so I'm halfway facing him. It becomes quiet, and I start to doubt us again. We always have something to talk about. Well, usually I'm the talker while he listens.

"Rube, alright? Does she know *me boys* there?" Gus asks while keeping his eyes on the road.

I relax.

"No, she has no idea," I say, beaming with excitement.

"She's going to kill me once she sees him. She was super upset with me that I couldn't stay the weekend," I explain, feeling bad but I know once Ruby sees Quick she'll forget all about me.

Gus asks with concern laced in his voice. "She gonna be alright?"

"What, with Quick being there or dealing with Brody without me?" I question, not knowing what he's asking.

"I mean with her cunt of an ex. I know Quick will take good care of her. He's *doting* over her pretty hard," Gus explains, looking over his shoulder as he switches lanes.

Once he changes lanes, Gus looks over at me with a smile. Good-god, he's gorgeous with his fire engine red hair totally disheveled with curls going every which way. His beard has gotten longer since I've been gone. I'm speechless.

"Wat?" Gus laughs.

I smile, shaking my head. I don't want to tell him that I'm over here listing all the things I want to do to him as I am undressing him with my eyes, but the look in his eyes tells me he knows... exactly what I'm thinking. I've missed him.

"Doll, you're freakin' me out, not talkin'," Gus says, grabbing my hand and giving it a squeeze before lacing his fingers through mine.

I look down at our hands intertwined. I don't want him to let go, so I place my other hand on top, locking his hand between mine.

"I've missed you," I say nervously. I don't lift my head to meet his eyes. Instead, I keep them focused on our joined hands.

Gus squeezes my hand in response before saying in a husky voice, "Yeah. We have a lot to discuss."

Just hearing those words my heart skips a beat as it fills with anticipation. I look up to see him watching me, but something out his driver side window catches my eye.

I scream, "Shit! Look–" but it's too late.

A car T-bones into us, crashing right into Gus' side door. The last thing I see is the fear in Gus' eyes before everything goes black.

CHAPTER TWO | IZZY

Pain.

That's what I feel.

Pain so indescribable radiates through my body.

God, what happened to me?

I try blinking, but my eyelids won't move.

Jesus — the pain.

The pain is so severe it consumes my whole being.

Help me.

I take a deep breath, but my lungs protest with a cough. I try lifting my eyelids once again, but they're stuck shut. I start to freak out.

Where am I? What is wrong with me?

A panic attack builds inside my chest as it constricts. I reach for my chest but realize my hands are bound behind me. I try to move my legs, but they are bound too, throwing me into a full-blown panic attack.

I can't breathe. Oh, God, I can't breathe. Help me.

Something's over my head. I rub my face to the ground trying to move whatever's covering my face, and that's when I feel it. The right side of my face has its own heartbeat. The pounding intensifies. I get my left eye to open, but my right eye's swollen shut. Fuck, the pain is so excruciating that every muscle in my body feels like a million knives are being repeatedly stabbed over and over again throughout my body.

Someone help.

"Help." My voice cracks, sounding exactly how my jaw feels, like someone just shattered it but the instant my head begins to pound, all other pain subsides with this pain erupting across my forehead. I try to move my jaw side to side but can't. Instead, I just cry out in pain.

Please, help me. Please, God.

As memories start to flash across my hazy mind of what happened, I shake my head mumbling "no," over and over again fighting against my restraints. Thrashing around I use the pain to fuel my rage to fight, but as the pain becomes unbearable and I become light-headed, I stop my fight afraid I'll pass out. Exhaustion hits me first before I let myself succumb to the fear.

I've been taken.

"God, please - no." The words come out as a whisper even though, in my head, it's a gut-wrenching scream. My heart breaks at the memory of Gus unconscious, with blood pouring from his head while I'm being pulled from the car and thrown into a van full of masked men. And then the punch that knocked me out cold.

Tucking my knees back into my chest I continue to cry, begging for someone to save us. I pray Gus is alive. *Why me? Goddamn, my head feels heavy.* My memories are a blur. *Is this a bad dream? God knows I have them all the time. It's one of my worst nightmares, seeing Gus hurt trying to protect me and now it has come true. Oh, God. I'm all alone, and he's probably dead. Please let him be okay.*

I try to move when a tingling sensation starts spreading through the left side of my body from lying in this position too long. I try to stretch out my stiff, aching body but fail horribly when every inch of me feels like it weighs a hundred pounds.

Exhausted, I lower my head back down against the hard ground. Blowing out a low sigh I try to push my hair out of my face, but with the bag over my head, it does me no good but instead swirls the smell of vomit around. My hair smells of vomit.

Fuck, do I have vomit in my hair? Jesus my mother would be beside herself seeing me like this. Oh, my God. What. The. Fuck! How can I think of that right now? Of all the things to think about,

I'm fucking worried about what she would think of me if she saw me. Not if they're worried I'm gone or even about my wellbeing - no it's about what I look like.

I shake my head clearing all thoughts of my parents when something falls onto my face. I jolt my face around, and when the smell of vomit hits my nostrils full force, I lose it.

Dried vomit surrounds me, inside the bag, around my face. I shake my head more, but that only makes it worse, as vomit rises to the back of my throat, I'm about ready to lose it. The pain is too unbearable to sit up, so I tilt my head to the side and vomit the little I have left in me. When nothing else comes up, I'm left with dry retches as I keep attempting to vomit in the bag. Still, nothing comes up. A few more dry heaves hit me, but finally, they stop. My face hurts so bad that I don't care now that I'm covered in my own vomit. I can't take it. I just want the pain to ease.

God, I'm a blubbering mess right now. I try to breathe in but I vomit more instead, and then the pain comes again.

Fuck!

I slowly breathe out and of course more pain.

I hear a voice from afar, and panic stills my body. I'm freaking out hearing things, but when another sound comes closer beside me, I hold my breath. Someone's in the room with me. Everything's black with this fucking bag over my head, restricting me from seeing anything, so I just stay still waiting - waiting for something to happen.

Sensing someone's near me, fear has my brain running in overdrive with 'what if' questions flying around, making my heart race building my anxiety with each second.

Is someone next to me? Behind me? Oh, God, standing over me or worse what if it's someone else that has been taken too?

I can't take the silence anymore. I need to know.

"Hello? Is anyone there?" I whisper hoarsely.

Nothing.

"Please, help me," I croak out, feeling the pain in my jaw. My body starts to shake uncontrollably, thinking no one's there and that I've imagined it.

Jesus, I feel like I'm losing my mind.

Still nothing until a few seconds later, a whistle.

What the fuck!

Suddenly, two sets of strong, rough hands pin me down. I scream, kicking my legs out only to stop when excruciating pain shoots through my right leg. A needle plunges into my arm, and I go limp begging for them to stop.

"Please... Please let me go," I plead from beneath the person.

Whoever injected me with the needle keeps holding me down, completely immobilizing me. I beg them to let me go as I uncontrollably sob until I pass out.

A loud noise stirs me from sleep and again vomit assaults my senses. I can't move my body. It's like I'm in a dream state of mind, or in my case more like a nightmare that I can't wake up from. I hear a door and sense movement around me, but with the bag still over my head, I still can't see anything.

A deep, demanding male voice, booms from across the room, "Is she awake?"

I freeze, holding my breath.

I want to jump out of my skin when another voice replies from right next to me, "What?" He sounds like he's old and tired.

I let out my breath slow and easy hoping they don't detect that I'm awake, but my fear overtakes my body, taking in too big of a breath, expanding my chest.

"She's awake," the American man, who's now right next to me, says. "She's breathing too heavily for her to be asleep. We need to move her, so get your men to clean her up and prepare her for shipping."

"Please. Let me go. Please," I say with a cry.

A door slamming shut is the only response I get from the American man who seems to be in charge. I still feel the other man hovering over me. I can feel his presence next to me and the instant I feel his fingers caressing my body, I gag holding back the vomit that's rising up my throat.

"Please, don't hurt me," I sob into the vomit filled bag.

"I take good care of you, *Conejito.*" His Spanish accent is thick with broken English. His voice is still low but what I thought was old now just sounds creepy. I think to myself; he isn't doing a very good job taking care of me, my arms and legs are bound, I have vomit all over me, my clothes are wet, and my body's shaking from the cold ground beneath me.

The man keeps caressing me, running his hands up and down the length of my body which is curled into a ball, like he's trying to soothe me. All I can do is plead with him and cry as my body is so beaten, I have no fight left in me.

I hear a few whistles before another set of hands land on me, I scream, but no sound comes out. I know what comes next - the needle.

Fresh air. I open my one eye to complete darkness. Excitement explodes inside me when I can feel my arms in front of me. *Thank you, God.* I'm still curled in a fetal position, so I slowly move a hand up over my swollen face gently touching it, assessing my injuries. My right side is twice its size making it impossible to see out of my eye. I try to lift myself up, but all my muscles scream in rejection, as my head starts to pound even harder. *Fuck!* I slump back down to the cold ground.

Breathe. Relax my mind. Calm.

After a few minutes of calming myself, I feel around the rest of my body. I have lacerations across my chest and waist. It must have been from my seat belt. I try to stretch my legs out but stop when they hit something metal.

"Shit," I hiss in pain reaching down to grip my ankle that is swollen as well. I don't know if all these injuries are from the car crash or from them taking me, but with my head still so groggy I can't remember.

Opening my good eye, I look around, and find it's completely black, not even a glimpse of light. I remember someone was in here with me before, I call out, "Hello?"

Using my left arm, I slowly push myself up onto my elbow, I need to drag myself to a wall or something. I take a deep breath and try to move but hit a metal pole. *Goddamnit!* Tears well up in my eyes when I realize I'm in a cage of some kind. I use a bar to pull myself up and scoot my body into a sitting position. Once I'm seated, I lean back against metal bars, tilting my head back I take in a few deep breaths.

Where am I? I need to be strong. I can do this…

Clearing my throat, I try again, ignoring the pain in my jaw, I call out a little bit louder. "Hello, is anyone there?"

Suddenly, floodlights snap on blinding me. I cower against the cage wall and instantly cover my face. I try to adjust my good eye by blinking a few times, but the powerful lights are shining directly on me, making it impossible to see anything. I keep blinking trying to adjust them to the light. When I can finally focus, I look down and notice my body is bruised and dirty with cuts and scrapes all over me. Using my hand as a visor, I scan out a bit farther around me. I see that I'm inside a small animal cage.

No. No. No…

My lip quivers, the tears start to fall down my face as dread fills my chest.

I'm all alone, but I feel someone is watching. I startle, throwing my hands over my ears as "Firestarter" by Prodigy blares loud, echoing throughout the room. I try to curl my knees up to my chest, but the right side of my body is banged up pretty bad. I extend my right leg out and curl it around my left leg as I sit there covering my ears and eyes waiting for someone to return.

I can't even think straight with the music so loud. It's been two songs and still nothing. Frustrated, exhaustion sets in when the next Prodigy song begins to play. I can't take it and cry out as I curl back up into a ball laying down on my side.

Finally, the music and the lights turn off. *Thank God.* I roll to my back and slowly blink my one good eye, praying that one of these times when it opens that there will be light to see. But no... there's only darkness.

Now that the loud music has stopped, I can try to get my mind working again. I need to remember more, my mind is a fog, and the only memories I do have are of Gus unconscious, all the blood around his head, and the shattered glass everywhere. It's like it's on repeat in my head.

How long have I been gone? Is he still alive? Surely someone saw the accident and would help him. So many questions with no answers have me freaking out. I sit up having a panic attack, and I can't breathe. My chest starts to constrict, and I feel my heart racing.

Gasping for air the floodlights flip back on blinding me. I move onto my knees, ignoring the right side of my body as the pain ignites through my arm and down my side all the way to my foot that won't lay right. *Goddamnit. The pain.* I try to take a few deep breaths as I lean down putting my head between my legs, but instead I end up smelling urine on my leggings. *Oh, my God. I can't take it.* The smell mixed with the pain, I feel nauseous. Leaning to the side, I grab the cage bars and stick my throbbing head between them and throw up.

Please. Fucking stop.

"Please," I say with a broken voice as I slump down covering my face from the scorching lights.

Thinking of Gus, anger erupts inside of me as I clench my knees, holding myself in a fetal position crying out, "Someone talk to me. Who the fuck are you?"

With no response, I continue my verbal tantrum releasing my frustrations. After my fit, I lay there crying for me, for Gus and that's when the lights flip off.

"Goddamn it. Quit fucking with me," I yell in pain, out into the darkness, knowing whoever is watching me can hear what I'm saying.

Sick motherfucker.

Exhaustion envelops me, and I tell myself repeatedly that I can do this.

Someone will find me. I can do this.

CHAPTER THREE| IZZY

PAST - ONE YEAR AGO IN MADRID, SPAIN

"Gin, get your perky little ass in here so I can do your makeup," I yell from the small bathroom we're trying to get ready in.

The only thing I haven't liked on this European tour is the small bathrooms. The first thing I do when checking into a hotel is scope out the bathroom.

At a young age my parents, the socialites that they are, had me trained to always to look your best. Their version of 'your best' and mine were two totally different things. They wanted me to be the pageant girl. You know the little girl with the platinum blonde hair with a blue ribbon, pastel knee-length dress, and a pearl necklace. Yeah, that was me for a while until modeling was forced on me. My mom being a model herself had me lined up to follow in her footsteps.

Obviously, I rebelled at a very young age, and I knew what was best for myself. I used to dye my hair, just to piss them off. But, now that I'm older, I keep it blonde with crazy updos and wild braids.

Don't get me wrong I love my parents, but they're as stiff as a board. Thank God for my music and that I'm actually good at it. Otherwise, they would have forced me to continue modeling.

"I'm coming," Ginger mumbles, coming into the bathroom and sitting on the toilet.

I smile down at her. "I think we should do the smoky eyes on you with your hair slicked back on the sides. It will look hot as fuck with your black dress you're going to wear tonight," I explain while looking her over, fidgeting with her hair.

Ginger's flawless pale skin attributes to her natural beauty. But when you apply just a touch of makeup, it just magnifies it. Her father nicknamed her Snow, like Snow White with her sleek black hair, five feet two inches, and muscular frame. The girl is a total badass, and with my help, she'll be picking the men off one by one tonight.

"Iz, you do your thing, girl. You know I love whatever you do." She smiles at me before looking down at her phone.

"Gus and B will be here in thirty minutes," Alexandria yells from the other room.

We both answer in unison, "Okay."

"I don't understand why my father doesn't want us going to this club. It's like one of the hottest clubs here," Alexandria says irritated, grabbing her clutch, putting her stuff for the night into it as we finish getting ready.

Alex's father Luc is the owner of the record label that Ginger and I DJ for and is very protective of her. This year-long European tour has been all planned, orchestrated and calculated to the minute, so that she's safe and secure. Total opposite of my father who didn't even ask who I was traveling with or where I was going. A pain sparks in my chest before I can shake off the feeling of rejection. I hate feeling like someone doesn't want me.

"Gus said something about he doesn't get along with the owner," Ginger replies, picking at her fingernails while I apply eyeshadow.

Ugh, just hearing his name drives me batshit crazy. That mountain of a man has me all twisted up. Time to have some fun.

"Well, I'm ready to have some fun and dance!" I say, grabbing my cocktail off the bathroom sink and taking a long sip.

I feel like I'm these girls' big sister, being that I'm older than they are. When I first met them, both were very quiet. Alex being more the only child introvert kind of thing. But Ginger, now she's quiet but not in the 'I'm shy' kind of way but in more of a 'I'm sizing you up' kind of attitude. She's a badass undercover for sure.

But with a little Izzy spaz added to the mix, we all balance each other out and have become very close.

Half an hour later we're all in a VIP booth dancing our asses off to "Ghetto Kraviz" by Nina Kraviz. I look around and see all our security. Luc spares no expense when it comes to his daughter. Brant, Alex's personal bodyguard, is extra stressed tonight and is staying close to her. I haven't seen Gus in a while and to '*not*' see him - his six feet three inches, fire engine red hair - is saying a lot because I can usually spot him anywhere in a club.

Damn, that man gets my lady bits going. Too bad I'm just a job to him because if that fine ass specimen of a man showed any interest in me, lordy-lordy, I would jump on that and not let go.

As I'm looking around for Gus, I see a big group of men stalking toward the DJ booth, and I notice one of them is a DJ from our label named Dominic. I've never actually met him or played at the same venue, but I've heard of him, and he's good. Plus, there's something about a man that carries himself with such confidence that has me wanting to follow him anywhere. I'm all about dominant men that know what they want. He's Russian too which is hot as fuck. I'm sure that's why he's here, to see the Russian DJ that has been playing most the night.

"Let's head up to the DJ booth and introduce ourselves," I suggest, hoping the girls will go for it so I can meet the sexy Russian.

I turn to see the girls are laughing. "What? Did I say something funny?" I laugh back at them finishing my drink and setting it down.

"Girl, you're boy crazy. Every place we hit you're all up on those DJs," Ginger giggles, sounding drunk.

Alex hardly ever drinks but Ginger likes to let loose once in a while, and I guess tonight is one of those nights. No wonder Brant's so stressed. I think those two are hitting it on the down low. She hasn't been with one man since I've known her. I know she was hurt pretty bad from some guy back home, but like I tell her 'you just need to catch another *ride* before hers runs out of gas.' Maybe she listened to me and is getting some from Brant.

"I like boys. Yes, I do, *but* I like men more, *and* you know what I like even better? Hot Russian DJs." I laugh jumping up and down trying to get them excited to go with me up on stage, but the look on their faces is a no go.

I pout. Still nothing. "Damnit where is Eva when I need her?" I declare, pouring myself another shot before I head to the DJ booth alone. Eva works for Spin It and is just as crazy as I am.

"Make sure you let B know what you're doing. He's all bitchy tonight," Alex informs me while bouncing around to the music.

I head toward the stage after telling Brant where I'm going, and just as I'm about to round the corner to the stage entrance, I smooth my dress down making sure my jewels are all intact, and my signature Princess Leia side bun twist braids are secure.

"Izzy? Is that you?" I turn to see three young girls headed my way.

"Yes, I'm Izzy." My heart jumps for joy that I'm getting recognized more. That is why we did this international tour, so we could get our name and music out there. So far it's been huge for me, and these girls just made my night.

"Are you playing tonight?" They beam with excitement at the idea of me playing.

"Sorry, ladies. I'm here just having a good time," I reply apologetic.

"We've seen you like three times. You're badass. Can we take a picture with you?" one of the girls asks, but all three pull out their phones.

"Of course," I smile.

"Here let me help you." The thick Russian accent has me quivering with just those few words.

As I turn, the girls scream out, "Dominic." I smile one of my seductive smiles toward him, nodding my head.

Each girl takes their turn taking a photo with me and then I offer to take them with him. After the girls run off excited, it leaves me with the Russian hottie. I'm a bit disappointed when I notice I'm the same height as him with my two-inch heels on. I'm five feet nine inches in flats and I hardly ever go anywhere without heels. I'm the same height or taller than most men. It has been the story of my life.

"Good evening Isabella. We've never met, but I'm Dominic." He extends his hand taking mine and bringing it to his lips for a kiss.

Good-god. Hearing my formal name roll off his tongue has my nipples hardening. I usually don't like my full name, but he makes it sound so damn sexy.

"Hi, nice to finally meet you. Please call me Izzy. I've heard your stuff — it's good." I smile, noticing he still hasn't released my hand.

"Would you like to join us on stage? I'm here with some friends celebrating a birthday," Dominic explains, pulling me up the stairs when I nod yes.

Goddamn, his accent has me humming with desire. These damn foreign accents get me every time.

"Izzy!" We both stop instantly hearing my name called out. Gus appears out of nowhere looking like he wants to murder someone. I panic, worried there has been a fight or something happened with the girls. I release Dominic's hand and turn on the step coming face to face with my Irish beast. *My Irish beast - where the fuck did that come from?*

He's eye to eye with me, and *I'm* on a step. *Fuck me.* My lady parts tingle instantly. *Please tell me you want me.*

Gus peers over my shoulder and I notice Dominic hasn't left me but instead has moved back down the step right behind me, towering over both of us.

Holyshitballs. I'm being sandwiched by two mega hotties.

I giggle.

"The girls are worried about ya. They *dinna* see ya on stage," he says with no emotion on his face as if he's bored.

Ahh, he's doing his job… Always the job.

I feel a sharp pain tug in my chest. The things this man does to me but I'm not even on his radar. He has been driving me nuts all tour with his grumpy, non-talking, Irish ass.

"Hello, Gus. I've got some friends up here. She'll be safe with us. I'll walk her back over when she's ready." Dominic's deep Russian voice booms with authority.

My body is electrified being in the middle of these two domineering men, and only one wants me while the other is doing his job protecting me. The thought of them both taking me has me licking my lips.

"Iz… I think ya should come back with me," Gus says, sounding irritated.

"Nah, Dominic's friends will watch out for me. I'll be back over there in a few after I have a couple of birthday drinks with his friend." I smile tapping him on the shoulder all cheerful as I normally do.

When I don't see a change in his expression, I turn to Dominic, who reaches for my hand again, guiding me to his friends.

I want a man who wants me, who will take charge and fight for me. I guess I know who really wants me.

Dominic releases my hand placing it on my lower back, guiding me to his friends, he whispers, "You have nothing to worry about. I will not let anyone hurt you, *Zvezda moya.*"

The way his deep voice comes out so smooth dripping with his accent and to end it with something in Russian. A word that just rolls off the tip of his tongue sounding so sexual I almost trip.

Jesus Christ that was fucking hot.

"What did you call me?" I ask breathlessly.

"I called you, my star," he purrs.

Holy shit.

CHAPTER FOUR | IZZY

"Wake the fuck up!"

I startle hearing a male voice barking at me. I wince in pain, trying to get up. The floodlights powering down on me again blocks me from seeing anyone or anything, but I can hear the men around me.

Focus Izzy. Listen to the voices. Try to figure out how many men are here.

The room is all dark except where the massive lights are shining on me, making it impossible to see the outer area of the room.

"What the fuck happened to her face?" a deep rumble comes from across the room.

I lift my good arm up to grip the bar, pulling myself up into a sitting position while keeping my head lowered. "Please help me," I try to plead with a hoarse voice to the man who sounds concerned for me.

"There was a car crash when we snagged her," an unfamiliar male voice explains, sounding far away.

"Did the car crash put all those marks on her body?" the demand comes again from across the room.

Please, God. Let this man help me.

"She's a feisty little cunt that's for sure, and she wouldn't shut up," the same male voice replies.

"Look we got her, and she's here like we agreed," a familiar voice speaks up near me, letting me know the American man from the other day is here.

I open my good eye, but the floodlights are too bright. My

mouth's like a dried up sand pit, and when I go to lick my lips, it's like rubbing sandpaper together.

"Get her some water - you fucking idiots. If the package is damaged in any way, they won't be happy with your work and they sure as fuck won't pay," the man from the back says with anger.

No one says anything, only irritated huffs and grunts sound around me.

"Has she been violated?" the man in charge asks.

"No," the American says, but I murmur, "Yes. I have."

I don't think anyone has fucked me, but I have been violated by whoever is fucking watching me and plunging that needle into me.

"No. She has not," booms a voice loud and clear from behind me, making me jump.

Oh, God, it's the creepy Spanish man.

A tanned, muscular hand reaches around me from behind, handing me a water bottle.

His English is broken but hearing him come off so aggressive has me cowering.

"Well, something has happened to her besides a fucking car crash," the deep rumble comes out hard, and he sounds closer. Like they're all closing in around me. The man's accent is thick, but I can't figure out from where. All I'm concerned with is drinking the water.

I can't open the bottled water, and after a few tries, a hand reaches in grabbing the bottle from me.

The Spanish man growls something in his foreign language.

I try to peer out of the corner of my good eye but only see a dark, muscular arm reach back in handing me the open bottle.

"Look, man. We did what you asked. She's here, so what the fuck are we doing with her?" the American man says irritated.

"I want you to feed her, tend to her wounds, clean her up, keep her secluded from the others and you better pray her face heals before they get here. She will be shipped out in a week."

"Another week? What the fuck? We need to get her out of here

- no, fuck that - out of the country and soon," a man's voice from earlier grunts from somewhere close beside me.

"Do you have a problem with my orders?" the man clipped, sounding lethal.

"No, but if her Russian boyfriend or her security guard–" A shot fires. I scream as a body falls to the ground with a thump right next to my cage. I hold my legs to my chest dipping my head down to cover my face and see the body on the ground. I'm on some kind of table. My cage is off the ground because I can see the man lying there dead. I close my eyes and cry. I'm so fucking scared.

"What the fuck!" the American yells.

"Do any of you motherfuckers have a problem with my orders?" he pauses.

Silence.

"Good, because I don't want to hear another fucking word about her or her people. Is that clear? The less said, the safer everyone is."

Still, no one says anything, but I faintly hear the Spanish man cursing under his breath behind me.

My people. Russian boyfriend. Security team. If Gus is hurt will they come for me? Will the club look for me? Beau will - but what if Gus is dead or in the hospital. Oh, God.

"Do not violate her again or you will pay the price. They want her untouched. Clean this fucking mess up. And clean her up - she has a high price on her head," the man demands from across the room. "This girl is of the utmost importance, she means something to someone, that's why I have all of you watching her, so don't fuck this up. No one - and I mean no one - is to enter this room but one of us five. None of you are to leave this building or speak to anyone here about her. If anyone is to breathe a word, they'll find out. I will be in touch soon. Don't fuck this up."

Five? There are other men in here besides the American, Spanish man, deep rumble guy… so that leaves two more depending on if he is counting the dead guy.

25

Courage rises from God knows where, but I ask, "What do you want? Who are you?" I try to get my questions out, but a door slamming shut across the room lets me know the man has left.

Am I invisible? Can anyone hear me when I talk or am I talking to myself and thinking I am saying it out loud? Fuck!

"Jesus Christ," the American exclaims.

I feel two hands on my shoulders pulling me back against the bars. Pain shoots through my right shoulder. "Please don't," I cry.

A string of Spanish words escapes his mouth as he breathes down my neck. I clench my eye shut, trying to calm myself.

"Mig, leave her alone. Get her some food and more water."

"*Si Jefe,*" Mig replies. I hear a few whistles and snapping of fingers, so I don't know who all leaves or not but one thing's for sure, the Spanish man they call Mig never leaves.

After a few moments, I sense the creepy man near me, watching me. Goosebumps take flight over my body making me shiver. I'm lying on my side curled up into a ball again. The lights are turned off, but this time there is a light shining behind me. I'm too exhausted to move or try to see what is behind me, but I know he's there.

"Eat. *Conejito.*"

Is he calling me... Bunny?

As a sandwich is tossed next to my head, I let the smell of peanut butter and jelly assault my nostrils. My stomach growls sending a jolt of energy through me, so I reach up grabbing it.

I need my strength, I tell myself as I bring it to my dry lips.

"I take good care of you, *Conejito,*" he says next to me sounding creepy as fuck, letting me know he isn't going anywhere.

The thoughts of what the other guy said, about my people coming for me has my mind stirring with hope and shuts out all thoughts of what the sick fuck means.

Will someone come for me if Gus is gone?

CHAPTER FIVE | IZZY
PAST - SIX MONTHS EARLIER

Gus pulls up in an SUV just as I'm locking my parents' house, where I've been visiting before I head out on my six-month tour. Gus unfolds his ginormous body from the car heading over to grab my luggage. *Fuck me till Tuesday. Goddamn, I've missed seeing him.* There isn't a day that goes by that he doesn't take my breath away.

I watch as his enormous body stalks toward me with his broad shoulders framing his massive chest, along with his thick biceps. *Fuck me.* I lick my lips. What gets me even hotter is his fire engine red hair, scruffy beard, topped off with his emerald eyes. Goddamn, my lady parts are tingling. *Shake it off, Rogers. He's your bodyguard, not your boyfriend.*

"Hiya, good looking." I smile greeting him, but the look on his face is anything but happy.

Great! I get grumpy Gus. Yay-me.

Once we both are settled into the SUV and on our way, I can't take the silence and ask, "Okay, what's going on? I can't handle grumpy, stressed the fuck out Gus. I need to know what has your panties in a bunch. Are you mad you had to come babysit me or what?"

The look on Gus' face has me leaning back into my seat, and I can't even see his eyes behind his sunglasses, he just looks enraged.

"Wat the *fuck* ya say? I don't babysit ya, for fuck's sake," he says, seething with anger before turning to look back at the road. "Something happened back home, and we don't know if it has anything to do with ye girls. We're bein' cautious." His accent is thick, another hint that tells me he's upset. Gus grips the steering wheel making his knuckles turn white, so I let him calm down a bit before drilling him with questions.

"Why are you so mad - what happened?" I ask in a low voice, hoping not to piss him off more with my questions, but I need to know.

Gus lets out a long sigh, rolling his shoulders back as if trying to release some tension before he starts talking. "Another girl was taken from Club Touch. She looks like Gin. We're just taking precautions. I told them I'd take care of ya. I'm stressed out - not mad."

"Jesus Christ, that *is* bad. Fuck, here I thought you were just your grumpy self," I say, ending with a low laugh and trying to hide my fear. I left New York to come home for a bit to get away from all the drama that happened to Ginger - but now it is happening again. *Shit.*

Ginger was shot just a few weeks ago while saving Alexandria from being kidnapped. I thought everything was solved and that Emmett, the guy who took her, was killed.

"Are we all in danger again?" I ask nervously.

Gus reaches over grabbing my hand with a squeeze and says to reassure me, "Iz, don't fret. I won't let no cunt ever hurt ya."

My heart swells, exploding with excitement that he wasn't irritated he got stuck with me. *But damn him, why can't he say this to me as a boyfriend and not my bodyguard?* Gus mistook my long face as worried and shakes my hand. "Seriously, don't fret. I gotcha."

I give him a small smile and look out the window.

He makes me so confused. Any time I have ever mentioned us being more than what we are he stops the conversation, saying I have a boyfriend. Which I did, or I guess I do. We haven't officially broken up, but it's been over for a while.

Dominic smacked me around a couple of times during sex, and when it started happening outside the bedroom, I called him on it saying we needed time apart, but he flipped out. He scares me every time I try to say we need a break. I know it's over between Dominic and me, but getting him to understand this is where I'm having issues.

The rest of the drive was good. We always fall into a good conversation. Once he relaxed and started being my normal Gus, and we start talking shit to each other, the drive went much faster. The banter between us always makes me feel good. We're so comfortable with each other and can talk about anything except us.

I've always wanted Gus, but the problem is him not wanting me back. Until recently, he has always been irritated, grumpy or just downright pissed off around me. I've been feeling our connection, and it's definitely something more. Gus has been letting his guard down a lot with me, so I know he feels it too.

Gus is usually a quiet guy in group settings but if you're one on one with him, he opens up. He doesn't like to talk much, but I guess I talk enough for both of us. He's worked for BB security for years now and is one of Beau's main guys. He only started to relax around us girls when we went on the European tour last year with Alexandria. Beau didn't trust anyone to head that operation besides Gus and Brant.

That year-long trip sealed the deal for me. I fell head over heels for the man I can't have. We fought like cats and dogs, but that's what captivates me. Everything I do seems to do the opposite to him, turning him away from me. I'm one spoiled bitch and I usually always get my way. But when it comes to men, I pick the bad boys - the ones that are complete and total fucking assholes. I always think they'll take care of me and be domineering in the bedroom, but they all end up being abusive dickheads.

I want someone to want me, cherish me, not my money or my social connections. I'm outspoken, crazy loud and off the chain most of the time so to want a dominant man is unusual. Most would think we would clash, but I would give anything to submit to someone worthy. I need someone to dominate me, put me in my place. I love that 'take charge' kind of guy.

I thought Dominic was that person at first, but he was just a very bossy man. Not one that wanted to take care of me, but one that wanted to control me and push me around. The story of my life.

"Don't open the door and don't leave. Do ya hear me, Iz?" Gus bellows from the doorway of our motel room.

Gus pushes my buttons, and he doesn't want anything in return. He infuriates me because my sexy, sassy, charming ways don't persuade him, and it only makes me want him more.

I flop down onto the bed and reply annoyed, "Yes grumpy." He's so bossy. It makes my insides tingle. I dream about him ordering me to my knees, demanding I perform all kinds of naughty things.

Yummy.

I decide to take a shower while he's being all ex-Marine, scouting the area. We've never been alone in a hotel before. We've been alone in a car, like the office but nothing like this, overnight in one room. Someone is usually always with us, and we always have separate rooms. Usually, us girls have a room, and the boys have their own.

My insides are all messed up with anxiety. I know he won't do anything because I 'technically' still have a boyfriend. And... he's never really said he's into me. I'm pretty sure it's in my head, or I imagine it when I think he's flirting with me. Anything he says I usually analyze it, hoping it means something different - you know like he loves me and wants me to have his babies - but as usual, I'm wrong. Because, Gus is the perfect gentleman with a hardcore accent, badass Marine attitude and the looks to make any woman, buckle to her knees. I just wish for once I knew what was going through his mind.

I jump when I hear a knock on the bathroom door.

"Ya done? I gotta use the loo," Gus barrels from the other side of the door.

I smile. "One second." *Game on.* I wrap a towel around my wet body and open the door, knowing damn well this tiny little towel is not covering all of my five-foot-nine-inch body.

Gus stands towering over me looking hot as fuck. I cascade my eyes up his torso until our eyes lock. Hoping for some sign that he's affected by my *non*-attire. I smile. "All yours," I say in a playful voice.

Gus doesn't move or respond, but instead, he just stares at me. Jesus Christ. The man could be a fucking Queen's Guard, he doesn't flinch. I couldn't read him if my life depended on it, but lordy-lordy, the zing that electrifies the air between us is undeniable. He has to feel it too.

Seconds feel like minutes, and his stone stare never falters. He's going to reject me again, so I lower my eyes in defeat, and as I move to go around him, he grips my elbow.

"Izz..." he groans my name as if it pains him to say it.

I stop moving forward but still don't look up, keeping my eyes focused on my toes, hoping I don't cry. I hate rejection, especially coming from him.

Gus demands, "Isabella, look at me." Gripping my chin and lifting my face, so we're eye to eye. I'm shocked hearing him use my full name. He never uses my full name. That mixed with his tone has me searching for a glimpse of what I feel. My body ignites, as hope floats through me under his touch and stare.

"Ya've got a man," he states. "Lord knows I do want ya, but I just can't," Gus says sounding conflicted.

Holy shit! Did he just say he wanted me? Holyfuckingshitballs!

When I try to protest about Dominic, he lifts a finger to my lips silencing me.

"Call me ol' fashioned, but in *me* eyes, you're spoken for. I watch everything, every detail and I know wat ya want *and* need. I just can't give it to ya right now. Not until *you're* truly ready and available," he says in a firm voice that tells me there's no negotiating.

Frustration swirls through me - I feel something - he feels something. I don't understand. I'm so mad he has my emotions all over the place. I hate being rejected, especially from someone that *wants me*. I can't take it, so I go to lower my face so he won't see the tears building up in my eyes.

"Isabella, *d'ye* look away from me." His stern, domineering voice has my body humming back to life. I clench my towel tighter around me, rubbing against my hardening nipples.

"Fuck's sake, are ya listening? I do–" He stops mid-sentence and looks up at the ceiling murmuring in his native tongue before looking back down to me, glancing a little farther down at my breasts for a split second before sliding them back up to lock eyes with me again. "I do want ya, but to prove *you're* not ready, let's try something, I want ya to lie on that bed." He points to the bed nearest to the bathroom.

My heart skips a beat. *He wants me to get on the bed... holy shit.* I look up to see he has a devilish smirk on his face. I move to take a step, but he stops me, saying, "Wait, not until I tell ya to go, now I want ya to lie on that bed and twiddle yerself," he says with a gleam in his eyes. My eyes widen in shock that he's talking to me this way. I still haven't spoken a word, I don't know what to say. He chuckles, and says, "I want ya to do this while I use the loo." I snap my face up as disappointment spreads across my face. I was hoping he was going to watch me touch myself, or something. Fuck, anything... I'll take anything to be closer to him.

"Isabella, listen to me. I want ya to do that while I *shag meself* off in the loo *thinking of y–o–u*," he says the last part slow, making his point.

"But, I don't—" I try to interrupt, but he continues.

"Sweet Jaysus, let - me - finish. I'm going to *shag meself* off thinking of ya, *cos* Isabella, you're beautiful. Christ, I want ya so goddamn bad, but you're not mine - *yet*," he says, his voice deep and raw.

I'm in shock. My mind is still on repeat that he said he wants me - that I'm beautiful - he wants me. I blurt out, "What—" but snap my mouth closed when I see his face harden with irritation.

He continues, "Fuck me, for this exact reason." He runs his hand through his disheveled curly red hair that I yearn to put my fingers through. "You. Are. Not. Ready. Do ya understand?" he asks, sounding frustrated.

My mouth slightly opens, but nothing comes out because my brain's still catching up. *Wait! He said shag meself. Shit... He's going to jack off in the shower thinking of me!*

When I don't say anything, Gus leans down with a smirk across his beautifully bearded masculine face, and slowly says, "I want y–o–u to answer m–e. Did y–o–u un–der–stand wat I just said?" I shake my head. Gus stands up tall throwing his head back with a full belly laugh.

Laughing he says, "I *dinna* think so. We've got stuff to discuss but now is not the time. All ya need to know right now is *you're* used to certain lads, and I'm the complete fuckin' opposite."

I don't understand what he's talking about.

Gus must read my mind because he starts ranting, irritated, holding up one finger. "Ya can't be alone." He throws up another finger. "Ya date cunts that ya *think* are wat ya want, but really ya have no idea wat that is." And another finger. "Ya've never been with a real dominant before. But, you're goin' to learn the true meaning of wat one's supposed to be like when you're mine. Now..." He drops his hand, crossing his arms over his enormously hard chest. "I want ya to go lie down on that bed and twiddle yerself. Think about me *shaggin' meself* off. Do y–o–u understand me? Answer me *yes* or *no*. I want to hear ya say it."

He must think I'm a true fucking blonde because I'm seriously having a hard time believing he wants me to do this. I blink a couple of times. My pussy starts to spasm just thinking of him touching himself. When he quirks an eyebrow, I reply, "Yes."

"Brilliant. Now, the last thing, do y–o–u understand *why* we can't be together right now?" Gus asks, but this time he sounds amused.

Fuck no, I don't understand. I want to scream it at him, but his gaze has me frozen. I shake my head but remember he wants the word, so I reply, "No."

Gus is losing his patience and says slowly again, "Y–o–u have a boy–fri–end and are not ready to be with me. I want ya..." Gus takes a step forward wrapping his arm around my waist pulling me up against him letting me feel his enormous erection pressed against my belly. I gasp, almost dropping my towel. "I've wanted ya for donkey's years, but ya've been with Dominic, and lastly, ya need to understand a few things about me if ya decide ya want to be with me." His voice is husky and deep with desire. I want to reach up and kiss him, but I'm spellbound looking into his eyes.

Ohmyfuckinggod, he wants me. Donkey's years? What the fuck?

"Donkey's years? Understand what? What does that mean?" I interrupt.

Gus chuckles. "Donkey's years means a very very long time, and I like things a certain way." He tightens his grip around my waist rubbing our bodies together against his hardness. I moan but don't say anything. *Damn...I'm shocked into silence for once.*

"Isabella, ya need to learn to listen to me. Ya need to quit trying to seduce me or manipulate me... it won't work. I won't cave. I don't want to have this conversation again until after yer single."

Jesus, the way he says my given name, the way it rolls off his tongue has me dazed.

"But..." slips from my mouth, as he releases me stepping into the bathroom with a smile.

"Now go lie down and do as I ask." Without another word, he

shuts the door leaving me speechless and completely, utterly, aroused.

What. The. Fuck - just happened?

I stand there for a few minutes trying to figure out what just happened between us. When I hear the water turn on, I snap out of my stupor, I did what he asked and twiddled myself, and as I orgasm, I call out his full name, Aengus. Knowing damn well he could hear me, and I prayed he climaxed right along with me.

True to his word when he came out of the bathroom, he was back to calling me Iz, and it was like that conversation didn't even happen.

I couldn't sleep. My mind replayed the conversation over and over again, trying to figure out what he meant by understanding a few things. I get the whole - I have a boyfriend thing, but I need to figure it out because one thing is for sure, I want him, and I want him bad.

CHAPTER SIX | DOMINIC
DAY IZZY'S TAKEN

"Yeah?" I grunt into my phone.

"Boss."

"What! What do you want?"

"Someone took her. I can't find her!" one of my men yells, sounding out of breath.

"What the fuck do you mean you can't find her?" I snap my fingers alerting my personal *byki* to remove the *suka* that's sucking my dick. *"Hvatit!"* I growl at the bitch enough and the good little cunt withdrawals her suctioning lips from my cock just in time - my bodyguard grabs her arm pulling her up to escort her from the private room.

"She –"

I cut him off, slipping my cock back into my pants. "Explain to me how you lost her. She just flew home. What do you mean you lost her?" I seethe into the phone.

"Boss, I didn't lose her, men took her. There was a car accident, their car was hit hard, and the Irishman was unconscious when a van full of men rushed up grabbing her."

I yell out, what the fuck, *"Ty che, blyad!"* I shoot up off the couch, furious at the thought of someone touching what is mine. I become more enraged yelling, "Where the fuck were you when this all happened?"

"Boss, we jumped out of the car and were rushing over when we saw the van roll up. It was a hit for sure, the driver of the car that hit them jumped out and left with them. Boss, it happened so fast and by the time we got back to our car they were gone."

"B'lyad!" Fury like I've never felt before explodes through every cell of my body. *Someone took Zvezda moya.*

"Motherfuckingcunt!" I yell into the phone. My *byki* moves back into the room closing the door to my empty suite here at my family's strip club. I take a deep breath. "Was it anyone you recognized?" I demand through gritted teeth.

"No, Boss. I called Kirill asking for help. He said he would look into it."

Fuck, Kirill! If anything, he would be the one to do something like this to get back at me for not producing more women. I've been back in Russia dealing with legal shit, and I've had to account for my actions to my family. They're not too happy with me. I've cost them a lot of money.

Being here has put me at risk of exposure. I've had to double my work here, and in the states, while I've been gone. When all I wanted to do is rush back to New York to be with my star.

My crazy little star. Fuck, she's the only bitch who's been able to put up with my shit and has those long fucking luscious legs. Just thinking about them has my dick stirring to life.

"Boss?"

Goddamnit, I need her.

"What do you want us to do?"

"Find her. I'm on my way."

I hang up the phone, grabbing my gun and jacket as I head for the door, dialing my uncle.

CHAPTER SEVEN | GUS

PRESENT DAY - HOSPITAL

Beeping.

*Mother of Christ my fucking crown hurts like a cunt... Isabella.
I need to get to her.*

Suddenly I hear muffled voices all around me, so I try to concentrate on them, but my head pounds and all I can think about is Izzy.

Is she okay? Did she make it out of the accident?

"Izz..." I try to say, but my throat's too dry, and I can't finish.

"He's awake," a male voice near me says, and then more men are chattering.

I want to open my eyes, but they're too heavy. I try to push them open but stop, wincing in pain from the pounding in my head.

"Redman, it's Shy. You here with us, brother?"

My head is groggy, but I know Shy, he's the president of the Wolfeman MC. He called me by my road name. One they gave me when I became a prospect.

I groan.

"Gus, man, it's Beau. Do you need a nurse?" Beau, my boss, the owner of BB Securities and one of my closest friends asks.

"No." Again my voice comes out raspy and dry, making it hard to speak. I attempt to open my eyes again, this time they crack open, but the bright lights shine down on me, making me squint. I grunt, "Water. Lights."

"I'll get some water," Luc says from somewhere near me.

"Quick, hit the lights," Shy orders next to me.

They're all here and not with Izzy. I don't hear any women here. Heaviness builds in my chest as I start to worry.

"Gus, open your mouth, I have some water," Luc says as I tilt my head toward him.

I take a few sips and let my senses take over evaluating my surroundings, and everyone's mood right now is dread and anger.

The room's full of my brothers, both from my security team and my club. I close my eyes and take a long deep breath as I try to contain my emotions. Something bad has happened to Izzy, I can feel it in my bones.

When I reopen my eyes, I say, "Where is she?" I pause to clear my throat. "Tell me everything."

The look on everyone's face has me both panicked and furious at the same time. It's Beau that speaks up first. He's always the one to stay calm and level-headed. Probably why he's the owner of one of the most sought after security companies in the world.

"You were in a car accident. A van came up behind the car that hit you, men with masks took her and the driver of the car that hit you," Beau explains.

I look around the room at Shy, Quick, Mac, Beau, Luc, and Dallas, the men I call brothers, and become irate. *Why are they all here and not out looking for her?*

Sensing I'm agitated, Shy continues, "We have every person we know looking for her. We're all here right now joining forces and regrouping. We'll get her back," Shy states calmly, trying to keep me calm because he knows what I'm thinking.

I'm about ready to snap, and I never lose my shit. I'm usually the one that is calm and holding it together out of all of them. It was what I was trained for in the Marines. I need to keep it together. I close my eyes taking a deep breath, trying to ease the pounding in my head, I ask, "How long?"

"A *few* days," Beau answers hesitantly.

My eyes pop open. Fuck being calm, I grit out, "She's been gone a *few* bloody days? Wat the fuck does that mean?" I look around the room with all eyes on me and what I see is worried faces staring back at me. "Get me the fuck out of here - now," I demand, gripping the side rail to pull myself up, but my head feels like it splits in two. Which ignites shooting pain throughout my body, letting me know I won't be going anywhere, anytime soon. I yell, "Mother of Christ!"

Everyone yells at the same time for me to chill out and lay back down.

"I'm calling the nurse," Luc says.

"Gus, man, you can't just get up," Beau says calmly.

Fuck me and his calmness.

"Brother, easy. We got this. Let us fill you in on all the details. We'll get her back. You need to stay calm," Shy demands roughly.

"Fuck off. Stay calm my arse. She. Is. Mine," I say through gritted teeth.

Grá mo chroí. She's the love of my heart. I need to get her back.

Shy replies, "We know brother. We know."

"I never should have left you. It's my fault," Quick says from behind the men. Everyone turns to him, but it's me he's looking at with broken eyes.

Jaysus Christ.

I don't understand and ask, "Wat did ya say?"

"I shouldn't have gone to LA. I would've been with you. I could've—"

I cut him off, "Ah, stop. Ya could've been killed or hurt, just as I am. Don't be an *eejit*. It's not anyone's fault." I take a few deep breaths so I can keep it together and let Quick know it wasn't his fault. I say calmly as I look around the room, "It's no one's fault. They blindsided us. It could've been anyone with her." I pause a second before continuing, "Fill me in from the beginning, starting with me, when I can get out of here?"

I'm not going to be able to do anything if I'm laid up in here. For the next few minutes, I lie there listening to them tell me about my injuries, but it's not anything I can't handle. I've had several concussions while in the service.

Beau and Dallas both go into detail about the search for her, telling me they've been working with the police and FBI. They tried to contact Dominic, her ex-cunt of a boyfriend, but he's still in Russia. They've talked to people inside of Benito's crew and still nothing. Beau said the rest of the boys from my security team are on their way back from the UK tour. I guess when Brant told Alexandria, one of Izzy's best friends, that he was headed back to help look for her; she freaked out wanting to come home too. With everyone talking and telling me what has been done, or what is being done, I still haven't heard anything good.

"I've put in a call to my uncle," Luc states next to me and the room goes completely quiet. I turn my head in disbelief. He hates his uncle or at least that's what I understood from conversations. His uncle is a very powerful man and is said to be one of the main Italian Mafia Bosses. We never talk about him, so I don't know details, the only thing I know for sure is that he hates him.

"Why?" I ask, confused.

The pain in my head intensifies with so many questions firing off with the 'why's.' *Why would he call him now? He didn't call him when his own daughter was being threatened, so why call him now?*

Luc pushes his shoulders back, crossing his arms over his massive chest. The man isn't small, and he definitely can hold his own, but right now it's all about his demeanor, it's lethal, letting us all know how he feels.

"This is serious. We have no real leads. I've called in several favors trying to find her, but so far no one has heard anything." His thick Italian accent bleeds through each word as he expresses his concern.

"Do ya think he's involved? Why call him? I know how ya hate him." I hold his stare letting him know I'm serious and want answers. No one ever questions him about his personal shit, but he just made it my business.

"Nah, but he has more resources in that world than we do, *yeah?* Izzy's my responsibility. She's one of my girls."

I don't like him calling Izzy his girl, I growl, "She's mine."

Luc turns his body to fully facing me. "Ya work for me. I pay ya to watch over her, *yeah?* She's my responsibility. *Capisci?*" Luc states in a matter-of-fact way, standing his ground.

"I quit then. She's my girl. I told ya that no one would be watching her but me. I told ya already," I seethe.

Luc keeps a straight face and doesn't show any emotions to what I've just said. I just quit, and he just stands there like nothing.

Beau laughs. "It's about fucking time you pulled your head out of your ass, brother."

I don't break my death stare with Luc, but I answer him, "She's the one... my *one*. Always has been." Just as the words leave my lips my song for her plays in my head. "The One" by Kodaline. I need to get her back. I need her to know how I truly feel about her.

Luc drops his arms and smiles. "*Yeah?* Like we didn't know that. *Whaddaya* think we are, *fuckin' pazzo?* We've known since ya came back from Europe. Why *you've* been denying it... has us all wondering if *your* fuckin' head needed to be checked."

Shy says jokingly, "Maybe getting your head rattled made you come to your senses, but we're just glad you're finally gonna claim her."

"Get me the fuck outta here."

CHAPTER EIGHT | IZZY

It's been three weeks since Gus and I returned from Ginger's place in West Virginia, and it feels like a lifetime ago. The few days we stayed at the clubhouse were the best days of my life.

It was like Gus and I had finally connected. It was amazing to see him relax and have fun with no events or people to manage. It was nice for a change. Usually, he's planning our night by arranging cars, who will secure what area, the layout of the place. Always work mode and never just hanging out.

When it was just the two of us, he dropped his guard a few times, showing his attraction for me by telling me to do things to myself. He even admitted he wanted to be with me but couldn't. He was testing me I think, and I was completely willing. It drove me crazy that he wouldn't give in. He always said I needed to understand him, be ready and I was spoken for, or some shit about me needing to learn to be alone before I could submit to him. It was all bullshit that drove me nuts because anyone around us could tell something was going on. I denied it to anyone that asked because I'm determined to win him over.

But it all came crashing down once we returned to New York, where Dominic was waiting impatiently for me. Smothering me, demanding attention, I tried to break it off with him, but he wouldn't have it. He became crazed with jealousy.

We're on tour for the next few months, so I'm trying to make it work, especially since Gus has cut me off since returning. Dominic knows I've been pulling away and wanting out of the relationship, which just makes him more aggressive and needier for sex. I've tried to make every excuse in the world not to have sex, but he gets mad, and I end up giving in. Lately, it's become even rougher, to the extreme of leaving marks.

It was like the minute Gus dropped me off at my studio he changed back to his grumpy, bodyguard mode. Yes, Dominic was there waiting for us, but I was just hoping Gus would have stayed and fought for me or some shit. I felt like I lost him as he closed himself off, keeping his distance from me. It's been hell these last few weeks.

Dominic and I fight more than we get along. I feel alone. Alexandria and Maddox are so happy and in love they're inseparable. Brant's all pissy without Ginger and is so far up Sasha's ass I just ignore them. Ginger's been healing, but thank goodness she is finally returning home. I'm so unhappy, but I won't show it or let anyone see how I really feel. I always have my happy face on, but when I catch Gus staring at me I know, he sees right through me. I don't hide that I miss him. My heart both jumps to life and breaks at the same time. He doesn't want me.

Every time Dominic and I get into a fight I hear Gus' voice in my head telling me I need to be alone and not go from guy to guy, or that I need to figure out who I am. I would always tune him out by the end of his speech because I like having someone around and I don't like being alone.

Today we're all in Los Angeles, my hometown. I'm over the moon excited to have all my friends here. I was bummed to hear my longtime friend, Ruby, is out of town with her husband Brody, but having Alex, Ginger, and Sasha here is amazing.

"Why do ya let him talk to ya like that?" I jump with a yelp hearing Gus behind me.

"What the fuck, Gus?" I say holding my chest. He scared the shit out of me.

I look around to see where Dominic is, noticing he's outside the store chatting it up with Maddox, Quick and Shy, Ginger's man and one of his guys from their motorcycle club. Not wanting to bring any attention to us I turn back to looking through the rack of clothes. Ginger and Alex are wandering around the store looking at clothes themselves, so they didn't hear me yell.

"What are you doing here? I thought you guys were headed back to the hotel. And how the fuck did you get in here?" I ramble, asking him surprisingly.

"I'm headed back now but wanted to check on ya. Answer me, Isabella," Gus demands, using my full name. He knows damn well what it does to me. It's like showing a kid a piece of candy but saying they can't have it. Using my full name is him telling me he wants and misses me, but nope, I can't have him!

Motherfucker!

I still keep my back to him when I answer him nonchalantly. "What do you mean?"

Two can play at this game. He thinks he can just sneak in here all ex-Marine style and demand answers from me. Well, he needs to think again. I know damn well he's fuming about how Dominic acted at lunch today. Dominic tried to ruin it by flipping out at the restaurant because some dude bought me a bottle of Dom Perignon.

"Iz, I can't take much more of prick boy talking to ya as he does. I'm about to lose it. I thought ya were leaving him?" Gus states behind me, gutting me as he questions why I haven't left Dominic. I try to keep my focus on the clothes racks in front of me. I'm sure he's watching the guys outside.

"I know. I will talk to him," I answer him, feeling defeated. When I really want to say, '*You're right. Save me. Kick his ass, and I'm all yours.*' Yeah, right!

"Why—" he cuts himself off, which pisses me off, and I turn around to face him.

"Why… Why - what, Gus? You've barely spoken to me since we got back from the clubhouse. Why worry about me now?" I start off sounding bitchy, but my emotions get the better of me leaving me sounding desperate. I hate it.

Gus grabs my wrist, looking murderous and says, "Why

worry? I fuckin' worry when the *dirtball* puts his *cunt* hands on ya. I left ya be so ya could deal with *ya bull shite.* Ya need to figure it out soon before I handle it for ya." He turns my wrist up exposing my marks.

I gasp, pulling my hand back. Before I can recover to say something, he's walking out of the back door, leaving me speechless with tears pooling in my eyes. I take a few deep breaths, trying to calm myself before the girls see me. I look back down at my wrists which are covered with jewelry. The girls know we have kinky sex, so they don't ask anymore, but as of late it's been less sex and just him being rough with me. Gus noticed.

Fuck!

Jesus, I'm like a ticking time bomb ready to detonate. I can't keep standing here in the VIP. I'm losing control of myself. My bouncy, happy-go-lucky self is cracking. Ever since Gus left the store, I've been crazy bitchy. I flipped out on Dominic when we got back to the hotel, which led us into a full-fledged fight and I left before it got physical. I went up to Ginger's room to get ready and pull myself together. I need to hold it together until we get home where I can break up with him.

But that's not what has me losing my shit. Oh... no... it's Gus. It's *his* behavior since he left the store that has me in an uproar. Seeing him in Ginger's suite all dressed up. He *always* wears black and usually cargo pants, or whatever shit security guys wear, but not tonight. Tonight he has on gray slacks with a red button-down shirt and dress shoes.

God, he reminds me of the guy that played Leonidas in the movie *300* but with wavy red hair. He always has some kind of facial hair either a beard, a goatee or like tonight he has a five o'clock shadow. *Sexy as fuck.* And he was laughing and drinking while relaxing with the guys. Like he did with me in West Virginia. It was a slap in the face. I played it off, laughing it up, but inside I was flipping the fuck out. Usually, he's quiet, stressed about the night or some shit to make him grumpy.

Oh, but not tonight. Nooo.

Right now, here at the club, Quick and Gus have goddamn *girls* up here in the VIP. Jealousy like I've never felt before has erupted inside of me. I'm about ready to explode. I want to beat the shit out of the girls *and* him. I know he's pushing my buttons, but I can't take it. My buttons are motherfucking pushed.

I've never seen him with a woman. My heart jumped out of my chest when they brought them up here. I'm trying to contain myself and be professional, but I'm bouncing around this VIP like I'm on crack.

Dominic's stewing in the corner, watching my every move. I have to tell him it's over, but I'm scared. I don't want a huge scene, but I also don't want to be alone with him when I tell him. He won't listen to me, so something needs to happen in order for him to get it through his thick head it's over. I'm afraid of what he'll do if I cut him off. He's batshit crazy.

I look over to see Dominic watching me as I move to get my stuff. I need to get the fuck out of this VIP area.

"You headed up to the stage?" Ginger asks when I grab my music.

"Yeah, it's almost time," I say softly. I don't want to say much more with my emotions on the brink of explosion, as I try not to look at Gus standing next to the fucking bimbos.

"You ready?" Dominic asks from behind me.

Fucking great. Yay me! I think to myself as I turn to face Dominic with a smile. "You betcha."

Dominic places his hand on my lower back and guides me through the crowd toward the stage.

God, if only I knew back then what I know now about Dominic, I would have never gone with him on that stage back in Europe. I would've taken Gus' advice and went back to the girls. But, I didn't, so here I am, walking with a fake smile on my face like we're some happy couple.

Fuck me till Tuesday. That's what my best friend Ruby and I would say when we were fucked. She hates being called Ruby Tuesday, so we came up with 'Fuck me till Tuesday' when shit is about to hit the fan. The good kind or bad, it's just our saying now.

God, I miss her so much! I wish she was here and not with her fucking husband.

"I'll be right here with Brant and the guys," Dominic says, leaving me at the DJ booth with Sasha.

I plaster my fake smile on before answering him, "Okay, sounds good."

I can finally relax and go to my happy place with my headphones on, and a massive crowd in front of me grooving to my beats. Life is so much simpler. Music is my lifeline, and without it, I would be lost. I can escape, clear my mind of all the negative and be happy. Since I can remember music has always been my escape. Parents fighting - put headphones on. Parents ignore me - put headphones on. Boyfriend's being a dick - put headphones on. It's always music that saves me.

I look over to watch Gus in the VIP with those cunt bitches when I feel a hand on my arm which startles me for a second. No one is supposed to be in the DJ area, so it takes me off guard. I smile at the man, and before I can reach my hand out to say hello, Dominic's pushing him. The guy says something, and Dominic has him on the ground by the throat.

Shocked I scream, "What the fuck, Dominic?"

I notice two of Dominic's New York friends that I didn't even know were here, rush from out of nowhere, grabbing two other guys that are trying to pull Dominic off the man, and before I know it, a full-blown fight is happening on stage. I try to move away, but someone is shoved into me. I'm yelling at them to stop.

That's it!

I can't take it anymore.

I'm done.

Tears start falling as I scream at everyone and everything in my life. I completely freak the fuck out.

Fuck my life!

Suddenly I'm pulled into a massive chest. I pound against whoever is in front of me, crying and yelling, but when I hear Gus' smooth deep rumble, I stop fighting but continue to cry, letting it all out.

After that, it's all a blur. The police. Dominic being arrested. His verbal assault on me and some guy I didn't even fucking know. All I'm concentrating on is Gus' voice. His calm words, keeping me together. His strong arms are holding me, comforting me. I don't even know how we got back to the hotel. I'm just lost in my own thoughts crying.

"Isabella," Gus says softly.

The noise is gone. The lights are gone. The people are gone.

"Isabella, ya alright? Answer me." Gus shakes me gently, trying to get me to focus on him.

But I can't - I can't do this - my mind has cracked. Too many things are rushing through it that I can't focus.

"Isabella, look at me for fuck's sake." Gus starts to sound panicked.

When I don't say anything, Gus lifts me up, cradling me against his chest before sitting back down with me on his lap. His large hands caress me as he rocks me back and forth.

"I've got ya," he says kissing the top of my head, hugging me tighter.

I whisper, "I'm sorry," through my sobs, hoping he'll hear me.

"I'll take care of ya. No more doing it alone." Gus glides his hand down my back soothing me. My sobs grow louder, as I cry into his massive chest clenching his button-down shirt.

"Ya've got me now. I won't be leaving your side." Gus' sweet and smooth voice is music to my ears.

"He won't let me go. I've tried, I promise I tried when we got back. He won't," I say, sobbing against his now soaked, snot-streaked chest.

"Oh, he will. I'll promise ya that." Gus grips me tighter letting me know I'm safe.

CHAPTER NINE | IZZY

Wrapping my arms around my tattered legs, I hunch over them, resting my swollen face on my knees. I try to calm down by taking deep breaths. It won't help me if I have a full-blown panic attack.

I repeat, whispering to myself, in a shaky voice, "I can handle this."

But my subconscious tells me I can't take much more. It's been at least a week, and I'm still in a cage.

Alone.

Beaten.

And most of all...

Pissed. The. Fuck. Off.

Who will visit me today?

When the door opens and the floodlights flare up, I huddle against the bars. Even with my blindfold on I can hear the buzz of the lights come to life and the heat of them pounding down upon me.

"*Conejito*," Miguel says from afar.

I don't answer hoping he'll go away, but when he pokes me a few minutes later, saying my pet name again, I moan in frustration.

I feel like it has been weeks since the bossman left the men to deal with all the shit. Miguel blindfolded me before they moved the dead body. Then he and a few other men held me down while cutting my clothes away. I tried to fight and scream, but it was useless. They proceeded to hose me down like a caged animal.

Once they finished cleaning me up, Miguel tried to soothe me while drying me off. Caressing me, touching me everywhere as he told me that if I behaved for him, he would protect me from the others.

He informed me that as long as I didn't fight or make trouble, that he would be good to me and he would take care of me. At first, I thought he was fucking crazy. Which I'm sure he is, but now I believe him because he has been the one to feed me, bathe me and keep the other men from touching me. He's the only one that is allowed to 'pet' me as he calls it.

"Behave. Men are coming to see you today," Miguel states from beside me.

I still don't know how many men are around, but Miguel is the only one that speaks. I asked why, but he didn't answer. I was instructed to leave the blindfold on, and if I was to try and take it off, I would be punished. The less I fought, the easier it would be on me. I did try to lift the blindfold once because of course, I don't listen. I was hit with some kind of switch several times on my back, and he blared Prodigy over the speakers for hours. I haven't touched the blindfold since, plus he taped it to my head making it secure.

I have kept quiet for the most part only asking irrelevant questions like, what does *conejito* mean. He explained to me how he has been watching me for a while. He thinks of me as the Energizer Bunny, so he calls me his little bunny. I was right about it meaning bunny.

I'm not that energizer bunny now though. I've regressed into myself. I've always hated being alone. That's why I date so much and like domineering men. I want someone to take care of me. I want to be someone's everything. I have everything I want in life but love. I hate being alone.

I know it stems from feeling neglected by my parents. They always seemed to be too busy with work or worried about what everyone thought. Until my best friend Ruby came into my life, I felt alone. You wouldn't know it from looking at me because I was trained at a young age to look and act perfectly. Never show my weaknesses.

Ruby has always kept me balanced between all the crazy men I've dated. She truly is the only one that has been by my side through most of my life. I hated it when she met her boyfriend, who is now her soon to be ex-husband. He took her away from me, making me feel alone. I became out of control but thank God for my music. It's the only thing that keeps me sane.

"*Conejito*. Don't ignore me. You *do not* want to make me mad today." Miguel's broken English comes off harsh, bringing me back to reality, but I still ignore him. I wonder who else is with him.

I used to ask about the other men, who I only know by smell or sounds. They don't speak to me, but they're a bit more aggressive with me. Their hands are rougher, bigger and not as forgiving as Miguel's.

One man smells of tobacco and whiskey. He must have a glass or bottle near him at all times because he reeks of it. I even asked for a drink of whatever he had, but Miguel always seems to know because he says no from somewhere in the room.

Then there is another man that whistles a lot. I think because right before he touches me, I hear a whistle, they both feel like the same man but different. I still haven't figured it out. Either one or two, they're big men compared to Miguel. I can tell by the sound of their heavy breathing and the way their feet shuffle around. Then again, I'm not an expert on sounds, but in my head, I'm thinking they're heavy men.

The question I do seem to ask every day, but it never gets addressed is, "What is the guy in charge going to do with me?"

I cried for what feels like days when I asked about Gus, and Miguel told me they left him for dead. That I needed to forget him, he wasn't coming for me.

A door opening again with two male voices muffled has me sitting at attention. I still cover my face from the heated lamps.

"As you can see, she's secure here with no entrance except the door we just came through. The door behind her is just a bathroom and a kitchen. She's secluded and secure as promised." The voice is that of the American man bellowing through the room. He hasn't been here since the big bossman was here. I wonder who he has brought to me today?

Shoes I'm not familiar with sound across the floor. I've been focusing on voices, sounds, breathing, and most of all the sounds of shoes walking around. Hearing him approach I wait for whoever it is to speak but when no one says anything, I pull my legs tighter into my chest readying myself for anything.

I hear the snap of a finger along with a bunch of shoes shuffling around me.

"Don't hide from me, *suka*," a deadly voice filled with hatred demands, as he calls me a bitch.

And that accent... I'd know that accent anywhere... Russian.

My heart picks up, but I don't move. I keep my swollen face hidden.

I cry out in protest when hands grab both of my arms pulling them through the cage slits, pinning them so I can't move. "No, let me go," I whimper in pain, crying, but my words are ignored as my head is yanked back exposing my swollen face. My chest heaves with each breath as I hiss, feeling the pain throughout my body.

The Russian demands, "What is this?"

I can smell Miguel's breath behind me, letting up on my hair, but it doesn't ease my pain.

"There was a car accident when they snatched her, but I assure you no one has violated or hurt her," the American man replies, and for the first time, I hear a slight hint of nervousness in his voice.

The Russian sounds amused. "Who hit her face?"

I try to focus on the Russian's voice, hoping for any recognition, but all I hear is hostility.

This time it's Miguel stating the facts. "He is dead."

"How?" the Russian who now sounds inches away from me says.

"He mouthed off to Bossman himself, and he shot him."

A tisk-tisk sound comes from the Russian.

"Lucky, I wasn't here. This cunt is nothing to us." His words dripping with disgust.

Who is this person? Why me?

I can't hold my tongue. I squeak out, "Why?"

Miguel pulls harder on my hair trying to warn me to keep my mouth shut, but fuck that. I want to know why this man doesn't like me. What have I done to him?

The Russian's accent is thick, laced with so much anger, "Why? Why you ask me?"

I whine, "Please."

"You messed with the wrong man, my cousin. You made him a pussy."

My temper spikes at what he says, and I fire back without thinking, "Who the fuck is your cousin?" I know Miguel will punish me, but I'm confused. The only Russian I know is Dominic, and he's no pussy - he's one mean son of a bitch.

The Russian clears his throat, spitting, he says, "*Suka...* in time. You will know why when I return."

As I listen to the American man lead the Russian out the door, fear consumes me.

Everyone holding me lets go, releasing my arms, I pull them into my chest as I ball up against the cage wall leaning my head on my knees.

"*Conejito,* I told you to behave, that men were coming to see you today." Miguel's voice is filled with what sounds like sorrow, but I know he's just like them - a monster.

I panic hearing the word men, not man.

"There are more?" I mumble into my legs.

"*Si Conejito.* I can't protect you when you speak out."

"If you want to protect me, let me go. Help me escape," I plea to him as I cry holding my chest.

I don't know how long I sit there crying, but when I hear the door open again, my body goes rigid against the cage wall.

"Miguel!" yells Bossman.

Oh, God. No. No. Not another.

Someone's with him. I can hear more than one pair of shoes. The lights have been bearing down on me all day, so I don't move from my spot. I don't acknowledge them at all. I want this to end. To be a bad dream and wake up in Gus' arms.

"*Si Jefe,*" Miguel's voice soars next to me.

"How's our little bunny, as you call her, today?" The bossman tries to humor whoever is with him, but it just makes my skin crawl.

"Sh –she's better than before," Miguel stutters, sounding nervous.

Why is he nervous? Who is here?

"Is she asleep? Why hasn't she moved?" the new man asks, and again a familiar accent has me lifting my head, but this time it's an Italian accent — his voice's warm and smooth like Luc's.

"What happened to her?" The man sounds infuriated.

"When the men took her, she was in an accident. My men here have been taking care of her since she has been in my care."

"Who here hit her? That's not just an accident, that is brutality," the man states.

"He's dead. I killed him," Bossman announces, sounding proud of what he did.

With the sound of footsteps approaching closer, I pull my legs to my chest cowering away from whoever is approaching.

"She hasn't given us any problems for the most part. She's very subdued and easy to control," Bossman explains enthusiastically.

My anger starts to build, and I want to flip out, but a hand grabs the back of my neck warning me.

"When did you say she'd be up for auction? She *is* exquisite and just what I'm lookin' for - very beautiful. I leave for Italy in two days," he says to the bossman. I feel him staring at me. He's the first one ever to come this close to the cage. I want to rip my blindfold off and look into his eyes, but the hand gripping my neck has me submitting.

"The auction's in a day's time. I have four buyers coming from afar. I must say you coming here and showing interest all of a sudden has me questioning why? I know we're old friends, but our business is always of *other sorts*. You've never shown interest in this side of my business," Bossman questions the Italian, but I hear something off in his questioning. Like he either fears the Italian or he doesn't trust him.

I hear a couple of whistles and a few finger snaps. *What're they doing?* I hear feet shuffling around me. I start to panic and my breathing increases.

Miguel releases my neck, and I turn my head to the side trying to listen if he moves away, but I don't hear footsteps. Miguel reaches in pulling my elbows back sending shooting pain through my right shoulder. I cry out as someone ties them securely against the bars.

"No, it hurts. Plea—" I cry out as my head is jerked back.

"Shh behave," Miguel whispers into my ear.

I try to calm down, but tears soak my blindfold as I whimper in pain. Miguel whistles again. "Good *Conejito.*"

He must be happy with my submission because he releases my head, but I'm still pinned to the bars. I slide my legs out in front of me scooting my butt back so my arms are not as tight. I tell myself over and over again that I need to comply, not to freak out, that it will only make it worse.

"Magnificent," the Italian says impressed.

"Yes, Miguel here is one of my best trainers," Bossman praises Miguel. They all seem to be surrounding my cage now.

I flinch with a yelp as the Italian man replies only inches away from me. I feel his breath on my neck. "You ask why all of a sudden I'm interested in your women? Well, you've never had a swan this beautiful before. She isn't your normal girl. It's her blonde hair." I flinch again when a smooth muscular hand touches the swollen side of my face. "I bet her eyes are as blue as the Caribbean Sea." He touches my blindfold covering my eyes and then gently runs his fingers down through my hair continuing down my back. "And this smooth milky skin." He slowly moves his hand back up my side - sending goosebumps across my body - over to my breast cupping it.

I freeze, but my rapid breathing has my chest heaving up into his grasp. I bite my lip whimpering trying to hold back my vicious words that are at the tip of my tongue. "My cock's hard just looking at her, and she's filthy." Taking his hand from my breast, he snaps his fingers. I let out the breath, thinking it's over. "I hope you clean her up and make her look presentable for tomorrow," the Italian says, moving around to the front of my cage.

Two hands grab my feet pulling them out to the sides, spreading my legs. I scream in pain when they yank my right leg. I try to kick them, but my right ankle is wrenched, seizing all movement. I'm sobbing yelling, "No please," over and over again.

"You say she has not been fucked or assaulted in any way? She *is* clean, *yeah*?" the Italian asks.

"Yes, that's why she's going for so high. She *is* fresh. No drugs and no one has tainted her. Miguel's the best."

Miguel pulls my hair yanking my head, exposing all of me. My legs are spread apart as I cry in pain. "Yes, a swan she is." The snapping of fingers and a whistle has Miguel reaching around me slipping his fingers into my panties, moving them aside.

"No. Please," I beg Miguel.

The Italian's intake of breath is loud and heavy. He's in front of me looking at my pussy exposed for all to see.

"Fuckin' exquisite. Perfectly, pink. I will want to fuck her as soon as we leave here. No matter the price, I will pay. She will be mine," the Italian man says with a lustful voice.

"Yes, we'll have to see. There are four other buyers very interested in her as well," Bossman says excitedly.

I'm sobbing with my head jammed back. Miguel grips my hair even harder, letting me know he isn't happy. I don't understand. *I'm complying.* But then two long fingers slide through my folds before dipping into my pussy, right next to Miguel's fingers that are holding my panties aside, I know he's furious that this man is touching me. I plead with Miguel.

"Please. Make it stop. You promised. Please." I can't hold back my body from shaking. The pain, the assault on my pussy has my body fighting against itself. The Italian obviously knows what he's doing as he gently and slowly finger fucks me.

I need to close my mind off. I need to think of something else.

Gus. I need to think of my Aengus. It's him touching me.

"Oh, she will be mine. I will make sure of it. You know when I want something, I get it," the Italian says with a determined voice. I can hear his breathing increase with his fingers. I try to wiggle my ass to move.

Be calm. Close off my mind. Think of Gus touching me. Think of anyone but this fucking creep touching me.

There are a few whistles before I hear the bossman clear his throat.

"Yes, well we'll have her clean and primed for you. You've had a taste, but it's time we go. I'll add you to the list." The man sounds both happy and irritated at the same time.

"Yes, a taste indeed. She's sooo responsive. I can't wait to have my way with her," the Italian man says as he lets his fingers glide in and out of me a few more times before removing them.

My body betrays me, giving him the satisfaction of thinking I want him but my mind's locked on the memory of *Gus* touching me and how *Gus* made me feel. The Italian man doesn't leave just yet as he grazes a hand up over my breast, slipping it into my bra cupping it, as he sniffs what I'm sure are his fingers from my wet pussy. "Fuck me. She's the one. She will be mine." He pinches my erect nipple before turning away.

Hold it together. Don't fall apart. I'm okay. I can handle this.

As the men head out to leave, Miguel's hand covers my pussy, shielding it, and when the men are completely gone, he slides his middle finger through my folds slipping it into my pussy. I cry out, "no" but he just keeps his finger lodged inside my vagina, not moving it.

Close my mind. Don't think. Block out everything. Go to my happy place... Gus.

"I need to cleanse you of his touch," Miguel breathes into my ear as he keeps me pinned. "You're wet. Did you like him doing that to you, *Conejtio?*" He slides his finger out slowly.

"No, please stop," I beg him, but my body continues to betray me.

"Your body tells me different. Do you like it when *I* do it?" Miguel's voice goes lustfully low.

No. No. No... only Gus - only my Aengus.

Miguel slips two fingers inside me, and I keep crying out no, over and over again, hoping he'll stop. I try to move my legs, but the men holding them are strong, and the pain is unbearable.

Be strong. Block it out! Don't fall apart.

He pumps them faster hitting my sensitive spot. He's experienced and knows what he's doing. He slips three fingers in, and his palm rubs against my clit as his fingers glide in and out of me, fucking me. I try to fight it. I can't block it. I'm falling apart. This is sick. Fuck. How sick am I to feed off the pain and pleasure? The hate I have for these men, but my body gets off on the pain and assault they're doing to my body. I cry even harder.

"Do you want me to make you come?" Miguel licks my shoulder taking a bite when I hear whistles.

"Please. Stop," I keep begging, shaking my head no but my breathing increases, I tense up as my body reacts on its own building its climax.

"We have a few minutes before Bossman has the videos back on," he says.

I feel a larger rough hand on my breast, pulling it out of my bra, tugging, pulling and gripping it before wet sloppy lips suck my erect nipple. I grit my teeth together as he force fucks me, and I come hard contracting around Miguel's fingers, while he keeps finger fucking me.

God, please. Block it out, Izzy. Don't fall apart. It hurts. I'm falling. Please make them stop.

I lean my head back and pray. Pray that the assault on me will be over soon. Pray that I can block it out so I can take my mind elsewhere. Just then I hear a door open. *Thank you, God!* All the hands release me instantly except Miguel who takes his time removing his fingers, placing my panties back. As soon as my legs are free, I slide them up against my chest as fast as I can to cover myself.

"Miguel!" shouts Bossman.

"*Si Jefe.*" Miguel's voice is rough with desire.

"When that motherfucker comes back, I want one of your men watching him at all times. I don't trust the son of a bitch, but he's by far one of the deadliest men I know. There's a link too." He pauses, and I hear fingers snapping, "But I don't think he knows that. I want you watching him. I don't give a fuck what happens to her *after* I get paid. Do not let her out of your sight until *I* get paid. Do you understand?"

"*Si Jefe,*" Miguel replies.

"Now, leave her alone. Do not fuck with her anymore. I saw what you fuckers were doing. Don't think I actually stop the fucking video when I bring them in here. I just tell them that. Don't make me fire your fucking ass. She's going to be one of my highest sales all year!" Bossman booms with excitement as he leaves.

Miguel curses under his breath before he speaks to the men in a low, swift voice using Spanish, so I don't understand.

I have my head leaning back trying to calm my breathing.

When hands grab my arms, I plead with them, but to my relief, they're cutting my ties, releasing my arms. I cross them over my breasts curling into a ball on the cage floor. I can't take much more. I'm falling apart. And just then, the song, "I Fall Apart" by Post Malone pops into my head, and I start to chant it in my head as I rock myself, letting the pain soar through my body blocking everything else out.

CHAPTER TEN | GUS
PRESENT DAY · WOLFEMAN MC CLUBHOUSE

I'm going out of my mind. She's been gone too long. I've been out of the hospital for a day, and I feel like I'm losing it. All I can think about is that I failed her. That she's scared, needing me and I can't find her. Waiting isn't one of my best fortes. The men have been working night and day. Quick and now Brant haven't left my side. They're worried I left the hospital too soon, but I assured them I would be fine. I try to hide my pain. I just needed to be here in case they find anything out.

"Here, drink this." Brant hands me a pint of Guinness as he sits next to me at the clubhouse bar.

"Thanks," I say, grabbing the glass from him and taking a long pull from it.

Brant seems different since he returned. His hair's longer, face unkept, not like before when he was clean shaven.

"B, ya alright?" I ask him.

Brant laughs. "You're asking me if *I'm* okay?"

I don't laugh back but instead look him dead in the eyes. "Yeah, I am. Ya seem different. Been worried about ya brother."

Brant looks away, lifting his own beer to his mouth and taking a long pull just as I did. He looks lost. Ever since Sasha was taken and Austin was killed, he hasn't been the same.

"Any word or new lead on your *one*?" I question.

He doesn't turn to look at me but answers, "I know she's alive. There have been some sightings of her, but it seems I'm always too late."

"Do ya need my help?" I offer him.

Brant leans back with a full-hearted laugh. "Gus man, I love you, brother, but we need to find your lady first."

"We got company," Quick yells from across the club.

Brant springs to his feet and when I jump up my head explodes with pain. I falter back against the bar trying to get my balance as stars take flight in my vision.

"Redman, you good?" Shy asks, approaching me from the side.

"Yah, I'm good."

"Who the fuck is that?" Quick exclaims.

The clubhouse has TVs throughout the building with surveillance cameras. So anywhere we are in the club we can see what is going on in the other rooms and outside. Right now, we're all looking at a TV showing us the front of the building where two SUVs have pulled up, and so far five men have exited the cars.

There's at least ten or more of us here, and we're all armed. Brant's the only non-member here.

"Who the fuck are—" Quick starts to say, but we cut him off.

"Christ. It's Frank Mancini," I say with a stern voice.

Brant husks out, "Motherfucker."

Everyone looks at both of us saying in unison, "What?"

"It's Frank Mancini - Luc's uncle," I answer as I head for the door, putting my gun back in my holster.

As I walk through the door, Brant at my side and my brothers following behind, I try to keep my shit together.

"Frank Mancini," I greet him as we walk out to meet him.

"You're Aengus Stone, and you're Brant Bolton, am I correct?" Frank looks between the two of us as he approaches, surrounded by men. But Frank is not one to hide behind his men as he leads them to stand in front of us. He's just as big and brawny as any of his guards. And goddamn he could be Luc's twin brother with how much they look alike.

I reach my hand out to shake his, "Aye."

After he shakes Brant's hand, I turn to introduce Shy and the others.

"Now that everyone is acquainted, I need to have a chat with you. And preferably not out here, *yeah*?" Frank surveys the parking lot. "I will have a few of my men stay with me while the others drive around."

Shy isn't too keen on welcoming anyone, especially one of the head mafia leaders into the clubhouse. "Is this little visit in reference to Izzy?"

"Why the fuck else would I be here?" Frank retorts sounding irritated.

"I'd rather not see or deal with my nephew, and I know you" —he points to me— "are involved with her, so I'm here with my news, plus you're not being watched yet."

Shy and I exchange a look before Shy announces, "This way," turning to head back into the clubhouse.

Frank turns to his men and starts barking orders in Italian. I'm blown away by how much Luc resemblance Frank. I've seen pictures, but the way they move and their demeanor it's exactly the same. When he turns to me, noticing I'm evaluating him, he smiles. It's a devilish smirk, one that's definitely deadly.

"Don't worry, Aengus. I've found your beautiful swan," he says, walking by me following Brant.

Once inside Frank, Shy, Brant and myself sit at a table with Quick and Dallas standing watch behind us with Franks two bodyguards. Four of our guys are still standing guard outside. Shy sent a few of them to check the garage and perimeter. Mac's at the White Wolfe dealing with business stuff.

I'm amped up, ready for a fight. He knows where she is but doesn't have her.

Frank sits across from me with a smirk. "It took me a good hour to lose my tail. My nephew has many different people watching him, at all of his buildings and even your girl's place. I didn't see any watchers around your clubhouse...yet." Frank pauses. "But once they link her to your clubhouse, I'm sure you'll have just as many. So, that's why I came here."

I'm about to lose it and blurt out, "Where is she? You said ya found her?"

"I did, but I need to explain what I know before ya freak out and rush out of here, *yeah*? Ya need to be smart about this and have a plan before ya run in there guns shooting. *Capisci?*" Frank says in a calm voice, waiting for us to settle down."

Fuckin' hell he sounds just like Luc. It's scary how much they resemble each other.

"So... you *don't* know who took her, but you *do* know where she is?" Shy asks leaning forward, placing his forearms on the table.

"Yes, she was taken by someone else and given to someone I do business with once in a while. When my nephew reached out to me, I was intrigued. He hasn't contacted me in years." He pauses looking around the room. "I went looking for your little swan, and sure enough this guy had a beautiful package waiting to be sold to the highest bidder."

I say through gritted teeth, "Sold? When?"

Frank gives me a look that probably scares a lot of people, but I don't fucking care. He knows where she is and hasn't told me.

"I went today to check out the merchandise. I wanted to see if it was really her because this guy has a lot of women. He tries to tell us they are these beautiful packages, but they end up being some junkie." He pauses, crossing one of his long legs over the other and resting his hands in his lap. The man projects lethal power to the fullest, and any man should be scared of him, but right now I don't fuckin' care who he is. I want my girl.

"I tried to get out of him who took her, but he evaded the question. He started questioning me why suddenly I wanted to buy this kind of merchandise from him since I don't deal in slave trafficking." He looks around the room, his eyes falling on me when he begins speaking again as he explains, "I actually *am* against it, but I think I *persuaded* him that I *really* wanted her for myself." He pauses again, taking this time letting each of his words sink in.

The fuck does that mean? I keep my eyes locked with his, but every nerve in my body tells me to hit the bloody cunt. I don't like his little innuendo he's saying. I'm about ready to ask what he had to do, but I stop myself.

Frank breaks eye contact first and continues, "But, he still must not trust me since he had me tailed and either him or whoever took her is having everyone watched, I'm sure until she's sold and shipped away."

"So... you saw her with your own eyes?" Shy questions.

Brant immediately follows with, "And you know where she is?"

"Is she alright?" I ask right after.

Luc answers, "She's pretty banged up from the car accident *they said*, but no one has touched her since the one guy that roughed her face up was shot dead. She's stripped of clothes except for her undergarments. They *showed* me and assured me she hasn't been tainted by any of *them* or drugged. They've blindfolded her in a cage, but the man who's looking after her even told me he has been watching her himself and no one has raped her."

This cunt prick and his innuendoes have all my fuckin' red flags flying high, but I still don't say anything.

Brant stands up. "We need to get her - where is she?" he demands as he starts to pace around us.

"That's the thing. She's in a highly secured building near the docks. She's tucked away in a back room with four men guarding her. There is only one entrance and no windows. That's why I said ya need a plan before barging in there because they're not some everyday hoodlum - they're professionals.

This guy has the backing of all the families, and they keep his whereabouts a secret for a reason. He's what we call a gatekeeper. He deals in everything and with everyone. They call him Bossman. That's why I can't figure out who took her and who's having all of us watched. It could be the Cartel, Iranians, the Bratva, Triads or the Yakuza... Who the fuck knows but whoever it is, they want her gone."

Dallas moves forward like he's going to say something, but Shy speaks first.

"So why *are* you telling us? If the families keep him safe," he asks the question I'm sure we're all thinking, wondering what his angle is here.

"My nephew has never asked for help." He pauses, looking down at his clasped hands before continuing. "Like *never*, so for him to ask me for help is huge for my family. How could I say no, he *is my* blood, no matter how he feels about me," Frank replies seriously.

"I love my nephew, and if she means that much to him, then she means that much to me, *yeah*? Now, I told him I'm flying back to Italy in two days. I'll keep these men on a goose chase. I'll stay away from my nephew. Everyone knows we don't speak but for me to just show up when one of his girls goes missing has put a lot of my associates on high alert, putting me in a compromising position, especially since I haven't found out who took her yet. They've kept their silence, but I'll find out, I assure you."

I stand up fast. "I'm not waiting two fuckin' days to go get *me girl*."

Frank sits back folding his arms across his massive chest as he looks up at me. "Eh, did I say ya needed to wait two fuckin' days? I'm here to fuckin' help ya, so calm the fuck down. Now let me fuckin' finish."

Everyone tenses in the room. I know we're all on high alert ready to fight whoever took Izzy, but I need to calm the fuck down. I feel light-headed, so I sit back down gripping my head. "Jaysus Christ."

Frank gives me a minute before he continues, "Now the day after tomorrow is when the auction will be held for all the women that are there, and your girl's one of them. He has four buyers plus me coming to bid on her and multiple online buyers. We need to figure out a plan. If you don't want any bloodshed, I can try to buy her, but it will be a bit costly, and not guaranteed. Plus, again, it puts me in a compromising position. I'd rather not be involved."

Brant announces, "We need to speak with Luc and Beau. We'll need to come up with a plan."

Dallas finally speaks up, "If you can give me the location, I can hack their system and figure out the layout of the building. We need to sit down, go over all the details and survey the location."

Frank grins up at Dallas. "Now I like the way you think son. Who are you again? I know all of my nephew's security, but I have yet to look into your clubhouse."

Shy tenses up. "I'd rather you keep us off your radar if at all possible. We don't need any more problems."

Frank looks taken back by his remarks but chuckles. "Micah, I know about the important ones. Don't think I didn't look into you all when Alexandria was going through her shit." Shy's jaw clenches hearing Frank use his real name.

Brant buffs up pushing his chest out. "Then why didn't you get involved then?"

Frank looks amused. "My nephew didn't ask, and it seemed you all had it under control. I just watch from afar."

Fuck this motherfucker. I grit my teeth holding my tongue before I say something I'll regret.

Frank stands up grabbing his phone from his pocket. "My nephew knows how to get ahold of me and my car is here so just keep me informed, *yeah?*"

We all stand up, but Dallas speaks up first. "You haven't given us any details or locations."

Frank snaps his fingers, and one of his bodyguards pulls out a folder handing it to Dallas. "Make sure you tell my nephew all that I have done for him, and I'll wait for your call."

As we walk Frank out, everyone's quiet, but right before Frank steps into his SUV he pauses and says over his shoulder. "Your swan is very beautiful. Hopefully, you don't lose her again."

I take a step toward him, but Brant stops me, grabbing my arm.

"Worm, get everyone on the phone and tell them to get here. We'll need everyone, and they need to be here now. We don't have that much time," Shy barks over his shoulder as he moves up to stand next to me. "B, call all your people. We need everyone on this. Get everyone here and let's get your girl back," he says, grabbing my shoulder for reassurance.

"We still don't know who took her," I seethe.

"We'll just have to ask the cocksucker that has her, won't we? You don't think that son of a bitch doesn't know who she is? Fuck that, he knows, and he's watching us too, making sure we don't find her before he can make millions off selling her to some third world country. At least we know she's okay. We'll get her back, brother. We just need to be smart."

"Fuck me!" Quick groans beside us.

We both rasp out in unison, "What now?"

"It's Firecracker, and she's on one. I've been evading her calls all week trying to keep her from finding out that Izzy has been taken." Quick shows us his phone. It's a text from Ruby.

I just found out my BFF has been KIDNAPPED. You fucking bastard. That's my best friend!!! I knew something was wrong, and you said NOTHING. Guess I know why you haven't been answering — club business my fucking ass. I'm on my way, and you better pray to God that I don't see you. Don't worry I won't be calling you anymore, you fucking bitch.

I look between the two of them and when Shy looks at me, I bust up laughing. For the first time since she has been taken, I bend over gripping my pounding head and laugh my ass off.

"Ha-ha laugh it up bitches, but she's coming straight for you two," Quick grunts, walking back into the club with his phone to his ear.

Shy who's still laughing slaps me on the back. "Come on. Let's figure this shit out."

I stand up holding my head trying to calm the shooting pain when Worm comes out. "Prez, Wolfe's already on his way from what Storm just said. I guess Snow talked to him and told him they should all be here for Redman, so they're all on their way except Hawk and a couple of prospects."

We both turn to our secretary of the club, Worm. Shy booms, "Great, that puts them here tonight, now we just need the intel."

The next few hours are crazy with both sides of my life coming together to help. I know Izzy isn't officially my girl, but everyone knows she's mine. I try to contain myself while they go through the motions of building a plan. Shit, I'm usually the planner who coordinates everyone.

I have always been the one to calm them down when something has happened, but here I sit about to lose my shit again over something as petty as I won't be the one to carry her out. They think I'm not healed enough.

Fuck that.

I don't say anything. I just sit and listen. Maddox brought in his full team which means Ethan is here working with Dallas on all the computer stuff. Those two are the best hackers I've seen. I look over and see the team leaders, Beau and Chad, along with Mac. They keep everyone in control and calm.

When the girls show up, it's a fucking madhouse. Alexandria and Ginger are fuming about Ruby not being told. They're all a fucking mess, which makes me feel a bit better about how I'm reacting to all of this. They're at the bar drinking with the bartender Maze, who just got here to work. I need a drink. I should go join them. Luc and Shy are in the office talking. Everyone is talking at once. My head feels like it's going to split open and my vision has gotten blurry a few times today. I know I should say something, but I don't. I need to be here and not in the hospital —

nothing a drink won't cure. When I push my chair out, I stand up and grab my head in pain.

"Christ," I wince in pain.

"You good, brother?" Quick says, sitting next to me.

When I raise my eyes to look over at him, I see stars, and I sway, grabbing the table for balance.

Quick stands up followed by Brant.

"You need to rest and for once in your life, let us help you. I promise once we figure shit out and form a plan, I will come get you, but brother you need to rest. Go lay down. You're not going to do any of us good if you're passing out," Quick says firmly with Brant nodding his head in agreement.

"Gus man, I will check in on you, but you need to rest. You're here and not the hospital, but if you don't listen to us, you'll be right back in there, and this time we'll leave you," Brant says, folding his arms over his chest.

"I'll send Stitch in there once he gets here and have him check you out, but for now you need to lie down," Quick says.

I look around, and everyone is hustling and talking amongst themselves. I know they're right, that I'm no help in this condition, but it kills me not being involved.

"It's not a request. Don't make me get everyone involved over there." Brant motions to everyone behind him.

"Yah, I'll go lie down but don't fuck around an leave me." I grab the back of my neck trying to ease some of the pain.

"I promise you, brother, once we know the plan, you will know the plan," Quick says, crossing his heart like a dipshit.

I laugh and turn toward the hallway of rooms to go lie down for a while.

CHAPTER ELEVEN | IZZY

I don't know why I pray every day and night. I feel like he isn't listening. It's completely black again, and since the floodlights are off that usually means no more visitors for today.

Miguel and the guys have left me alone since their assault. I've been singing the Post Malone song, over and over again, in my head. Like he says, "There are so many thoughts going through my brain," that I can't stop dissecting my life as I sing it over and over.

I ended up crying myself to sleep just thinking about all the fucked up shit that I've put up with in my life - with relationships, my career, and my family. I really am falling apart from the inside out. I feel completely torn apart.

I woke up laying on my back on the cold cage floor. My eyes are throbbing, and I want to open them. My swollen eye seems to be better, and I want to try to open it. I'm scared they're watching me, but I need to try and blink. I lift my blindfold just a tad bit from the bottom, and sure enough, I can see nothing with my good eye, so it is dark. I slip my fingers under it feeling around my bad eye before I lift the blindfold a bit higher so I can blink. It's still swollen and crusty, but I can open it. Relief and hope fill me.

"*Conejito.*"

I scream hearing my name and drop my blindfold back down, covering my eyes.

"What did I say about you removing it? Do you want to be in trouble?" Miguel's creepy voice comes from behind me. *Jesus Christ, he's a fucking weirdo.* Who sits in the dark watching someone?

"I'm sorry. I thought I was alone. My eyes hurt and I needed to blink a few times. That's all I was doing. I wasn't removing it," I explain, hoping he'll let me be and not turn the lights back on.

"Do you want my help? I can remove your blindfold for a bit. Let your eyes breathe while the lights are off," he says smoothly.

Really? What is he up too?

I turn my head to the side, leaning toward his voice as I plead, "Yes, please may I open my eyes for a bit? I can't see anything, and I promise to put it back on," I say to him, trying to keep my voice neutral, and not let him know I'm creeped out by him and most of all skeptical as to why he wants to help me.

When he reaches into the cage, I prepare for him to touch me, knowing he will use this as an invitation to feel me, and sure enough, his hands start at my arms gliding up over my shoulders before he grips my neck. I let out a sharp hiss as his hands tighten around my neck in a chokehold. "I want you to shift your body toward me turning your back to the camera and doors," he whispers into my ear before releasing my neck. I gasp for air and turn my body as best I can, grabbing the bars I pull myself up, but the pain in my leg hurts.

"Sit down. Lean your body to your left facing the bars," Miguel instructs softly in a low voice. I do as he says.

"Don't try anything funny. We have eyes on us at all times," he says inches from my face in a whisper tone.

"Why are you helping me?" I whisper.

"I feel bad about letting people touch you. I should've protected you and said no," he says sounding remorseful as he caresses my cheek, down my neck, to my collarbone and then back up.

He didn't say he was sorry for assaulting me, but I don't mention that, instead I try to keep the bile down from his touch.

"Why do you sit in the dark watching me?" I plead with him for answers.

"I'm protecting you. You are mine. I don't want any of these men touching you or hurting you. I can't allow that to happen, so I sit and watch. I mean look at what happened today while Bossman was here. Just think if he or I wasn't around," he says like it's nothing and part of me feels bad for thinking he was an animal, but my subconscious still tells me not to trust him.

I nod my head, and his hands slide up the back of my head so he can remove the tape around the cloth before untying it. When the blindfold falls from my face, the air hits me, and I blink a few times. I feel free, not confined and even if I still can't see, the weight is lifted — excitement courses through me.

"Thank you," I say as I move my hands from the cage bars to my swollen face. I feel around touching and probing.

"Does it still hurt?" he asks.

"How do you see me?" I question.

"I have night seeing gear so I can see you."

I laugh at his broken English, "You mean you have night vision glasses?"

"*Si.*"

I run my hands through my hair and surprisingly it's smooth. Miguel brushes it and keeps it feeling smooth. "Why do you pet me and brush my hair?" I ask hoping to get him to open up. I need him to trust me and then hopefully I can get him to help me.

"I train women to be obedient, so when they have a new master, they're compliant. You're my pet, and I'm here to take care of you," he answers me like it's no big deal that he's a slave trainer and that he sounds completely fucking crazy.

Miguel keeps touching me with one hand caressing my body up and down my side. I try to control my thoughts and face since he can see me and I can't see him.

"You're very submissive but very stubborn. That's why you're so lonely. You don't know what you want."

I don't reply to his comment because really what can I say, it's kind of true. I think of Gus and what he has been telling me these last few months, how I'm not ready to be with him. That I need to learn to trust him and let go but each time he tests me I rebel, never truly giving up my control to him. I'm in shock of his appraisal of me, and he continues.

"Most people are that way." He pets my hair.

"Are you like that?" I murmur.

He laughs. "No, I need control. I feen for it in every aspect of my life. Either someone is giving it to me, or I'm taking it, but training girls I get it all the time." He cups my face. "Once a girl breaks, and she truly gives up all control, it's a beautiful circle of giving and taking."

I'm so lost in his words, thinking of what Gus has told me and listening to him, they don't seem to mean the same thing. I'm so lost in my thoughts of Gus that I don't realize I've moved even closer to the edge of the cage pressing my face to the bars as he touches me. As he moves both his hands through my hair, I freeze when I feel a pair of lips brush over mine. I try to pull back, but Miguel grips my head holding me securely against the bars. When his tongue slips out licking my face, I scream. Pushing against the bars I try to get away from him.

"*Conejito*, I thought you wanted me, no?" Miguel releases me laughing.

"You sadistic fuck. What is wrong with you?" I cry out, wiping my face as I scoot back to the other side of the cage.

"You think I would fall for your sweetness?" He laughs sounding like he's possessed. "Oh, I like your sweetness alright." I move to the center of the cage hearing him move around.

"Why are you doing this? I thought you were nice," I cry, and tears fall from *both* my eyes. It feels so good. I blink a few times letting the tears run down my face. I start to laugh at myself. Of all things to be thinking of right now, I am fucking happy because I can feel my tears run down my face and actually cry. How fucked up am I?

Miguel hears me laughing and stops laughing himself, "What is so funny?

I laugh harder. I've lost my motherfucking mind.

Hands reach in from behind me, and I cry as loud as I can. "*Conejito,* time to put the blindfold back on before you get into trouble."

I start to laugh again. "You mean you will get into trouble. You took it off of me," I spit out.

As my arms are wrenched back, I feel another pair of hands around my face. *What the fuck?* Are they all in here just creeping on me with night vision? Who is this fucking guy that doesn't speak? I feel like I'm losing my mind.

Miguel murmurs a string of Spanish as he tightens the blindfold in place. "Don't remove it, someone is coming," and just like that, both hands are removed and within seconds the lights beam down on me. My skin heats instantly.

Jesus Christ. What the fuck just happened?

I sit there huddled up with my knees to my chest waiting for something to happen. All I hear is the buzzing of the overhead lights, but then I hear them... yelling coming from outside the door. It's men arguing and they seem to be getting closer.

"What the fuck?" Miguel sounds from behind me just as the door swings open.

"Guess who's back, and I brought a gift for you," the Russian man from earlier booms from the door.

"What the fuck did you do to her, Kirill?" Dominic's voice radiates with fury.

"Dominic?" I say barely audible, turning my body in the direction of his voice.

He found me. Oh, thank God he found me.

I cry out begging, "Please, Dom. Get me out of here."

He replies, "*Zvezda moya,* I will take care of everything,"

"*Net, Kuzen.* You will not," Kirill says, gritting out each word sternly. "We gave you several chances. You cost us money. The cunt must go."

He just said cousin - Dominic is his cousin. So, he was talking about Dominic being a pussy. How can this be happening?

79

"Net, Kuzen, let her go, this is between us," Dominic demands, sounding just as powerful as Kirill.

"Kuzen, we had it all until you fucked it up with this *suka,"* Kirill's voice drips of hatred calling me a bitch.

Had it all? What is he talking about?

Dominic fires back, "We still have it all. You're acting fucking crazy."

"Kuzen, it's over. Your lies and betrayal are over. You lie to everyone," Kirill screams like a madman. "Tell her! I want to see you tell your *Zvezda moya* the truth."

My mouth opens, and before I can think to shut it, I blurt out, "Tell me what?"

Dominic growls, *"Kuzen."*

"Net! Not until you tell her everything. Tell her why you're here. How you knew where this warehouse was."

"Kuzen, hvatit!" Dominic shouts enough, warning him to stop.

Shit, he's involved. Did he know they were going to take me?

His cousin doesn't listen to him because he keeps ranting, "Net, tell her how she's payment for *all* those girls you didn't supply us with because *she* and her *cunt friends* got in the way."

I have too many questions running through my head to stop myself from yelling, "What is he talking about?"

Kirill huffs, "Don't be stupid, *suka.* Think... All your problems stem from dating Dom."

Shit.

My mind starts shooting off the memories of when Alexandria was taken by Emmett. The warehouse full of girls. Emmett and Dominic were roommates, but—

I gasp. "I was his alibi."

It's all starting to make sense, each time a girl was taken, I was his alibi. I'm lost in my thoughts so I don't hear them talking to me or fighting. I'm just in shock, trying to remember everything, when Miguel grabs my neck, I snap out of it and scream in pain.

"Get the fuck away from her, NOW," Dominic growls from across the room.

Miguel doesn't move, instead he reaches in and grabs me around the neck in a chokehold. I panic, grabbing at his arm, but he doesn't squeeze too hard. He just holds me up against the cage. I still claw at his arm hoping he'll release me.

"Motherfucker," Dominic yells.

Kirill's sadistic laugh echoes around the room as he calls out, "*Net. Net. Net. Kuzen.*"

I hear men shuffling around as they yell in Russian. I hear fighting erupt nearby, when two shots are fired, and Miguel releases me. I know something bad just happened, so I pull my blindfold off to see what's going on, but the lights are too bright.

"Dominic…" I cry out. "Please… where are you?" I can't see anything. I can only hear men grunting as they fight and yell in Russian.

Kirill's evil voice yells over all the noise, "Tell your *suka* how you set up her friend to be taken. How you hired those bikers to help *you* get them off your ass."

"No," I say, falling against the cage, this all can't be real.

Kirill laughs vindictively, "Oh, yes. It was him the whole time. All those girls that were taken - it was him."

Dominic took those girls from the club. He was at each of those clubs but… I was with him every one of those nights. Am I that oblivious to what's going on around me that I would miss something like that…How could I have missed it?

"*Kuzen, hvatit!*" Dominic yells breathless, struggling against whoever has a hold on him.

He has to be lying. I would've known. He is crazy, but he wouldn't do that. I have to believe it was a lie and yell, "You're lying." I try to defend Dominic, hearing him fight near me. I hear Dominic talking, but they're all speaking Russian so fast, and I can't see anything. I yell, "Dom, where are you?"

It's Kirill who responds going on another rant, "Believe it *suka*, it was my dear *kuzen* who sent those hands. It was he who sent those letters. It was all *him*. Right *Kuzen*? Tell her you thought up all of this to save your ass from my father. Tell her!"

I hear Dominic struggling for breath. "*Hvatit!* Let me up, and I will tell her... to her face," Dominic grunts out.

When I hear snapping near me, I look around. I move into the center of the cage so I can try to see who comes close. I see Dominic being held by two men and they release him as he walks toward the cage. His face is all bloody. "Dominic, oh God," I cry, reaching toward the bars. He doesn't say anything as he reaches into the cage pulling me up against him, holding me.

"I'm so sorry, *Zvezda moya*. This *is* all my fault. It *is* because of me that all these things have been happening to you. I'm so sorry."

I cry, not understanding how he could have been behind all of this. "How? Why?"

Dominic takes a deep breath, and says, "I'm the nephew of Vladik Petrov, and my family's the Russian Bratva."

I lean back so I can see his face and when I see the truth etched across his face, I know it's true. I ask, "What? How did no one know?"

"My last name was changed to Malitzki when I came to the states so I could start my empire here."

Kirill spits, "*Net,* you mean our empire that you fucked up because of *this cunt.*" He laughs sarcastically. "Like I said *suka,* you made him into a pussy. He's done."

Dominic's eyes are filled with remorse and sadness. I shake my head at him, and say, "What do you mean because of me? I don't understand." My voice is barely audible.

Dominic says something in Russian, never taking his eyes off me.

"What *Kuzen*? You don't want your *little star* to know the truth? That you wouldn't give her up, so you fucked up everything we had just to keep her?" Kirill's voice drips with disgust.

"I don't believe it. You couldn't have done all those things. I know you," I say trying to convince myself. I stop once I see the sadness and defeat in Dominic's face, confirming what I know his cousin is telling is the truth. I lean back shaking my head saying, "No. No. No…" as I begin to cry. "All this because of me?"

"Yes, *suka*. Now you know why you were taken. He's obsessed with you, and he would never let you go. I'm taking everything away from you, so you know how it feels," Kirill explains.

Dominic turns to yell at his cousin, pleading with him in Russian, but when his cousin replies slowly, it's bad. Dominic turns back to face me, his face turning paler with each word that comes out of Kirill's mouth.

His eyes are filled with so much pain. "I'm so sorry, *lyubov moya*. I –"

A gun goes off, and Dominic goes down as a bullet shatters his skull, spraying blood across my body.

I scream, reaching for him as his body falls.

"Oh, God, no. Please no!" I cry out, closing my eyes.

When I hear Kirill making a tisk-tisk noise close to me, I open my eyes and see a pair of shoes next to the pool of blood forming around Dominic. I don't move or look up. I keep crying as I look at the lifeless body of my ex-boyfriend.

"See *suka*. You did this. This is on you. Now you will be sold and treated like the whore you are." Kirill spits on me before he leaves me lying there crying.

How could he do this? I knew he was possessive but to do all that stuff? How could I have not known? Dominic is gone… Gus is gone… Who will come to get me? Everything has happened because of me… All the things of how and why filter through my head until I pass out from exhaustion.

CHAPTER TWELVE | IZZY

I wake to Miguel calling my name. I'm afraid to open my eyes and see Dominic laying there dead. I don't move or say anything, but instead, I just lay there completely still.

"You need to get up. We need to prepare you for the auction," Miguel says from behind me.

Still, I don't move. If they want me to do anything they'll have to do it themselves. I'm done. Fuck them. I know they won't kill me. I'm worth too much money.

"I know you're awake. Don't test me *Conejito*. You won't like the outcome," Miguel threatens me, and still, I lie there.

When two sets of hands grab my legs and arms, I lay there not even fighting them. I just let them pull my limbs subduing me from moving.

Miguel starts speaking Spanish fast and loud. I hear feet shuffling around, but my eyes are closed. I don't want to see what they're going to do to me. Suddenly I'm being pulled from the cage, as they drop my legs to the ground before they handcuff my hands in front of me. I open my eyes, Miguel's standing in front of me as one of the other men holds me up.

"Hello, *Conejito*. Are you going to behave?" Miguel asks with a smile. If I wasn't already in shock, I would have been from seeing his face. He has scars all over his face like knife marks or maybe even scratches. Brown eyes so dark they're black with long dark oily hair. He's a tall man but with a slender body.

He takes hold of me while the other men move around me. My legs are too weak to hold me up and cramps are starting to shoot through them from being stretched out for the first time since I've been captive.

"You're not going to talk today?" Miguel taunts me with a smile.

I just stare at him emotionless, without a word.

Hands wrap around my waist from behind me, holding me up again so Miguel can let me go and take a couple of steps back to look me up and down. "You need a shower and fresh clothes."

I close my eyes and just wish this could all be over with. What if I fight? Will they kill me? I won't let anyone own me. I will kill myself before I become a slave. I begin to start thinking of all the ways I could kill myself while Miguel reaches down grabbing my feet as they carry me off.

We head through a few hallways with a bunch of doors lining them, making me think of the clubhouse and all the rooms they have down their hallways. Tears pool in my eyes thinking about Gus. Is he dead too? Did I get him killed too like I did Dominic?

I start to cry as they lay me down on a cold concrete floor. When I hear running water I know I'm in a bathroom. I can't really tell from where they laid me down without lifting my head or moving, all I can see is it looks like a big gym or jail style room with a bunch of shower heads. The water continues to run as if they're filling a bath. I close my eyes and just listen, so many feet shuffling around, like sandals scraping along the concrete.

"We'll put her in the side room with the bath. I'll wash her so you can get the other girls washed and ready to go," Miguel orders, but to whom I have no idea. The nonspeaking man still hasn't revealed himself to me. I've only seen figures and bodies, I haven't seen anyone's faces except Miguel's.

"Up you go, *Conejito*," Miguel says lifting me up and placing me into a big metal tub. The warm water feels like heaven against my aching body. I close my eyes, hiding the pure bliss that overcomes me by soaking in this bath.

I'm completely submerged in the metal tub when he slowly

removes my bra sliding it down my arms to my hands that are handcuffed together. He lifts my arms up over my head to the back of the tub. When I hear a clicking sound, I know he's cuffed me to the tub unable to move. Next, he slides his hands down my body ripping off my panties. My first reaction is to scream or yell at him, even fight him off, but I don't. Instead, I just lay there mute and motionless.

I want to kill him. Could I kill him? Would I kill him if I had the chance? Morbid thoughts go through my head of escape. *If I try to escape would they kill me... torture me... beat me...*

"What are you thinking about?" Miguel questions while caressing my body as he cleans it.

I don't answer. I will not comply.

I hear him move away from the tub and a door shutting, while I continue to keep my eyes closed. I'm determined to stay mute when I feel one of his hands start to pet my head.

"Open your eyes," he demands.

Still no response. I will not comply.

"Nothing?" Miguel says, sounding irritated.

Pain shoots through my body as he grabs my bad ankle. I scream in pain, thrashing my body around splashing water everywhere.

"There she is," he laughs pushing my waist back down, pinning me in the tub.

I shoot daggers with my eyes and growl at him. I refuse to say anything. *I hate him.*

A whistle sounds from behind me, causing him to look up.

"*Si*, keep a watch. I'll be just a minute," Miguel answers whoever's behind me.

He uses one of his hands to pin me to the bottom of the tub, while moving his free hand down my chest gripping one of my breasts full handed before pinching the nipple, tugging on it. I try to wiggle his hand away, but his grip on my nipple tightens causing me more pain.

"Tisk-tisk. Behave now." Miguel licks his lips, biting down on his lower lip as he starts his assault on me. I hiss, gritting my teeth to hold back my screams. He's provoking me, and I will not comply.

Do not comply. Close off your mind Izzy. I chant to myself trying to clear my mind.

"I've wanted this pussy since the first day I laid eyes on you, *Conejito,* but someone was always watching," he whispers, leaning forward putting his weight on me, making it harder for me to move. "I've jacked off thinking about fucking this sweet pussy of yours." Licking his lips making a sucking sound. I close my eyes and try not to break. *I will not comply.*

"I'm so fucking hard right now. I think I'll let you watch me jack off as I make you come." I want to headbutt him, but it will only make this worse, so I concentrate on the pain. I open my eyes when I hear a door open, but a second later it closes.

Miguel stands up looking down at me as he unbuttons his jeans pulling his erect cock out. He sits next to the tub, stroking himself, watching me with crazed eyes. I turn my head and look away.

Block it out. Be strong. Do not comply.

He reaches into the tub grabbing my ankle pulling it out and cuffing it to something. I growl, not saying a word. With his dick hanging out he moves around the tub grabbing my hurt ankle, and I cry out in pain as he secures it. I'm floating in the water with my body suspended. I start to panic, thrashing around making noises like I'm a caged animal.

Miguel just smiles licking his lips. "Yes. Yes. This will work for now." As he moves toward my face, I freak out thinking he's going to stick his cock in my mouth, but instead he splashes water on my face. He grabs my throat with his left hand as he strokes his cock with his right.

I gasp. Miguel leans down and kisses me, taking the last of my breath. I can't breathe. My eyes start to water and haze over. I'm consumed with fear.

"Are you scared, *Conejito*?" I hear him pumping himself faster. He releases my throat, I gasp and choke for air. Miguel tilts his head back in complete ecstasy, pumping his cock harder. He leans up next to the tub placing his cock next to my face. His fingers start to turn white as his grip gets tighter around his shaft.

Be strong. Close off my mind.

"I can't wait to be inside this sweet pussy of yours," he says, grabbing my throat again. He moves his cock close enough to my face that it starts to rub up against it with each stroke. "I'm going to come all over you and in you." His voice is laced with malice and desire. I feel light-headed, and my vision is starting to blur, but I keep them locked with his soulless eyes.

"Hmmm, I could just let the life drain from you." He leans down and kisses me again before releasing his grip, as I gasp choking for air. He stands up closing his eyes, pumping himself, breathing harder with each pull. His body tenses as he begins to grunt. I can't move.

When his eyes fly open, they're wild and possessed. I shake my head as he takes a step toward me.

"You are mine. It's time to mark you," he says breathlessly.

He grips my face, forcing my mouth open. He leans over touching the tip of his cock to my lips as he continues to jack himself off. I try to shake my head, but his grip on my jaw has my head pinned to the tub. He cries out his release as warm semen ejaculates from his cock in my mouth and on my face. I start to gag as he tightens his grip on my jaw, preventing me from closing my mouth or spitting it out.

He slows his strokes. "Fuck, that was good." He closes my mouth, holding a hand over my mouth and nose, forcing me to swallow. Once he releases me, I gag trying to throw up, while he puts himself back together.

Be strong. Hold on.

"That was just a taste." He slides his hand down between my legs, cupping my mound. "Once you're sold, I'm going to carry you to the back" –he slips a finger into my pussy. I close my eyes, and I try to shake my body— "and prepare you" —two fingers glide in and out of me— "for your new owner, *but*" —he increases his jabs. Finger fucking me, he adds another finger. "Before that, I'm going to fuck you—" I can't take much more, opening my eyes I glare at him while I wiggle around welcoming the pain in my leg and ankle as he continues. "So fucking hard my cock will split this tight little cunt in two." My hips are splashing around as he tries to stretch me using four fingers now. Water is going everywhere, but he just stays firm against me holding me in the water.

A whistle has Miguel huffing in frustration, but this time he doesn't look up. Instead, he keeps his eyes locked on me, keeping his fingers moving in and out of me. I break the stare, closing my eyes as tears start to stream down my face.

"Mig!" shouts the American man from the other room. I never thought I would be happy to hear his voice - Miguel whistles in response, unrelenting in his continual assault on my clit. I'm going to come. I try to fight as he twists my nipple with his free hand, flicking my clit one more time. I groan. "That's it come for me, *Conejito*," he grunts.

I cry out my release as he rubs my clit, moving his fingers in and out a few more times. I drop my head back exhausted from the fight. My body goes limp, feeling defeated and broken.

A whistle comes before the door flies open. "Miguel!" the American man yells.

Miguel doesn't take his eyes off of me, and says in a subdued voice, "*Si Jefe*, she's all clean." With his fingers still inside me, he smiles, wiggling them one last time before slowly pulling them out of me. He pulls his hand out of the water to his lips, sucking his fingers. Miguel then looks up at the man behind me and says, "All done."

"I've been calling you. We need to get her out there," the American man orders.

"*Si*, right away sir," Miguel says, uncuffing me from the tub. I sink to the bottom lifeless. He broke me. I want to die. I can't be someone's slave.

Once lifted out of the water, everything moves fast. I hardly have time to process what is happening. There's a line of women, freshly showered, all in white linen dresses, with white slippers. Most of the girls were functioning, but you could tell they were high from whatever drug they were given, making them compliant with whoever was in charge of them.

Miguel won't let anyone touch me as he combs my hair and dresses me in a matching dress and slippers. I still haven't spoken, but I look at him with dead eyes. I can't stand or walk due to my ankle and leg still being injured so he carries me. A lady came in to fix the women's clothes and hair before shuffling us out of the room.

"Soon this will all be over with, and you'll be on your way to your new owner's home," Miguel chuckles as we walk. "After you're sold, you will say goodbye to me, *Conejito*. It will be a memorable goodbye." His voice is filled with menace and no remorse. Still, I say nothing. I don't think I have any life in me anymore.

We're all lined up, heading down a few more hallways before entering another big room, it looks like a gymnasium with a stage. The lights are bright, beating down on us again, so we can't see anything past the area we're standing.

The lady leads the line of women with Miguel holding me at the end. We're told to stand shoulder to shoulder, like a lineup. We are called by number, one by one, to the circle at the center of the stage, ordering each woman to turn around slowly. A few women have a hard time making it to the circle, so the lady has to assist.

When my number is called to move to the center of the circle, Miguel mutters under his breath, "Don't try anything stupid. It will only make your life more hell." Before dropping my legs down to stand me up, he faces me outward. I stand on my good leg, limp in his hold. He maneuvers me slowly around as my head slumps forward.

I fight the tears, gritting my teeth so I don't say anything. I won't crumble or break like these other women when they were put on display for the sick fucks watching and appraising us. When my turn is done, Miguel picks me back up and hauls me back to the line standing me upright again holding me in place.

I hear commotion on the other side of the lights. Men's voices are rising, and a female voice is rising above them all. Miguel's grip around my waist tightens, pulling me closer to him. I know he can't see anything either.

Suddenly there's an explosion from behind us. We all turn around to see smoke coming from the hallway we just came from. Women start to scream as the smoke billows out into the room. Everyone moves away from the door pushing us toward the edge of the stage.

Miguel whistles but there's no whistle in response. I can hear men yelling and fighting beyond the lights, as more women and men rush toward us from the smoke-filled halls.

We're at the edge, Miguel tries to push the women forward, but there are so many of them. We are all trying to get away from the fire, with nowhere else to go they smash into us. Smoke has filled the stage, and I see my opportunity when he uses both his hands to push the women away. I slip to the floor so he can't see me. I crawl to the edge of the stage into the unknown and complete darkness.

Women are screaming and jumping off the stage as men rush around. I continue to move until I smash into the lower level filled with chairs. I hiss in pain but keep as quiet as I can. It's pitch black, I see the light at the top of the room, like a theatre. I pull myself up and try to walk, but as soon as I put weight on my leg and ankle, I collapse in excruciating pain.

Jesus Christ. Please.

Miguel is yelling, "*Conejito*, I will find you. You can't hide from me. I will find you." He whistles and yells at me again. It's mayhem with smoke filling the room. When another explosion goes off along with gunfire, I burrow myself under the stairs.

All I can hear is whistling, screaming women and gunfire.

Suddenly, I feel small feminine hands wrap around me, lifting me up. I look, but all I see is this mane of wild hair flying around as the woman practically drags me with her.

"Ruby?" I croak out my first word since yesterday. I must be hallucinating but, the hair, it...

"Let's go, Izzy. We don't have much time." Hearing my name, I gasp tripping myself, causing us both to go down. "Motherfucker, get up," the girl yells, pulling me up. Before I can say anything, she's throwing me over her shoulder, carrying me fireman style. She starts to move quickly through the smoke when I finally realize she's in a black silk dress with no shoes. I hear whistling, and I panic. Miguel is close, and he's going to capture both of us.

"No. Please. Hurry," I croak. Miguel choking me has left me with no voice.

God, who is this woman? I see two men in suits flank us, shooting in the direction behind us, but I don't know who they are. I try to stay still as she moves swiftly through the halls. It's so hard to see, and I can't tell if she is running away from the mayhem or straight for it. All I know is the yelling is getting louder.

"Izzy!"

Oh, my God.

I try to scream hearing Gus call my name from a distance. My voice is hoarse, and no one can hear me. *I need to fight. I need to get free. Gus is here.*

I start to squirm around, trying to get free. But the woman strengthens her grip on my arm and thigh causing me to cry out in pain. "Fuck Izzy, don't fucking move we're almost to them," she grunts out of breath. I stop fighting her as she keeps moving with me securely over her shoulder.

"Izzy!" Gus calls out again, sounding closer.

Gunfire erupts as one of the men goes down beside us. I feel a sharp pain in my shoulder just as the woman yells, "Goddamnit, Madd Dog!"

A second later we're falling toward the ground. "Gus!" I scream as we both hit the floor hard.

"Motherfucker! I'm hit." She rolls over to stand up with blood running down her leg and arm. The other man in the suit tries to pick me up, but he's shot in the leg as well. I turn to see who's shooting when I feel a burn in my leg. He turns, shooting, giving us cover, while she grabs my arm and starts to drag me down the hall. Yelling, "Anytime boys. I'm fucking hurt over here."

"Ghost!"

"Brant!" the woman yells back.

Hearing Brant's voice, I want to cry out for help. She falls down next to me with blood covering her shoulder and chest. I feel faint. "Don't you pass out on me," the woman says, meeting my eyes. It's then that I recognize who she is - I smile at her. She's the woman they call Ghost that saved Ginger, and now she's saving me.

"Izzy!" I turn to see Gus hovering over me like an angel.

I smile. "You're alive." My voice is barely audible. I try to clear my throat. "You came for me."

Gus leans down kissing me. "Always."

"Andy!" Brant cries out beside us picking up the now passed out woman.

Please, God let her be okay. Please.

More shots are fired as they pick the both of us up, holding us securely in their arms as they run for cover. I look down and see the white linen gown I'm wearing is covered in blood. It's all over me. I panic feeling light-headed. "I'm bleeding," I say, but it's a whisper. My head flops back, and before I lose consciousness, I see Quick and Shy surround us.

He's alive. He came for me. They all came for me.

CHAPTER THIRTEEN | IZZY

PRESENT DAY - HOSPITAL

Beeping.

Where am I?

I feel the warmth. I don't want to wake up from this dream. I don't want to go back to reality, or those men.

Wait, I was rescued. Wasn't I?

I feel someone touching my hand.

Don't move. Don't move. Don't move.

I keep chanting over and over again, praying he'll go away.

Maybe he'll go away.

Miguel never goes away.

He's always there.

He's always watching.

I need to comply. He won't hurt me if I comply.

I hear people murmuring near me.

Where am I? Think Izzy, think.

I need to remember.

Am I still dreaming? Pain. Where is my pain?

Something's wrong. I need to feel pain. It means I'm awake. I need to wake up so I can feel the physical pain. I need to breathe.

Wake up.

Oh, God. He's caressing me again.

Please stop.

I feel a hand running up my arm and cupping my face.

Shit!

Another hand swipes my hair away from my face.

He's always touching my hair.

It feels like spiders are crawling all over me. I can't take it anymore. I don't want him to touch me anymore.

Please make it stop.

Beeping. Loud fucking beeping. I try to speak, but nothing comes out.

"Iz?"

Aengus? Wait. My Aengus... I'm floating again. No...

I feel rough hands caressing me.

I feel his breath on my neck.

Oh, God, Miguel. He found me. Wait, didn't they kill him? I thought I was rescued?

My body starts to shake. I want to scream with fear. I need to get his hands off me. I feel a second pair of hands grab my legs.

No. No more needles. Please.

"Shh... relax you're okay," a male voice whispers into my ear.

Jesus, it sounds like my Aengus. But it can't be, no, it's Dominic. No, wait, it's Miguel. Oh, God why can't I think? Fuck, help me. I'm lost.

I hear feet shuffling across the floor.

Oh, no, are more of them coming?

I hear men yelling all around me.

They're here to take me away.

Loud beeping...

I shake my head.

It's a dream. I need to wake up.

"For *fuck's* sake, what's happening to her?" Gus' voice rings out.

It is Aengus, but he's so far away. Aengus, please don't leave me.

Loud beeping.

Goddamnit, I don't want to float anymore, I want to wake up.

Pain radiates up my leg.

Holy shit! It hurts.

I let a painful moan escape me.

Muffled noises sound around me. I panic.

I hear chairs shuffling, and loud footsteps coming closer.

Breathe, Izzy.

A male voice speaks, "Is she waking up?"

Oh, God. They're here to get me ready for the auction.

I panic.

Hands grab me, and my body starts to convulse.

"Isabella?"

Is that my Aengus? I'm so confused. Where am I?

I want to cry.

I want to wake up.

I want to be home and safe.

"Isabella, please. Come back to me," Gus whispers into my ear.

Is he really here? Did I imagine him?

I'm scared to open my eyes and see Miguel. I can't see him again. He's going to fuck me. Oh, God his fingers jamming into me over and over again.

I'm contaminated.

Save me.

I feel lips brush up against mine and I lose all control.

A guttural cry escapes me.

The beeping starts again, and it gets louder the more I freak out. I feel several hands holding me down.

Men are talking.

They're here for me.

A man growls...

CHAPTER FOURTEEN | GUS

"Christ, it's happening again," I blurt out, feeling hopeless.

Quick and Dallas help me hold her down so she doesn't hurt herself. The nurse comes rushing in, going straight to her monitors.

"Why does this keep happening?" I demand.

The nurse just gives me a look before tending to Izzy, injecting her with a sedative.

"For fuck's sake, will ya tell me what's wrong," I say softer, but I'm about to lose it.

"She needs to stay sedated to keep her calm."

"I understand that but what's happening to her when she shakes and starts to freak out? Is she having a seizure or what?" I run my hands through my hair frustrated.

"Sir, I'm sorry. She has been through some major physical and mental trauma. She could be dreaming, hallucinating, drifting in and out of consciousness, we won't know until she wakes up fully. All we can do is keep her calm until she decides to wake up," the nurse says, giving me a sympathetic smile before leaving.

"Thank you, nurse," Quick says as she walks past him.

Dallas sits back down pulling out his laptop, typing again.

"I can't take much more of this," I say, pacing around the room.

Quick leans up against the wall, watching me, trying to analyze my mood.

"Every time I touch her or say her name, she goes into a fit," I tell them frustrated.

"She needs rest, Redman. It takes time for her to heal - her body and her mind. Give her time," Quick says trying to calm me down.

"She needs to wake up," I grumble.

"Remember what the nurse just said, every person is different. We don't know what they did to her physically or mentally," Quick explains.

Thank Christ she wasn't brutally raped. The doctor did a full exam and saw no signs she was forced. They said most of her injuries were from the car accident. She was also shot when we rescued her, but it was a clean hit, going straight through her leg.

My body shakes with rage. "If any of those motherfuckers are still alive I'll hunt them down and kill them myself," I seethe.

"Got something," Dallas says from behind his laptop.

We both move toward him waiting to hear what he has to say.

"Okay, I've been researching since her last episode. I've read about people being medically sedated or coming out of surgery. With her medical diagnosis and the doctor's theories, it has me thinking." Pausing he looks up. "I believe we all need to leave the room."

Both Quick and I say together, "What the fuck?"

Dallas stands up taking his baseball cap off, bending it between his hands before putting it back on. "Look she's had mental and physical trauma." He starts pacing around like he always does when he's thinking. "It's like PTSD but different, because she isn't awake. She could be going in and out of consciousness as the nurse said but when you touch her or say her name - she kind of freaks out right?" He pauses for me to answer, so I nod my head. "Okay, so maybe we're triggering her PTSD, and she's hallucinating thinking you're them or maybe she can't get to you or who the fuck knows. Whatever it is, it's causing her to freak out. Maybe if we leave her alone, she'll wake up."

"I'm not leaving her alone in this room. She was stuck in a fuckin' cage, alone," I growl my frustrations but know deep down he might be right. Neither of them says anything. I've dealt with PTSD being in the service, but this is something totally different.

I feel helpless. "Christ!"

We're all standing at the foot of her bed in thought when the door flies open, and in walks Ruby, and by the look on her face, she's in full Firecracker mode followed by Gin and Alex.

They look like they're on a mission to fuck shit up, or someone. Dallas and Quick take a few steps back, but I stand my ground. Ruby points her finger at Quick. "Get the fuck out. Now."

Gin and Alex move toward Izzy's bedside. Quick smiles at Ruby and I can see he's ready to get her all riled up. He's about to open his mouth, but I interrupt him, "Not here." Without taking his eyes off her, he grabs her elbow and shoves a very disgruntled Ruby out the door just as Shy and Maddox enter the room.

The two of them laugh seeing Quick lead her out of the room, but once they see my face, they both ask, "What happened?"

"She had another episode, and they sedated her again," I explain, turning toward Izzy lying in bed. I reach out, touching her foot that's now in a cast. Gin and Alex are on either side of her bed holding her hands. Alex is murmuring in Spanish.

"Damnit, we always miss her trying to wake up," Ginger says softly.

Dallas clears his throat. I ignore him.

He clears his throat again. This time Shy asks, "What the fuck is wrong with you?"

Dallas is usually the quiet one, just watching and listening. He's the evilest one of all. He's more dangerous than all of us put together, but you would never think that by looking at him. He has a smaller build than most of us, but it's his computer skills, street smarts and his fighting abilities that make him untouchable. The only thing that ruffles his feathers is being the center of attention.

He clears his throat again. "Gus."

Shy snaps, sounding irritated, "I asked you what the fuck was wrong? You tell me."

Shy and Maddox are sitting in chairs while Dallas stands in the corner. I blow out a breath in frustration, turning toward them and say, "He thinks she's having PTSD while going in and out of consciousness, but different. I'm usually touching her or talking to her when she has an episode. He thinks we should leave and let her wake up on her own. That she might be thinking we're them or something traumatic, making her freak out." I finish hoping they think it sounds crazy cause I don't know if I can leave her.

"You're right, Dallas," Ginger says softly from behind me.

I turn around. "So you're saying I'm making her have these seizures or whatever the fuck they are?" I ask defensively.

Shy stands up, moving next to me facing his girl. "Angel, explain."

She smiles softly, "No, Gus, not like that. When I was hurt, and they had me sedated. I didn't know what was real and what was a dream. Especially in traumatic situations, you drift in and out, kind of like a dream-state, and it took me a while to come around. She was taken by men, maybe hearing men's voices is confusing her. It was Alex's singing that pulled me out, to be honest with you." She looks over to Alex who is holding Izzy's hand with tears in her eyes.

Jaysus Christ. She's right.

I take a deep breath, rubbing my hands over my face and up through my hair while looking up at the ceiling.

"You okay, brother?" Shy asks, putting a hand on my shoulder.

"No, I'm not. I just got her back, and you're telling me I have to leave her alone," I say defeated.

Ginger moves to the end of the bed, reaching out to grab my arm, "She's not alone, and once she's lucid and knows where she's at, it'll be fine. As soon as she wakes up, we'll have you come in. I truly feel with everything she's been through, it would be easier having us girls here helping her come back to us." Ginger lets go of my arm just as Ruby storms through the door looking like she's been crying.

Ruby's face is a mirror image of how I feel inside right now. Sad, mad, scared and most of all lost. It hits me hard because I feel the same way. I reach out, grabbing Ruby. I pull her to me. She fights me at first, but then she lets go and cries into my chest. I hug her tight and whisper into the top of her head, "I'm sorry. We should have called ya. It was my call, not his."

I feel a few tears run down my face, as she looks up, they drop onto her forehead. "She's all I've got, Gus. Don't you ever keep her from me again."

I push her crazy hair away from her face and smile. "Not gonna happen again. I promise."

I kiss her forehead releasing her so she can go to Izzy. Not telling her best friend that Izzy was missing was wrong, even though we thought it was for the best. Looking up from Ruby to Ginger, I nod my head. "Okay, I'll leave the room, but I'm not leaving the hospital. I will get a chair and sit outside. I'm not leaving. I'll check in with Beau and the guys," I explain to the room.

Dallas loads his shit saying he's going to go with me and Maddox. Shy kisses Ginger, explaining he has some stuff to deal with, and he would be back to get her later. Everyone says goodbye, with a promise to call if anything changes.

As we're heading out the door, Quick walks up. I grab him and turn him around. "Give her some time. You're with me."

"But," Quick tries to argue but stops when he sees all of us men leaving the room.

"I'm going to head over to check on Ghost. She's on the other side of the building. B and Chad are with her," Maddox explains.

"Fuck. I'm sorry Madd Dog, I forgot to check on her after the surgery. I haven't left Izzy's room since she got back from having X-rays," I explain feeling bad.

"Don't worry. You have enough on your mind," Maddox says trying to ease my mind.

"I'll go with ya," I say, turning away from the elevator.

Everyone agrees, turning to follow Maddox.

"Has she woken up yet?" Shy asks from behind us.

"Yeah, B texted, told me to come help calm her down," Maddox says with a chuckle.

"Here we go," Quick says bouncing on the balls of his feet.

I smile remembering when I first met Ghost. She saved Ginger from Snake taking her. She single-handedly took down two men twice her size and that bitch Raven.

"She's batshit crazy, tiny as fuck and more lethal than most of us men. No wonder B's texting for help," Shy says dead serious.

Maddox chuckles. "Yeah, she doesn't do well with people even though she has the biggest heart. She would drop kick me for saying that, but the girl's one of the best. She's been Ghost for as long as I can remember. No one calls Andy by her real name. Chad was the one that actually tried to use her real name all the time, but he was almost hospitalized for that slip-up," Maddox laughs.

I remember having my doubts at the beginning of our plan but never again. She has earned my respect and protection for life.

Before we even enter her room, we hear her yelling at someone. "I don't want any fucking pain medicine."

"Jesucristo, what's all the commotion in here?" Maddox exclaims walking through the door.

I see a scared shitless nurse standing between Brant and Chad next to Ghost's bed. I laugh at the sight. She's fuming alright.

Her hair is frizzed out with massive curls flying all around her face. She truly looks like a mad woman.

"Jaysus, are ya fuckin' possessed?" I say jokingly as I try to hold in my laughter.

Shy smacks me in the shoulder trying to hold back his own laughter.

"Fuck all of you," Ghost yells.

"Ghost, what's the problem?" Maddox stands next to her bed with his hands on his hips. He's braver than us getting that close to her bed.

Chad, Maddox's head of security, turns to us and tries to explain, "Madd, we're trying to get her to take her medicine. She needs to take this antibiotic –"

Ghost interrupts him, "Fuck that. You're trying to dope me up so I sleep."

"What's wrong with that? We're all here protecting you. Sleep for God's sake. You've been shot three times. Take the fuckin' medicine," Maddox demands.

Ghost huffs, leaning back, wincing in pain.

"See ya need to relax lass," I try to help, but she sits up glaring at me.

"I don't like being drugged. It makes me paranoid," she explains looking at all of us men surrounding her bed. Each of us are easily over six foot, towering over her, and here she is ready to take us on.

Maddox takes a deep breath. "Ghost, you know I would never let anything happen to you. We are here to watch over you so you can heal. Trust in me, take the fuckin' medicine. Please."

Ghost leans back again placing her good arm over her chest, rubbing her bandaged shoulder, and after a few minutes she finally gives in, "Okay, but - he needs to leave," pointing to Chad.

"What the fuck?" Chad yells, throwing his hands up.

Ghost just sits there staring daggers at him, not saying a word.

"Fuck this. I'm outta here. I'll be at the apartment helping Ethan," Chad explains walking toward the door.

"Helping him do what?" she yells.

"None of your fucking business, *Ghost*," Chad yells over his shoulder as he walks out the door.

We all just stand there watching them fight. She's so busy being mad at us that she hasn't noticed Brant standing in front of the nurse as she puts the medication into her IV line.

"What's he talking about Madd?" she demands.

"Once you're healed we'll talk, but for right now who will you feel safe with in your room, or do you need us to sit outside in the hall?" Maddox tries to change the subject.

"I'm staying," Brant announces to the room.

She glares over at Brant. But, you can tell the medication is starting to kick in, as her body is more relaxed and her words are coming out a little slurred. "B, I don't need saving. You can go home."

"Didn't say you did. I'm just staying to make sure *you* don't hurt the staff. I'm here to protect *them,* not *you.*"

We all chuckle knowing he's serious.

CHAPTER FIFTEEN | IZZY

Silence.

Shit, the pain.

Thank God, I feel the fucking pain — it's all over my body. Please let me wake up. I try to move but holy shit! It hurts. I let a moan escape me.

I hear movement around me, the creaking of a chair, feet shuffling around me. I panic.

Who's watching me?

Suddenly, a soft humming surrounds me.

Music?

It's calming, relaxing me. Not like the screaming of Prodigy. My head is groggy. *Why can't I open my eyes?* I try to move, letting out a moan.

The humming stops.

No, please don't stop.

I groan in frustration as pain engulfs me, making my body shake.

The angelic voice starts to hum again, but I can't understand the words.

"Izzy," a soft voice whispers next to me while the humming continues.

"You're safe. Alex, Rubes, and I are here with you." The soft voice makes my heart fill with happiness.

When I moan, I hear Alexandria gasp, "Santa Maria."

The pain is too much. I can't take the pain. I feel tears sliding down my face.

I'm safe.

I hear a voice singing… *Alexandria.*

They *are* here. I try to move my hand when suddenly small feminine fingers slip into my hand.

"It's me, Rubes. I'm here." I squeeze, hoping my sister will feel it. When I hear her gasp, I know she felt it.

"You're safe. We're all here. No one will hurt you again. I promise."

I moan in response since I can't seem to talk.

Goddamn, the pain is too much. I can't move without knife wrenching pain slashing through me. My head hurts as my subconscious fights with the memories that start flashing back. *The car accident. Gus' head bloody. Blood everywhere.* I'm so overwhelmed. I can't take it.

I don't want to think about any of it. It hurts too much.

Ruby starts to ramble sounding worried, "Izzy, stay with us. You can't leave us girls. Stay with us. Feel us." Several small hands cover me, on my arm, leg, and head. They *are* here. I'm not dreaming.

Suddenly it feels like my head is going to crack as memories start flooding back. I remember everything.

Punch in the face. Being taken and the pain. God, the pain. The man that got shot, the American guy, and Miguel. Oh, God and his fingers. The whistles. Men always watching me. And...

I cry out, squeezing their hands.

Dominic.

Beeping starts up next to me, but all I can think about is the truth about Dominic and what he's done because of me.

Dominic is dead. It's all my fault. They'll blame me. I blame myself.

The beeping gets louder.

Jesus, all the people that are dead because of me. Anxiety fills my chest.

Oh. My. God. It's all because of me.

Tears stream down my face as I cry for everyone that has been killed because of me.

Jason, Austin, and Sasha.

It's too much as pain washes over me.

When I start to gain consciousness, I feel pain spiral down my leg. I hear Ginger whispering, I try to hear what she's saying. "She squeezed our hand, but she seems to be having nightmares and crying out. Alex's humming seems to calm her. When she started to come out of it she panicked, but the humming did the trick. I think she's finally coming around."

Who is she talking to? Frustrated, I groan.

The room goes silent, I hear feet shuffling, and heavy boots move toward me.

Ginger grabs my hand. "Izzy? It's Ginger."

I move my eyes around behind my eyelids. *Please, God.* This time I will be successful, as I try to open my eyes they crack open. Gasps come from all around me.

"That's it, Izzy. I'm right here," Ginger encourages me.

I want to cry, but I need to keep going. When they blink open again, tears escape making everything blurry, so I blink a few more times trying to look in the direction of her voice.

Blurry figures come into focus, but it's too bright.

I hear Ginger crying. "That's it. Open those beautiful eyes."

Suddenly, I smell him. *Gus is here.*

My heart races as I turn my head slightly away from Ginger, taking in a deep breath through my nose.

I hear a chuckle. "It's me, Doll."

Jesus, it's like music to my ears, hearing his husky deep Irish drawl that I love so much. He called me his Doll again. He's here. Tears run down my face, and I blink rapidly trying to focus my eyes. I need to see him.

Gus gently grabs my hand. "Easy Doll. Don't rush it. I'm not going anywhere."

Tears stream down my face as I squeeze Ginger's hand. She returns my squeeze before releasing my hand. "I'm going to go get the doctor and Ruby. She'll kill us both if I don't go get her."

I moan.

Gus moves closer, leaning into me. His freshly showered smell has me coming to life. He's truly here. I blink a few more times to clear my vision. I see his gorgeous emerald eyes staring back at me with tears sliding down his face. I smile.

"Doll. I'm sorry," he says painfully.

What? Why is he sorry. I want to scream at him that none of this is his fault. It's all my fault. I close my eyes letting the pain pass through me. When he clasps my hand, I squeeze back.

He clears his throat. "I can't function without ya. I need ya to come back to me," he says, wiping away his tears.

I open my eyes hoping he can read them and know I love him.

"I'm not," I say with a squeak but stop, needing water.

His eyes light up. "Don't overdo it. Let me get ya some water." He goes to move away, but I panic and squeeze his hand.

He stops. "Aye."

The door swings open and a rush of fresh air flies in along with my best friend. Wild hair is flying all around her face. She looks frantic with Alexandria and Ginger following in on her heels.

I start to cry again, closing my eyes with a smile. I'm going to be okay.

"Fuck me till Tuesday - she's awake," Ruby says with a shaky voice.

Still crying I try to laugh, but it comes out a cough.

"She needs water," Gus says panicked.

"I got it," Alexandria says, moving to the counter.

I open my eyes to see my bestie crying down at me.

I smile, "Hi."

There isn't a dry eye in the room hearing my scratchy voice.

Alexandria walks over teary-eyed, handing Gus water with a straw.

I take a few sips just as the doctor and nurse walk in.

"I see someone has woken up," the doctor says cheerfully.

I close my eyes, fighting off the pain and exhaustion. I don't want to sleep anymore, afraid I'll wake up, and this will all be a dream.

CHAPTER SIXTEEN | IZZY

Ever since I opened my eyes, I've been surrounded by people. My room feels like it has a revolving door with someone new strolling through it all the time. The doctor was the first to question me about what I remember, he was nice, only asking me yes or no questions. I was thankful he didn't ask too much. I think he knew by the panicked look on my face I wasn't ready to relive my ordeal. He explained he needed to ask me these questions to see if I knew where I was and what was going on. He told me about all my injuries. My right arm is in a sling, wrapped securely against my body, my leg is wrapped from being shot, but thank God it was a clean shot going right through me. I think my bruised ribs hurt the most. My right leg is in a cast from the knee down. My head is wrapped as well. I bet I look fucking amazing right now. The doctor increased my pain medicine after telling him I was in unbearable pain.

I haven't said much to anyone, I just smile instead. I feel like every single time I open my eyes someone new is waiting to see me. Everyone is tiptoeing around me, making small talk but no one has questioned me. I don't know what I'm going to tell them. I lean my head back closing my eyes, taking a deep breath.

I wish everyone would leave so I can talk to Gus. I know everyone means well, but right now I just want to be alone. You would think after being captive in the dark that being alone would be the last thing I would want. But with all the people coming in and out and all this attention, it has me anxious and jumpy. I feel like I'm going crazy.

My fear that Miguel or someone is going to take me again has me on edge. The only thing that keeps me calm is seeing Gus. Every time I close my eyes I have flashbacks of Miguel's voice or those damn whistles. I want to talk to Gus so bad, but where do I begin, what do I say to him? I'm at war within my own head about what to tell them. I want to ask so many questions, but I know they will want to ask their own questions and I'm not ready for that. When I think too hard about it, my head starts to hurt, and I become exhausted.

"Doll, you need anything?" Gus asks next to me. I turn my head to look at him, and when our eyes connect, I begin to cry. How am I going to tell him all of this has been because of me?

The room goes silent as I cry. "Why don't we clear the room and give her a few," Gus says to everyone but never breaks eye contact with me.

I hear feet shuffling, along with words of endearment from everyone that I love, but I don't have the courage to look at any of them right now.

"What can I do?" he whispers.

I don't answer. I can't control what I might say, and I'm too scared to tell him yet, so I cry.

"Take a deep breath," Gus says with a soft calming voice, soothing me. I take a deep breath looking up to the ceiling as I try to calm myself down.

"I can't talk about it," I say softly.

"Doll, no one is expecting you to," Gus answers, looking defeated himself.

The door slowly opens as Ruby slides into the room.

I give her a fake smile trying to hide my grief.

"Iz, don't stop crying because I came in. You don't have to be strong for me. I'm here for you," Ruby explains looking concerned.

"I know. I just can't..." I start to sob again as Ruby practically climbs into the bed hugging me.

"We got you," she says choked up as she holds me.

"I don't want to sleep. I'm afraid this will be a dream," I say, scared as my eyes start to get heavy.

"You need to rest. We'll be right here with you," Gus says next to me

As I lay there in my best friend's arms, holding the hand of the man I love, I let sleep consume me, as I pray it's not a dream.

I wake to an all too familiar voice yelling from the hallway. "She is my daughter!"

Fuck! My mother.

My eyes pop open in a panic hearing her voice, just as Ruby bolts from a chair next to me, heading for the door.

"Mrs. Rogers, please calm down," I hear the nurse say when Ruby rushes out the door.

I look around the room, and all the girls are up on their feet. Ginger and Alexandria move to my bedside protectively as Eva stands at the end of the bed.

"Fuck," I blurt out.

They all look to me surprised I spoke when the door flies open and my mother and father enter, along with Ruby, Luc, and Brant.

Shit! This isn't going to be good.

My mother stops dead in her tracks, gasping when she sees me, and my father supports her with a comforting embrace.

Jesus, she's so fucking dramatic. That's my mother for you, always putting on a show.

With her hands to her lips, she whispers, "Isabella, my poor girl."

I don't say anything. I just lie there and stare at her, wishing I didn't have to deal with this shit right now. I lay my head back against the pillow and take a deep breath, closing my eyes for a minute.

"Why was I not notified? I need answers," my mother sneers to someone.

Annnd. There is my mother dearest.

I open my eyes to see her staring daggers at Ruby and Luc.

"Mrs. Rogers," Luc begins but is cut off by my mother as she turns to Ruby.

"Why am I just hearing about her being kidnapped from you *after* she was found?"

Ruby just looks at her, and I know my best friend, she's taking her time responding so she doesn't snap on her. Ruby and my mother have never gotten along.

"You're not on her emergency contact list anywhere. Ruby is the only one that was called and that was after we found out where she was," Luc answers with confidence, not backing down from my mother.

"She *is* my daughter," my mother grits out.

"She *is* an adult," Luc fires back.

I watch Ruby and Luc stand next to each other squaring off with my parents. My father just stands there with his arm around my mother not saying a word.

"Stop," I croak out.

The room goes quiet, and all eyes go to me.

Shit!

I look to Luc and Ruby with apologizing eyes.

"Please, a minute," I say quietly. I need to be alone with them. I don't want them spewing their fake bullshit on anyone else but me.

Ruby reads my mind as always saying, "Let's give them some privacy."

Everyone starts to leave, moving toward the door as my parents move to one side of my bed. Ruby's about to leave when I stop her. "Ruby, stay."

My mother's head snaps to Ruby and then back to me as her face turns red with anger. I'm surprised she doesn't flip out and say something. She has always hated that I've picked Ruby and her family over them. Ruby has always been more family to me than my parents, so I chose her a long time ago after my mother demanded I stop hanging out with her. My mother has hated her ever since.

Once everyone is out of the room, my mother turns her attention back to me as she leans over the bed reaching out to touch my hair, but I flinch away, not wanting to be touched.

"You look terrible. Are you in a lot of pain? How did this happen? Do they know who did it? The police won't tell us anything." She rambles while trying to mess with my hair again.

I pull away again. "Don't. I'll be fine," I say in a dry voice.

Ruby grabs me some water.

My mother stands up straight, and for an instant, I think she is going to cry, but she snaps out of it. "William, I want her moved back home and call—"

I cut her off, "No. I'm not leaving."

My mother whips her head back to me. "You *are* coming home with us. You've had your fun living this DJ dream of yours, but you're coming home."

My head starts to hurt as anger builds inside of me, I take a deep breath.

"No. This is my home," I grit out.

My mother's jaw clenches, but it's my father who finally speaks. "Iz, we're worried about you. We just want to take care of you, baby girl."

I soften to his words, but it doesn't change my mind.

"I'm sorry. I will be—" I stop speaking when the door flies open making everyone turn to see Gus barreling into the room, and he doesn't look happy.

Thank you, God. I smile.

My mother turns back around ignoring Gus surveying the room.

My mother continues, "Isabella, you were kidnapped. I want you to come home so we can take care of you and protect you until we figure out who's behind this," she demands.

I take a deep breath, and before I can reply to her again, Gus speaks up.

"She isn't going anywhere with you. She's mine, and I'll be taking care of her," Gus says as he moves to stand next to Ruby with his hands on his hips.

"She isn't yours and where were you before?" my mom throws back at him.

"Aye, she is, and I will protect her," Gus answers, ignoring her question.

I'm stuck on the — she's mine part. When my eyes connect with Gus', I get emotional as tears pool up in my eyes.

Ruby steps back letting Gus move close to me so he can wipe away the lone tear that escaped.

My father clears his throat breaking our connection.

"Well, I want to be involved with all the details of what happened and what is being done. I want to know our daughter is safe," he says in an authoritative manner.

Gus turns to my parents. "I will fill you both in on everything, and I promise she'll be safe, but she needs to rest, not deal with all this stress, so please come with me, and I'll explain."

Gus leans down, and kissing my forehead, he whispers, "I'll be right back."

As my parents move to follow Gus out the door, I turn to Ruby. "Can we keep everyone but you and Gus out for a bit?" I close my eyes when she says yes and heads for the door, leaving me alone in my room for the first time since I woke up.

I open my eyes and take a big deep breath. *I'm going to be okay.*

CHAPTER SEVENTEEN | GUS

As I'm explaining to Izzy's parents the details of what happened, Ruby exits her room.

"We need to clear everyone out for the day. Izzy wants to rest with no visitors," Ruby says to me while ignoring Izzy's parents.

"I just got here. I'm not leaving. My daughter needs me," Izzy's mom exclaims.

Ruby looks about ready to lose her shit when Izzy's father wraps his arm around her. "She needs to rest. We can come back tomorrow."

I give her father an appreciative look because there is no way in hell I was letting this woman back in there.

"I think our girl has been through enough. We need to let her rest and not bring her any more stress. Yes, come back tomorrow and see how she is feeling," I say in my most polite voice because I need them all to leave. All I'm thinking about is — I will finally have some alone time with my Doll. Her parents weren't very happy, but when the nurse agreed, telling everyone that she needed rest they started to take off.

"Gus?" Ruby says from beside me.

"Yes?" I say, turning away from Izzy's parents.

"I'm going to head over to check on Bella, have dinner and get her ready for bed. I think it would be good for you two to have some alone time," Ruby says, grabbing my forearms affectionately.

I'm so grateful. I pull her in for a hug. "We do, thank you. You should take the night off. You don't need to come back. I'll stay with her. If we need anything, we'll call," I say, pulling back with a smile.

Ruby smiles in return and yells to Ginger to wait up, that she's going to go home with them.

Ruby hurries back into Izzy's room. I'm sure to say goodbye and grab her stuff. The hallway starts to clear out leaving Luc and Shy standing there talking.

As I walk up, they both turn to me looking tired and worn out. I can tell just by looking at them something is wrong.

"What's wrong?" I demand.

Luc as always takes the lead saying, "We've got a problem."

Mother of Christ!

Placing my hands on my hips, I look to the ceiling taking a deep breath.

"We still don't have a lead on who ordered the kidnapping. We're still trying to weed through all the men that were arrested but dealing with the Feds isn't easy. They're not giving up much information. Especially since we didn't include them in our plan until after we were already inside," Luc explains.

I run a hand down my face.

Luc continues, "It's a cluster fuck trying to figure out who's been pulling all the strings. I mean we have four different Mob families in custody but until someone talks, or Izzy tells us—"

I cut them off, "No. We're not pushing her to talk."

Shy speaks up, "Brother, the Feds and police are going to question her tomorrow. We've put them off as long as we can, but now that she's awake they're coming for answers."

Shite.

"Today they were trying to question several of the girls we rescued," Shy explains.

"Did we get anything from them?" I ask, hoping they can go off their statements and give Izzy a few more days.

Luc answers, "No, most of them are so drugged up that they can't remember much."

A whistle comes from down the hall getting our attention. Mac and Quick are standing with Ruby and the girls at the elevator.

Shy nods his head at them before turning to me. "We'll be back tomorrow. If you need anything just call. We'll try to stall the Feds. Just be with your girl. We'll handle things out here."

Another whistle followed by a few, "lets go."

I say goodbye to everyone and head into my Doll's room.

As soon as I have the door half open, I know something is wrong. Izzy's frantically trying to get out of bed.

I rush to her. "Izzy, wat are ya doin'?"

She screams, "He's here. I have to go. Please help me. I have to hide."

I instantly go on alert looking around the room as I make my way in front of her. No one is in the room as I move to stop her from getting up. She's got her left leg off the bed but is struggling to shift her body.

"Izzy, stop this. No one is here to get ya. It's just me." I grab her face making her look up at me.

My heart breaks seeing the fear in her eyes. She's completely petrified.

"Doll, look at me. You're safe," I say in a gentle voice, hoping it will calm her down.

"I heard him. He's here," she repeats herself.

"Who?" I ask.

"Miguel," she cries. "He's here. I heard him whistle to his men," she rambles sounding crazy as her eyes shoot side to side looking around the room.

The nurse rushes in along with Dallas and Brant as alarms are ringing from her pulling off her heart monitor.

"What's going on?" the nurse exclaims followed by Dallas saying, "What the fuck?"

"Help me get her back in bed," I say, lifting her left leg back up onto the bed.

Brant moves to the other side of the bed, but as soon as he touches her, she screams out. The nurse yells at him to move.

"Iz, no one's here but me and ya. Nobody's coming for ya. I won't let anyone take ya again," I say, trying to calm her down, but her body is shaking uncontrollably in fear.

Izzy repeats herself, "He's here. I heard him."

"Who does she hear?" Dallas asks from the end of the bed.

"Do I need to get security?" the nurse asks, looking around the room.

"No, we got this but help me move her so I can hold her," I plead with the nurse.

"Mr. Stone, that isn't a good idea," the nurse starts to say but sees Izzy shake uncontrollably in fear. With her eyes in a daze, she shuts up.

I lay on my side pulling Izzy into my chest. "Shh..." I hum softly, hoping to calm her down.

"He's here," she says in a low sob.

"No one's here. I got ya," I say calmly. It takes everything in my power to keep myself in check while I look over her still body, at my brother's. When Dallas locks eyes with me, I say, "Miguel's not here. They're all gone. He can't hurt ya anymore."

"I heard him whistling," she says choked up, lost in what I'm sure is a horrible memory.

Dallas pulls out his cell phone typing away, and I thank God he didn't leave yet. Hopefully, we can figure out who this Miguel person is. I want to hurt the cocksucker with every fiber in my body.

The fucking cunt will pay. I promise mo chroí.

I snap my head up realizing what she must have heard. Dallas notices my sudden movement leaning forward waiting for me to speak. Instead, I lowered my head placing my lips to her ear and say gently, "Iz...what ya heard was Mac and the boys whistling for Shy to hurry up from down the hall. Doll, I heard it too. It wasn't anyone here to get ya."

I don't know if she heard me, but I lay there holding her until her breathing evens out. Brant motions he's going to leave. We both give him a head nod as Dallas goes back to working on his phone and I keep caressing my girl while humming softly.

I'm wide awake, agitated, trying to keep my shit together but the beast inside is clawing to be released. All I can think about is this motherfucker and that I have so many questions running through my mind.

Is he dead? Do they have him in custody? Did he touch her?

My mind's like a fucking crazed man, with so many questions, but I keep my body relaxed while holding her against me. When her body folded into mine, molding perfectly against me, I knew she was finally in a deep sleep. I didn't want to let her go, but I needed to release some of this tension. I slide out from under her carefully placing her in the middle of the bed, before covering her with blankets.

I turn to Dallas and grumble, "Who the fuck is Miguel?"

CHAPTER EIGHTEEN | IZZY

My eyes jolt open, and I freeze when pain shoots through my shoulder. *Whistling, I was dreaming of Miguel whistling.* I try not to move my body so I don't wake Gus, who's hunched over my bed with his head and arms resting on top of it as he sleeps. Dallas is on my other side sleeping in a chair. *My protectors.*

I lay my head back trying to shake the funny feeling of being watched. I know no one is watching me in this room, and it's just my nerves. Hearing whistles last night sent me over the edge. I can't be taken again.

Dallas shifts next to me in his chair. Neither of them looks very comfortable. Dallas has his cap pulled down low over his eyes with his arms crossed over his chest.

"You gonna keep staring at me?" Dallas says from behind his baseball cap. His voice a low rumble barely audible.

I smile.

"Maybe. Pretty boy," I giggle.

Dallas lifts his head peering out from under his cap. "You good?" he says sounding concerned.

I nod my head.

"You gave us all a scare. Legs, I can't be having you going 5150 on us," he chuckles.

"Sorry," I say apologetically, with a smile. I love hearing them call me by my club nickname.

Dallas unfolds his arms, tilting his hat up showing his boy next door baby face. He clears his throat. "We're not going to let anything happen to you again." I nod my head as tears slide down my face. "He blames himself you know," Dallas says, his voice soft and warm, as he takes his hat off running his hand through his hair before putting it back on.

Before he can say anything else, I say, "He shouldn't. It wasn't his fault."

"I know that, but he doesn't see it that way. I know, for, a fact, he's never going to leave your side. Not for a long time that is," Dallas answers honestly.

I take a deep breath. "This's all because of me," I confess in a whisper.

Dallas leans forward placing his forearms on his knees. "You can't blame yourself either. It's those motherfuckers fault, not yours. But, don't you worry, nothing is going to happen to you again. Redman claimed you as his woman, so you have full protection from the club now. No one will be touching or getting near you without going through a handful of brothers first," Dallas murmurs softly as we both look at Gus sound asleep.

He has no idea how wrong he is, that I really am the reason for all of this. All because I thought some Russian DJ was hot. For a very long time, all I've wanted is this man in front of me to love me. I wonder if I was never taken would he have claimed me that day in the car? I look over to Dallas.

"Thank you for being here. You didn't have to stay. I'm sure your bed is more comfortable than that chair."

Dallas stretches. "Legs, I'm not going anywhere."

Gus' head slips off his arm jolting him awake. He looks from me to Dallas.

"Wat happened? Wat's wrong?" He sits up looking around.

Dallas and I both laugh.

"Good morning sunshine," Dallas teases as he stands up to stretch.

Gus stands up stretching his body before leaning over me, placing a hand on each side of my body. I hold my breath as he gets inches from my face.

"Mornin' Doll," he says with a grin before leaning in the extra few inches giving me a quick kiss on my lips.

Holy. Shit. Fuck.

It happens so fast I don't register what he's done until he's standing back up stretching again.

He just kissed me in front of Dallas.

I smile, lifting my hand to my lips. "Morning."

The boys start to talk about food and coffee while I just sit there staring at my man.

They decide Dallas is going to go get coffee and some food from the cafeteria. Gus sits back down turning his attention back to me. I'm still in shock from the public show of affection.

"Wat's wrong?" Gus asks, leaning on his forearms on my bed.

"You just kissed me in front of someone," I answer, sounding shocked.

"Is that a problem?" Gus questions with a smirk.

"Gus, I don't know what's happening. We never had our talk, and with everything that happened, I just don't know what to think," I blurt out in a rant.

Gus stares at me for a minute, and you can see he's amused by this little discussion.

"Doll, *yer me one*. Nothing's going to take ya away from me again," he explains while moving to lean over me, placing his face inches from mine.

"It's y –o –u and me, together. We can have that little talk later, but I'm not holding back anymore. *You're* mine now," Gus breathes out softly.

My insides start to do flips with excitement. He wants me even after all this has happened.

He doesn't know it was all because of me though.

"Where ya at?" Gus says, lifting a hand pushing my hair over my shoulder. "Your eyes are telling me that you're thinking about something bad. Ah, stop," he demands.

Tears pool in my eyes. The song "Say Something" by Justin Timberlake and Chris Stapleton starts to play on repeat in my head.

Say something. Tell him. Say something.

"I want you too," I croak out.

Gus' smile gets wide as he leans in placing a soft kiss on my lips once more. It's so fast. I want to cherish his lips but realize I need a shower. Desperately.

"I look like hell. I need a shower and toothbrush," I blurt out as he leans back laughing.

I smile at him and just as I'm about to say something the door swings open and in walks Luc followed by four agents.

Fucking Great.

Gus gets defensive right away. "Wat's this all about?"

"Gus, they need to ask Izzy some questions. They have some photos they want her to look at."

I watch as three male agents stand back as a woman agent steps forward.

"Ms. Rogers, my name is Agent Marquez. I'm very sorry to be bothering you, but we really need to talk to you about what happened."

I start to panic.

"Izzy, since you were taken we've been working with these agents. They've arrested eight men. They need for you to look at these men and see if you recognize any of them," Luc says calmly, letting me know they're good people.

"I didn't see anyone. They had me blindfolded most of the time," I blurt out.

The woman steps even closer to the bed. "Ms. Rogers."

"Please, call me Izzy. When you call me Ms. Rogers, I think of my mother," I say with a grimace.

She smiles. "Of course. Izzy, I know it will be hard for you to talk about this but the more you can remember the more it will help us lock these men away."

Say something. Tell them the whole story. Of course, that song "Say Something" starts playing in my head *again,* distracting me.

One of the male agents moves to stand next to Agent Marquez.

"Hi Izzy, my name is Agent Hernandez. I've been tracking these men for a couple of years. It's a huge break in our case when we found so many of them in one place. The more information we can get from everyone the better case we can build against them."

Gus moves next to me reaching for my hand.

I close my eyes, using his strength to help me move forward.

They're going to find out about Dominic. That it was all your fault.

Even though my mind tells me to confess I can't do it. I can't tell them everything. "Like I said. I was blindfolded. There was only one man they left with me twenty-four seven. His name was Miguel. He showed me his face the day of the auction, but he was the only one I saw besides the women. I only heard voices. If I heard them again, I would be able to recognize them but faces I can't help you," I explain, hoping they don't keep digging.

The agents huddle together looking through some paperwork in one of the agent's hands.

Agent Marquez moves toward me but stops. "Izzy, is it okay if I show you some pictures? See if any of them are this Miguel person you saw?"

I nod my head as she moves slowly toward me handing me the pictures. I only have one hand, so Gus takes them from her showing me the photos one at a time. I don't recognize any of them except one, and it isn't Miguel. It's one of Dominic's friends. I try to stay calm.

"I know him from my ex-boyfriend Dominic, but I don't know his name," I say, pointing to the picture.

The agents all look over at the photo, and Agent Marquez explains, "That is Kirill Petrov, son of Vladik Petrov, Pakhan of the Bratva."

"*Madre stronzo,*" Luc blurts out, crossing his arms over his chest, lifting a hand to his face as he turns away from us.

The agents don't react. Instead, they all keep their eyes trained on me.

"What? I don't understand?" I hide the panic that is pumping through my veins.

They know! Say something. Tell them what you know.

One of the male agents who hasn't introduced himself says, "None of these men are the man you call Miguel? What were their voices like? Can you describe them to us?"

"The man they called Bossman had a weird accent. Then there was the American man. An Italian man and a Russian man." I pause. Closing my eyes, I fight within myself to say Dominic's name, but I don't. I can't.

When I open my eyes, everyone is still staring at me, waiting for me to continue. "Then there was Miguel who was with me every day all day, he spoke Spanish with broken English or he would…" I pause looking up to Gus for support. When he gives me a supportive smile, I say still looking at Gus, "Or he would whistle to his men."

It's Agent Marquez who speaks first, "You say whistle? What do you mean?"

I turn to face her. "Miguel would whistle to someone but it wasn't any of the other men that came to see me. It was someone who was always with him but never spoke. There could have been two men, but I don't know. They only communicated by whistling or Miguel would speak in Spanish."

Tears start to pool up, and I look down to my lap trying to gain control.

"Ms. Rogers. I mean Izzy. I'm Agent Thompson." The man that's been standing in the back not saying anything moves forward with a stack of papers in his hands.

I peer up at him when he slips three more photos onto my lap. "I think these are the men you're referring to."

I gasp when I see Miguel staring back at me.

I point to Miguel's face as tears fall from my eyes and say, "That's Miguel."

Gus and Luc are at my side looking down, both cursing in their native tongue.

Agent Thompson speaks, "These are the Sanchez brothers." Pointing to them he says their names, "Miguel is the oldest and their leader. These two are his younger twin brothers, Jesus and Julio. Neither of them speaks." I have my hand covering my mouth to hold in my sobs.

He continues, "They're wanted everywhere and are on the top five most wanted list. The twins are known for snatching girls while Miguel subdues them, breaking them down before selling them off to the highest bidder. They're contracted and work for almost all the Mafia families."

Gus speaks up, "Why *dinna ye* show her these in the first place?"

Agent Thompson looks from me to Gus, "Because we don't have them in custody."

Terror rips through me as I cry out, "No!"

Agent Marquez speaks up, "Jesus was found shot dead at the warehouse, but these two are still at large." She points to Miguel and his other brother.

Luc snaps, "Well who the fuck do you have in custody?"

Agent Hernandez moves next to Luc and lays the photos on the bed naming the men.

"Kirill Petrov and two of his men. This guy they call Mighty Mike who I'm assuming is the American you heard. He's a big-time American smuggler. We've been after this guy for some time now, he has too many AKAs to list, but you know him as Bossman. These three men are linked to the Luciano family. Six men were found dead, all linked to some crime family, but no one important. We recovered fifteen girls alive, and five were found dead. The sting was the biggest we've had in years. Luckily we were able to recover some of the data from the computers and surveillance videos. We don't have much on Kirill besides being there, but the Bossman we're hoping to put away for a long time."

I'm stuck on the word surveillance.

Were they watching us? Will they see what they did to me? Oh, God, they'll know I'm not telling them everything.

I start to freak out.

"Izzy? Doll wat's wrong?" Gus leans down grabbing my hand.

"Kirill will be released?" I rasp out in a panic.

Agent Marquez speaks up, "Izzy unless you can tell us something linking any of these men to what happened to you then we can't keep them. The Bossman is the only one we have stuff on. With all the data and reports from Sergeant Andrea Mills, we're confident that we have enough to put Bossman behind bars."

Gus and I both say, "Sergeant Andrea Mills?"

Agent Marquez laughs. "You know her as Ghost. She's the woman that saved your life. She was sent in undercover to get you."

I look toward Luc, but he looks as shocked as I do. "She's an enigma to me. I knew her name was Andy, but like everyone else, we don't call her that unless you want to be hurt, so hearing she's a sergeant surprises me."

Agent Marquez laughs again. "Yes, she is one tough cookie. Luckily we know everything about everyone."

Everyone goes quiet for a few minutes, lost in their own thoughts, I'm trying to hold it together, but the terror consumes me, and I break, blurting out, "What happens if Miguel or Kirill come after me for revenge? What is being done to keep me safe?"

Gus moves to grab my hand. "Ah, one thing's for sure, I'm not leaving your side."

Luc chimes in, "I've increased my security around the girls. They'll be safe."

Agent Thompson lifts his hand before speaking, "Izzy, you and the girls are pawns in this game of chess. They will, and probably already have, forgotten about you. Nothing is linked to you. They wouldn't have any reason to come after you. It wasn't your fault they were arrested or killed."

Yes! Yes, I was! This is all because of me.

I stare at the agent and begin to cry, which I'm sure they are thinking is from relief, but I'm crying because no one knows the truth. I'm still in danger. Miguel is coming for me. I know it, I can feel it down to my bones.

"I have one question for you," Gus speaks up. "Who gave the order to kidnap Izzy? She doesn't fit the profile."

Agent Thompson looks at me as tears continue to stream down my face. "Do you know where your ex-boyfriend Dominic is, or have you heard from him?"

Both Luc and Gus swear again in their native tongue.

I shake my head and cry even harder. I can't say the words because they'll be a lie.

Agent Thompson states, "Well I think we all need to start by finding him. We already have agents looking for him."

He's dead! Say it!

The men nod their heads, but I drop my head and cry.

Agent Marquez says softly, "Izzy, thank you for speaking to us. I'm going to leave my card here with you and please don't hesitate to call me if you remember anything or need anything."

I lift my head taking the card from her and nod to the other agents as they leave.

I'm so fucked. I need to tell them. I need to tell Luc and Gus.

They'll be coming for me.

CHAPTER NINETEEN | GUS

I kiss Izzy on the lips telling her I'm going to walk them out and I'll be right back. Dallas should be back any minute with our food. She's too dazed in her own thoughts to even care, as she just nods her head.

I walk out the door and find Luc speaking to the agents in the hall. When they see me walk up, I know they're thinking the same thing I am — Izzy's hiding something.

"Sorry Gus for coming without warning but they thought it would be best just to show up, rather than prepare her," Luc says apologetically.

"I understand," I say to Luc but turn my attention to the agents. "So wat are ya not tellin' us?"

Agent Marquez smiles. "Well actually Mr. Stone, it's the other way around."

I get defensive, folding my arms over my chest. "I'm not hiding *shite* from *ye.*"

"No, you're not, but your girl is. Something happened in that warehouse, and she doesn't want to tell us," Agent Marquez says sounding worried.

Yeah, I caught that too. I confess to myself knowing they're right.

"It could be something, it could be nothing, but until we know, we can't help her. I know she went through some hard shit mentally and physically, but whatever she's hiding we need to know," Agent Thompson explains.

"Aye."

"Lucas, when was the last time you heard from her ex Dominic Malitzki?" Agent Thompson asks.

"It was a few weeks ago. I called him when Izzy was taken to see if he heard from her or anyone, but he never answered or called back. He's in Russia, hiding from his court dates most likely. I cut him from my roster and label. We had too many issues with him and fighting. When he started getting all *fuckin' pazzo* over Izzy we just couldn't take the liability. After his fight in LA, he went back home. He returned a couple of times but ended up in jail again for harassing Izzy. Why? Do ya think he has something to do with this? He wouldn't have her kidnapped and sold. He's *fuckin' pazzo* enough to take her and keep her for himself, but sell her - no fuckin' way," Luc exclaims.

I growl as rage ignites inside me just thinking of that cunt trying to hurt Izzy.

The agents look from one another like they want to tell us something but can't. I'm about ready to explode. "Wat are ya not tellin' us? We've been honest and straight forward with y'all," I demand.

"This is completely confidential, but we think you should know. Malitzki isn't Dominic's real last name," Agent Thompson reveals.

"Whaddaya mean it's not his real last name? I've done extensive background checks on all my DJs," Luc says sounding irritated.

Agent Thompson answers, "He was born Dominic Petrov, Jr."

"The fuck ya say?" Luc exclaims.

Mother of Christ!

I turn to look at Izzy's door seeing Dallas standing outside it with food talking to a nurse. Izzy's in danger, I can feel it to my core.

Agent Marquez says softly, "Lucas, you need to stay calm. When Dominic's father was murdered, Dominic was very young. Dominic Sr. was the head of the Russian Bratva at the time. When he was murdered Vladik, his younger brother, took over as Pakhan. He moved Dominic and his mother to the States and changed their names, giving them new identities to keep them safe with a fresh new start. We believe that Dominic has been running things here in New York silently with his cousin Kirill Petrov. No one has proof because Dominic is clean, never going near the business."

"Madre stronzo," Luc says, throwing his hand up in the air, turning around and gripping the back of his neck.

"It's been that cunt all along? With Alexandria and Emmett? So, he was the other person working with Emmett? Jaysus Christ," I say starting to put things together.

"We believe so, but again Dominic is squeaky clean, and Izzy was always his alibi. At first, we thought she was in on it or knew about it, but we've been watching and can see she was trying to get away from him for a long time. But now, we know she's hiding something. Maybe she knows where he is and just doesn't want to say?"

Luc's face turns red as he raises his hand pointing toward the agent, saying, "Maggie, ya've known this for how long *an* didn't tell me?" He pauses, placing his hands on his hips. "I've *always* helped ya..." Luc turns to the other men pointing his finger. "I've been good to all four of ya. How could ya keep something like this from me?" Luc looks furiously at Agent Marquez like he's been crushed by her actions.

Maggie? Sweet Jaysus he's on a first name basis with her. What the fuck?

Irritated, I rant, *"Fuck off - ye* know she had *nothin'* to do with that *shite*. The arsehole cunt wouldn't let her break up with him. He threatened her, put his cunt hands on her. That's when I stepped in, after the incident in LA." Defending her and completely ignoring Luc's plea to *Maggie*.

All the agents nod their heads, but it's Agent Marquez who takes point again and speaks, "Yes, we know. Izzy is innocent in all of this, but we're wondering if maybe someone is using her to get to Dominic. We haven't figured it out yet either but what we do know is she needs to have security around the clock until we can find Dominic. This little conversation never happened. No one can know about Dominic's true identity. Kirill denies he knows Dominic and he'll be out soon with his lawyers up our asses. We need Izzy to talk."

"Aye," I agree.

Luc's still standing there staring daggers toward Agent Marquez. He's definitely fuming. "What about the Luciano boys? Are you going to let them go? Or are you keeping something else from us? You know the Luciano boys wouldn't have been there if I didn't ask them to get Ghost in. I'm sorry, *Sergeant* Andrea Mills!"

Mother of Christ. Luc's fuckin' fuming.

Agent Marquez answers him, "We're still holding them for their protection and ours. We can't seem like we knew about your deal, so we're questioning them just like the rest of them. *And* we can't let them go too soon, or the other families will question it. They'll be released in due time though - you have my word like I said from the beginning. They don't know we're working together. Everyone is staying protected."

"Except *me one*," I blurt.

Luc adds, "And *Sergeant* Mills."

No one says anything as the agents stare at us.

"I need to get back in there," I say, turning toward Izzy's door.

Luc calls out, "I'll be in touch later."

I give Luc a nod before heading to the room. When I'm at the door, I hear a little girl squeal from down the hall. I turn to see Quick tossing a little girl in the air and catching her, making her squeal with laughter. Ruby is a few feet in front of them, looking straight at me. I smile, lifting my finger for her to wait a minute.

I peer inside seeing her sitting there with Dallas laughing and eating a bagel. Knowing the coast is clear, I pop my head back out giving Ruby the go-ahead to bring Bella in to see her. I walk to my chair next to Izzy, and I smile. "There's a big surprise coming in." I pause for the door to swing open and when it does, we hear Bella yell, "An-tee Iz. Qwak, put me down. I want my An-tee," laughing and pushing off Quick, who's holding her tight.

Izzy's face lights up as soon as she sees Bella. "Bella bug!" she says cheerful and bubbly.

Quick sets her down on the bed so Bella can hug her An-tee. Izzy's crying as she hugs her.

"An-tee are you okay? I've been worried. Mama said I couldn't come see you," Bella says sounding sad.

"I'm okay Bug. Mama was right — I couldn't see anyone for a while, but I'm better now," Izzy explains to the little girl.

While Izzy and Bella start talking about how Bella likes it here, I make eye contact with my brothers letting them know I need to talk. I tell Izzy we're going to give them some time together, and we'll be right outside the door. Izzy gives me a worried look but hides it when Bella starts pulling on her hair.

Once we're out of the room, Dallas and Quick become serious. "What's going on?" Quick questions.

"I saw you with the Feds. Did they question Iz? Luc looked like he wanted to murder someone," Dallas says, folding his arms over his chest and leaning against the wall.

I look around the hall and only see a nurse at the nursing station.

"We've got some major fuckin' problems, and we need to get the lot of us together at the clubhouse. Izzy and the girls aren't safe. We need to talk to Wolfe," I explain to my brothers and with each word that comes out of my mouth their demeanor changes.

"I've got Bella and Ruby with me. Will they be safe here? Are they in danger?" Quick demands.

"The girls will be safe here. This meeting needs to happen- like now. I'm gonna call Shy," I explain, grabbing my phone.

"I'll head over to the clubhouse and send a couple of prospects back over here to stand watch," Dallas says but I don't answer him when Shy answers his phone.

"What up, brother? How's your ol' lady doing today?" Shy asks sounding chipper.

"We've got a fuckin' problem. Like a big motherfuckin' problem. Call Wolfe in, yeah? We need all of us to meet," I seethe through the phone.

"You good now or do you need people?" Shy asks, switching from happy to all business.

"Dallas and Quick are with me. Need eyes on the girls, can ya get'em all here? We needs eyes on them while we meet. The boys also need to be there. *Shite* just got dropped in our laps that's gonna rock us all. We need all our forces working together again," I say, letting him know Luc and Maddox will need to have their crew at this meeting too.

"Got it. I'll make the calls. I'll send Alex and Snow your way with Mac and a couple prospects. You and the boys can drive back with Mac. Give me thirty."

We don't even say goodbye before hanging up.

"Dallas, call Maddox. Get'em and his boys to the clubhouse. Everyone has thirty minutes," I bark orders turning to Quick. "Is Ghost still here or was she released yesterday? Do ya know where she is? I need ya to find her if she's still here or call Brant to find her."

Quick nods, taking off in the direction of Ghost's room as he pulls out his phone. Dallas is already on the phone with someone when I pull my phone out and call Luc. "Have ye informed Beau yet?" I ask without even saying hello.

"I'm on my way right now," Luc answers sounding defeated.

"Get him and all our boys that we trust to the clubhouse. We need to let everyone know. We need to be ready and figure this fuckin' *shite* out, *cos*, all the pieces are finally coming together," I explain.

"Yah," he says in a really low voice.

"Luc, it's not *yer* fault for not knowing. We were all fooled by that fuckin' cunt. No one could have known who he was. All we can do is prepare. I have all the girls coming here. We're gonna put some prospects on them while we meet. Get Beau and the boys, meet ya in thirty."

"*Yah*, thirty minutes," Luc says before he hangs up.

As I stand there, I try to relax before I head back in there. I don't want Izzy to see me upset. Whatever she's hiding I'll deal with later, right now her safety is my number one mission.

My phone rings just as I'm about to head into the room. I see it's Brant, so I step back into the hall. "How's it going?"

"What the fuck's going on?" Brant barrels through the phone.

"Meeting at the clubhouse in thirty minutes," I say sounding irritated.

"Why are you looking for Ghost?" Brant questions me.

"Are ya with her?" I fire back not caring how I come across.

"Yah, we're in her room," he says in a low voice.

"Do ya know about her?" I blurt out.

"What the fuck do you mean, know about her?" he barks into the phone.

"Like her full fuckin' name B." I raise my voice getting heated with him.

"What the fuck do you mean?" I hear him from behind me. I swivel around seeing him march toward me while hanging up his phone.

I don't care who's around, I blurt out, "*D'ye* know she was Sergeant Andrea Mills? Who does she really work for?"

The look on his face tells me he didn't know either. I fold my arms across my chest. "Exactly. Wat do we really know about the lass, besides she's a badass who saves our women? Is she working for the Feds or someone else? How does Maddox know her? We need answers."

Brant's still shocked. "Sergeant?"

"That isn't even the biggest problem we have. It gets worse - believe me." I lower my voice trying to tame the beast inside me that wants to rip Dominic's heart out for bringing all this shit to our doorstep.

"Sonovabitch," Brant breaths out.

"Get *ya shite* together. We meet at the clubhouse in thirty. Shit's gonna hit the fan, and you're not gonna be happy. Luc took it pretty hard, but I'm sure you're gonna feel just as bad as I do." I try to relay how bad it's going to get.

"Gus, man, just tell me so I can get myself together before I have to deal with everyone else flipping out." Brant looks worried.

"Dominic Militzki's real name is Dominic Petrov, Jr. He's been lying to us this whole time," I blurt.

"Motherfucker," Brant snaps.

"Exactly."

CHAPTER TWENTY | GUS

An hour later I'm standing in our clubhouse office that's full of men waiting for me to speak. I've never been much of a group speaker. I've always been the one in the back planning everything but not today. Today, I'm about ready to tell them some earth-shattering news.

Everyone's seated around the tables, staring at me. I clear my throat. "This morning Luc and four federal agents came to see Izzy. They wanted to ask her questions about wat happened. Izzy explained she didn't see any of them except one man, and his name is Miguel. He's the motherfucker who took care of her twenty-four seven.

"The agents pulled out headshots for her to look at, asking if any of them were the fucker. She said none of the pictures were of Miguel but pointed to this picture, saying she'd seen him before."

I pull the mug shot out taping it up on the wall before continuing. "Now most of you were there with us when we raided the place and might recognize these men, but now you'll have a name to go with it. Izzy pointed this man out. His name is Kirill Petrov, son of Valdik Petrov, Pakhan of the Russian Bratva. She explained she knew him as one of her ex-boyfriend's friends but didn't know his name."

The room starts to get antsy with a little bit of chatter, but I continue. "The agents then asked her to describe what the men sounded like who were coming and going. She started with the man they call Bossman." I pull out another mug shot and tape it onto the wall. "This man orchestrated the auction. He's also known as the gatekeeper. He's one of the fuckers that the Feds want to take down. He's in custody, along with..." I turn to the wall and start putting a group of mug shots up as I name the men. "Izzy went on to describe an American man - who's known as Mighty Mike, an American smuggler. The Russian man she spoke of, we know now, was Kirill."

The room starts to get louder as the men discuss what they saw that day, but I ignore them, needing to get this out so we can discuss it, so I continue, "When she was describing Miguel, she said he whistles to his men and spoke Spanish. The agent then pulled out these three photos." I pause, taping three more mug shots up.

"I think I shot that fucker," Mac yells from the back.

I laugh, but continue, "These are the Sanchez brothers, they're on the top five most wanted list, across the world. When I asked the agents why they just *dinna* show her these first, their reply was 'they *dinna* have them in custody.' Izzy lost her *shite* hearing they're still at large. Miguel"—I point to his picture— "He's the oldest and leader of the brothers. These are his younger, twin brothers that don't speak. This one" —I point to Jesus— "Is dead." The room becomes noisy with all the men talking amongst themselves.

"I told you I killed the fucker," Mac laughs.

"Quiet. Let Redman finish so we can discuss this," Shy yells out to the room of men silencing them.

I continue, "Before the agents left, I asked them if they knew who put in the order to take Izzy. They looked at Izzy and asked her if she had been in contact with her ex-boyfriend Dominic. She shook her head no. The agents told us we needed to find him *cos* he was the only link they could find to all these men. The agents then told us that with Ghost's statement of events that they'll be able to put Bossman away but Kirill will most likely be let go. Again, Izzy lost her shit. Two of the men that had her are going to be released." I pause a second before continuing.

"Now after the agents were done talking to Izzy, Luc and

myself followed them to the hall to ask them a few questions. I knew they weren't telling us something and I wanted to know what it was." I paused taking a deep breath and look over at Shy.

"This man" —I pull out a mug shot of Dominic— "most of us know him as Dominic Malitzki, but it seems his real name is Dominic Petrov, Jr."

Shouts and cussing erupt across the room. Shy starts pacing and I know his brain is putting it all together.

I yell above everyone. "Dominic's father, Dominic Sr., was the Pakhan until he was murdered. Dominic Jr. was very young when it happened. Dominic Sr.'s younger brother, Vladik, took over after he died and sent Dominic and his mother to the States for their protection, with new identities."

"Goddamn," Beau blurts out. I stop moving around to face the men around the room.

"Seems the Feds have been watching Dominic for a while now, but he was squeaky clean. They think he was involved with helping Emmett traffic those girls and possibly helping kidnap Alexandria."

"Why would he help kidnap Alexandria when he was with Izzy? It doesn't match up," Chad questions.

"I don't think he helped plan Alexandria. Nah, that was all Emmett's psycho ass and not wanting anyone else to have her. I'm talking about the other girls they found at the warehouse. I think Dominic picks people like Emmett who he knows will run under the radar. They pull the girls in, and then Kirill takes over. Dominic was a successful DJ who traveled the world DJing at huge clubs where girls were a dime a dozen."

Everyone nodded their heads agreeing.

"No one in the Russian Bratva, including his own cousin, will acknowledge him to keep his identity safe. The Feds think he's one of the main men here in the States working side by side with his cousin. This has all been theory until recent. If the Feds *dinna* tell us about Dominic, none of us would have thought he would do this. Shit none of us ever would have thought Emmett was behind Alex's stuff. I think Emmett and Dominic falling in love with the girls is wat fucked their plans up."

I pause letting everyone catch up.

"We can't prove any of this, but I think Dominic was involved with everything that went down with Snow too. He was there and knew where we were going to be. Again, we just got this intel a little over an hour ago, but I have a feeling once we start researching we'll be able to put all the pieces together," I said, folding my arms over my chest.

"Do you think Sasha is linked to this as well?" Brant asks from the back of the room.

"As I said, brother, we need to regroup and look at these incidents in a whole new way. I think Emmett going psycho over Alex started the downward spiral for their business. Dominic's obsession with Izzy and getting himself thrown in jail put a big wrench in the plan, slowing down business. We can't ask Snake if he was working with the Russians now can we?" I paused turning to look at all the mug shots on the wall.

Someone asks from behind me, "So you think Snake was working with Dominic?"

"It had to be either Dom or someone that wanted paybacks, so they paid the MC to go after Ginger. Remember the letters? They all mentioned the same thing, that she took something from them," I answer.

Shy moves to stand next to me looking at the wall, he adds, "But what did Ginger take?"

Maddox chimes in moving to the front as well. "The girls from the warehouse? Emmett? Maybe, for her interfering - shit, really for all of us interfering with their business? Maybe, Dominic wanted payback?"

"But then who ordered the kidnapping of Izzy? If anything, Dominic would have taken Izzy for himself not to sell her off," I say, looking at Dominic's mug shot, wishing I could figure it out.

Dallas pipes up from the back of the room. "Or maybe Dominic's family is trying to teach him a lesson? You said Kirill was at the auction - maybe it was him?"

I turn around to face everyone. "Well no matter wat, someone's using our girls. Someone paid Miguel to snatch Izzy and sell her off. We need to find Dominic or Miguel to put all the pieces together. None of our girls are safe with these men out there." I point to Miguel, Kirill, and Dominic.

"Don't forget Sasha. We need to find her as well. I have a feeling she might know something. It's too coincidental she went missing the same weekend of Dominic's arrest and Austin getting killed," Brant yells, expressing his frustration.

Sasha going missing has really fucked him up.

"What a motherfucking cluster fuck," Beau states as the room erupts.

"What else you got?" Shy asks, leaning back in his chair.

Luc, Maddox, and Brant file into Shy's office closing the door.

"What's going on, Redman?" Maddox asks, taking a seat across from Shy, next to Brant, who's plopped in the chair looking defeated.

Luc looks just as defeated leaning against the door. I guess it's me leading this conversation too.

"The agents also informed us of some other information we *dinna* know," I say matter-of-fact.

"Motherfucker. Are you serious? What else could there be?" Shy asks, pinching the bridge of his nose.

I turn to Maddox. "Madd, how well do ya know Ghost?"

Maddox tenses but answers right away, "I've known her a long time. Why?"

"Do you know wat her real name is or any background information on her?" I ask while everyone else in the room looks to Maddox.

"Of course I do. She's a Ghost. What's all this about?" Maddox sits up looking irritated.

"Well, none of us in this room really know anything about her, except she's saved two of our girls," I say in a calm voice hoping to calm him down.

"I've known her for many years - enough to know she's loyal. Again, what's all this about Redman?" Maddox fires back.

Exhausted I blurt out, "The Feds told us today Sergeant Andrea Mills gave them data and a full report."

Maddox doesn't flinch nor does he seem to be alarmed by this, "And? What's wrong?"

"She's a sergeant? Giving full reports?" Brant rants, sounding hurt for not knowing himself.

Maddox turns to Brant. "She used to be a sergeant in the Army before she started working for me as a Ghost. And" —he turns to Luc— "You have your men give full reports all the time of what their shifts were like. I don't understand what the problem is or what you're trying to figure out here."

"I guess we're just surprised and felt the Feds were trying to tell us something like she's an informant of some kind. We don't know anything about her. We're just trying to make sure one of us knows everything about her. That's all," Luc states softly.

"I know everything there is to know about her. She's a very private person and for a good reason. I trust you three, so I'll tell you what you need to know to feel secure that she would die for any one of us and is in no way an informant.

"She went into the Army at eighteen, became a sergeant at twenty-one, left the Army at twenty-seven. I've known her since she was about sixteen. She doesn't let anyone" —Maddox looks over to Brant— "and I mean anyone, close to her and again for a good reason."

"She saw Chad for a bit, but he started to get too close. So she disappeared for months until I texted her to let her know what was happening with Alexandria. She's loyal to a fault and if any of you question her motives - don't, it won't be pretty. She's off limits, so no digging or researching her," Maddox says sternly.

Everyone in the room is silent.

"Well, at least we know where she learned her mad skills. I trust her, and I don't care if she's a Ghost or Motherfuckin' Teresa. She saved my Angel and went above and beyond to save Izzy. Her personal information is safe with me," Shy says, leaning back in his chair with a smile.

"She's a lethal lass that's for sure. Thank ya, Madd Dog for letting us know. I'm just freaking out and want to cover all my bases. Sorry, brother," I say in an apologetic voice, feeling stupid for thinking she would have been working against us.

"I understand Redman. Thank you for not mentioning it out there. Andy's very private, and if she found out everyone knows her past, she'd bolt," Maddox exclaims.

"I just can't believe that tiny ass woman is or was a sergeant. I was in awe of her before, but goddamn, now I'm even more fucking impressed. She's one bad ass bitch!" Shy laughs.

"You have no idea. The things I've seen her do have shocked the fuck out of me," Maddox laughs.

"I'm outta here. I'm headed back to the hospital. I've gotta pick her up," Brant blurts out.

"Where are you taking her?" Maddox asks protectively.

"She's going to stay with me until she heals," Brant replies, standing up.

Maddox laughs, "Does she know this?"

Brant says over his shoulder heading out the door, "No, but she will when I get there. She's in just as much danger as the other girls."

"She's the last person that needs protection. I feel sorry for whoever tries to take her out. Ghost will kill the motherfucker," Shy laughs.

"I've got to see this," I say, following Brant out the door. "B, wait up. I'm going to get a lift with you."

"Fuck, I guess we're all headed back to the hospital because I need to see this for myself too," Maddox calls out after us, laughing.

"Can we put a wager on it? Who thinks he'll talk her into staying with him and who thinks she'll kick his ass?" Shy calls out to the room catching the other men's attention.

"I'm up for a bet. What're we betting on?" Dallas says, walking up.

"Fuck you guys. I'm outta here," Brant laughs, yelling over his shoulder.

"Takin' bets on B getting Ghost to stay with him while she heals or kickin' his ass," Shy laughs.

"My money's on her kickin' his arse," I say over my shoulder to the men as I follow Brant out the door laughing.

CHAPTER TWENTY ONE | IZZY

It's been a little over a month since I was released from the hospital. My life has been completely uprooted and turned upside down. My parents, along with everyone else, decided I needed to move. So, I gave notice at my apartment and I've moved into Luc's building where there is more security. Gus told me I either moved in with him or I took one of the suites Luc had available.

I didn't fight them because, to be honest - I didn't want to be alone anymore. I didn't want any memories of Dominic. Ruby and I had been discussing getting a place together, and Luc explained he wanted all of us girls under his roof for protection. And, they've beefed up the security, making it a fortress, not that it wasn't before, but he hired more men.

It makes sense with Gus living there and all my friends. It's been overwhelming. Especially since my parents were in town to make sure I got settled, which just drove me crazy. They finally went back home yesterday. My father said he needed to get back to work.

Ruby has taken charge of everything for me. She's handled the rescheduling of my events at clubs, answered all my messages and emails. She and the girls packed up most of my belongings that I didn't want the moving service to handle. Since I couldn't really move around well with my injuries and of course my leg in a cast, I've been hanging out with my Bella Bug while the girls did most of the work. Having Ruby and Bella here every day has been a blessing.

Bella is such a breath of fresh air. I love having her around because it keeps people from hovering around me, asking me how

I'm doing or looking at me like I'm going to break. Instead, we play with babies, color or have imaginary princess tea parties. I don't have to think or feel anything around her except being happy.

Gus has been so loving and comforting, but I can tell he's holding something back, or at least that's how I feel. I'm sure it's all in my own head. Lately, I'm in my head *a lot*, over-analyzing everything, worrying too much, panicking over nothing, all because of what's going through my head.

Gus has been working endless hours during the day with the club or with the security team trying to figure things out. He doesn't talk about it, and I'm sure it's because he doesn't want to upset me. But every night he's here with me, he hasn't really touched me romantically besides giving me a kiss.

We haven't discussed what happened to me either. He tells me when I'm ready, he's here for me. He holds me at night and soothes me when I have a nightmare. I battle in my head every day about telling them what I know. I tell myself if they bring up Dominic again, I'll tell them. But the longer I go without saying anything, the more I think telling them will only make things worse.

Since the Feds came to my room, no one has mentioned anything. I've become quieter, not talking as much unless I'm with Bella.

I've been out in public three times and each time I've almost had full-blown panic attacks. Leaving the hospital heading to my old place, I felt like someone was watching me. I keep hearing Miguel's voice in my head saying how he used to watch me, that I was like an Energizer Bunny.

Gus tried to comfort me, telling me that I was safe. I wouldn't let Ruby, Bella or any of the girls drive with me in the car. I was too scared to have them near me in public. I didn't want anything to happen to them if someone came after me.

The second time I was in public was when we went from my old place to my new one. Again, I made the girls leave before me, and I rode with the boys. That time I wasn't as panicked, just a bit jumpy being surrounded by so many people. I feel so vulnerable now in public like anyone can get to me.

Miguel can get to me. He was always watching me.

When I think of Miguel, I start to shake, panicking, but Gus is always here with me, reassuring me I'm safe.

The third time was yesterday when I had a doctors appointment. On my way to the car after the appointment, I heard whistling, and I completely lost it. I started crying, yelling at Gus that Miguel was here. Everyone went on alert looking around for the threat, but Gus heard the whistles and found someone whistling at their dog.

Gus had to pick me up and carry me to the car with the men surrounding us. I couldn't stop crying, ranting that Miguel was going to get me. When we got back to our building, Gus carried me to my place, taking me to my room. I was hysterical. Ruby and Bella tried to come in, but I told Gus no, I wanted to be alone with him.

It took him a few hours to calm me down enough to fall asleep. When I wake up, it's dark. He's sound asleep, shirtless, holding me securely against him. He still has a firm hold on me. I start to cry silently, but this time it was because of how much I love this man. *My protector*. It is at that moment I promised myself I will tell him everything. I start thinking about everything I need to tell him when exhaustion takes over. I feel better knowing I have a plan before I fall asleep.

The next morning as soon as I open my eyes, I feel the emptiness. Gus isn't in bed with me anymore. My heart aches with his absence. I know I need to tell him. As I start to get up, my bedroom door opens with my big beautiful protector walking in with two cups of coffee.

I smile at him with tears in my eyes.

"Doll…" he says sounding concerned.

"I'm sorry. It's happy tears," I say choked up.

Gus moves to sit down on the bed, handing me my coffee. I grab it from him, setting it on my nightstand.

This is it. Say it. Say something!

I start to bob my head to the song in my head giving me the courage to fucking say something. I clear my throat. "Gus, I think I'm ready to talk."

Gus snaps his head toward me as he leans his body sideways, facing me on the bed. I try to move up against the headboard, wincing in pain.

"Doll... careful. Do ya need help?" He stands up, walking around to my side of the bed, leaning over he hugs me, lifting me up and pushing me against the headboard. With my arms around his neck, I lean in giving him a kiss.

He smells freshly showered. It makes my body want him - no need him.

Gus groans, releasing me. He looks conflicted. I bite back my insecurities that he doesn't want me. He hasn't tried anything with me since we've been home. I guess it's best because once I tell him everything he probably won't want me anymore anyway.

I take a deep breath, "Okay, sit. I need to get this over with so you can leave."

Gus' face becomes furious. "Why would I leave?"

"You will. Please sit down so I can explain." I pat the bed for him to sit down. Gus sits down facing me. He bends a leg, tucking it under his other leg that's hanging off the bed. I can tell he's preparing himself for what I'm about to tell him. I close my eyes, taking a deep breath.

Opening my eyes, I start off saying, "I just want to say I'm sorry I haven't told you this sooner. I understand if you become upset with me."

Gus' eyebrows crease and I know he's about ready to say something, so I hold up my hand and say, "Please, I'm going to be saying a lot and I'm sure you'll want to interrupt, but please let me get all of this out before I can't."

Gus relaxes his face, grabbing his ankle and knee. I can tell he's holding his anger in by how hard he's gripping as he tries to calm himself.

"It's all because of me," I whisper, looking down at my hands, wringing them together. "I was taken because the Russians wanted to get back at…" I pause. *Say it! Do it! Say it!* "The Russians took me because of Dominic."

A rush of relief escapes me. I don't look up yet but feel so much better now that I've said it. I take a deep breath and look up. Gus' face is like stone with no expression. His knuckles turning white from gripping his leg too hard, explains it all. Not wanting to lose my courage I continue, "Dominic was behind the girls being taken from the clubs. He was behind everything that happened with Ginger. He paid the MC to come after Ginger. He was behind everything because of me." I pause trying to keep it together. I clear my throat. "Dominic's cousin was mad at him - which by the way is the Russian Mafia - so they kidnapped me to get back at Dominic for costing their family money."

Gus clears his throat. "I don't understand."

I look at Gus with tears in my eyes. "The man I pointed out in the pictures. I knew who he was. I knew he was Dominic's cousin…"

Gus' face becomes enraged "Ya knew his family was with the Russian Bratva?"

"No… No!" I exclaim. "I found out he was Dominic's cousin when I was in the cage. See…" I pause again. "Kirill brought Dominic to the warehouse. They fought over me. Dominic fought to have me released. Kirill told me everything that Dominic did, how he tried to cover up his mess with the whole Emmett thing. How the family told him to get rid of me but he wouldn't." I take a breath and say, "They told him I was payment for all the money he'd lost. When Dominic fought back, they killed him right in front of me," I say with a shaky voice.

Gus says shocked, "Dom's dead?"

I nod my head. "Yes, the night before the auction."

Still shocked, Gus stands up and starts to pace the room. "All this happened in front of ya?"

I wring my hands together. "No, well yes. Once I heard Dominic's voice, I tried to fight off Miguel who was pinning me to the side of the cage. Once Dominic started fighting Miguel released me. I pulled off my blindfold, but the lights they had shining on me were so bright, that I couldn't see anything outside my cage. They released Dominic so he could come to the cage and then they shot him, right in front of me."

"Jaysus, Mother of Christ!" Gus exclaims, pinching the bridge of his nose. I don't say anything, letting it all sink in for him.

"So...you're saying Kirill, the Russian Bratva, took ya to sell ya off as a slave?" Gus' face is unreadable. I nod my head yes but don't say a word as I try to read his mood.

Gus starts to pace the room again. I let him, giving him time to think. He stops dead. "Did Kirill hire Miguel?"

I pause to think about it. "I don't know. Miguel said he was watching me for a long time. That I was always on the go like an Energizer Bunny, that's why he would call me his *Conejito*." I hear a growl, but I'm lost in my thoughts. "The first day when the Bossman was talking to the group about me there was someone else that said I was a feisty bitch when they took me. He was killed for talking back to the man." I pause shaking my head. "I don't know. Miguel said he was there to watch me and make sure no one touched me. He was protecting me."

Gus blurts out, "From who?"

I look up and say, "From all the men."

"Wat men?" he fires back, his voice filled with anger.

I sit there thinking. *What men? The Italian man? The brothers? Miguel? They all touched me. They all wanted to hurt me.*

"They all wanted to touch me..." I say almost silently.

Gus moves so fast he sits directly in front of me, placing his finger under my chin and forcing me to look him in his eyes, and asks, "Who wanted to touch ya?"

Tears fall from my eyes as I inhale through my nostrils thinking of all of them touching me. My lips quiver as I whisper, "They all touched me."

Gus lets go of my chin bringing both hands to cup my face, leaning his forehead to mine, never moving his gaze from mine, and says, "I'll kill every cunt that laid a fuckin' finger on ya, I promise ya that. Yeah?" I close my eyes as tears fall freely from them. "Look at me Doll. I will never let anything happen to ya again."

I nod my head.

"Did they?" Gus stops himself.

I know exactly what he's trying to ask, so I answer, "No... No, there were only two men that actually 'touched' me."

I tell him everything in detail. I explain to Gus what Miguel and his brothers did to me that night in the cage and then what Miguel did to me before the auction. When I tell him about the Italian man, Gus becomes tense, clenching his jaws together. I ask him if he's okay. He replies by shaking his head. I give him a few minutes to calm down.

"Isabella... You –are –mine. I know we still need to discuss us, but nothing is keeping me from ya. No one will keep us apart now. We're together, no matter if we have our little talk or not, you're mine. Thank ya for telling me everything. I know how hard this is for ya," he says in the most loving voice. I start to cry.

"I'm so sorry. I'm sorry I didn't tell you sooner. I'm just..." I whisper as my words get clogged in my throat.

Gus pulls back upset, he shakes me a little, saying, "Wat do ya mean? Why would *you* be sorry? This is all on them and they'll bloody pay."

A quiet sob slips from my throat and Gus pulls me into his chest, holding me tightly.

"Isabella, please don't cry. I'm here baby. I got ya," Gus chokes out.

I feel like a heavy rock was lifted off my shoulders. I feel so much better now that he knows. I take a few deep breaths against his chest. I silently say, more to myself, but it comes out as a whisper, "I feel so much better now that you know."

"Wat did you say?" Gus says softly.

I pull away from him, placing my hands on his chest, and say, "I've been scared everyone will be mad and blame me because everything happened because of me."

Gus inhales through his nostrils, closing his eyes for a split second as he tries to contain himself. "Isabella, this is not your fault. This is all Dominic. No one will be mad at ya. I promise," he states with a soft smile on his face reassuring me.

Exhausted, I let out a long shuddering breath as I lean back against the headboard.

Gus leans forward placing a kiss on my forehead. "Get some rest. I need to make some phone calls."

I laugh. "Told you that you were going to leave me."

Gus smiles. "I'm not leaving ya. I'm just going to the other room to make some calls."

I smile back at him and say, "I know."

Gus pauses, giving me a long stare and right when I'm about ready to ask if he's okay he leans into me. "Isabella..." he breathes, inches away from my face.

I exhale and as my mouth opens, Gus cups my cheeks pressing his lips to mine. We both moan once our tongues collide, deepening the kiss. I reach out needing to touch him, pulling him closer to me. Gus breaks the kiss, breathless, and says, "Sweet Jaysus, I want this..." Placing his forehead to mine. "But ya need to heal."

As always he knows exactly what I need. I nod my head in response. I don't know if I'm ready either, but I do know one hundred percent I want him too. I close my eyes and whisper, "I tried to block them out thinking of you. I thought of you all the time." I pause, opening my eyes to see his full of emotion. "I thought of the last night we were together. You kept me strong."

"I'm glad I filled your mind, *cos* you're all I thought about too. I can't live without *me one*," Gus replies choked up.

After another embrace and a passionate kiss, he stands. "I'll be back in a few. You should get some rest and come out when ya feel up to it. I'm sure the girls are waiting."

I nod my head, leaning back against the headboard. I'm exhausted, but I feel much lighter, and for once, since all this happened, I don't feel stressed, I actually feel happy.

Thinking everything will be okay, I close my eyes.

CHAPTER TWENTY TWO | GUS

When Quick and I walk into our small security office in the building, I see everyone's already here. After leaving Izzy's room, I called everyone that lives in the building to meet me. Once all the calls were made I checked on Izzy finding her sleeping so I told Ruby I would be back in an hour and where to find us if she needed us.

"Redman, this better be important - you just got me out of bed on a Sunday," Shy laughs. "You all know how I like my Angel in bed all day on Sundays."

"Trust me. Y'all want to hear this," I reply.

"Did you find something out?" Luc speaks up from across the table.

I sit down and blurt out, "Dominic is dead."

The room explodes in questions. I raise my hand to silence everyone and continue, "Iz told me everything that happened to her."

The men all become silent. I stand up and start pacing around. I can't say all this while sitting down. It's hard enough repeating what those men did to her. I'm about ready to finish but turn to Luc. "The part that really unhinges me is that she told me an Italian man touched her."

"*Madre stronzo,*" Luc shouts, kicking his chair out to stand, his body pulses with rage.

I continue, "She said he was there to see for himself if she was wat he was looking for. They put her on display for this man, and he called her his swan."

Luc paces, clenching his hands and murmuring in Italian, and the only thing I can understand is *uomo morto* - dead man.

Shy pounds his fist on the table. "That cocksucking, motherfucker!"

I let my brothers vent as I continue, "She said he fingered her and fondled her breast."

Another string of curse words escapes Luc as he becomes enraged.

I still continue, "Kirill told Izzy that Dominic was behind everything that happened to Gin. She didn't get details, but Kirill said it was all because of Dominic. Now Dominic's dead but Kirill and Miguel are still out there. We need to figure this *shite* out. Is Kirill going to come after any of our girls again? He knows wat Ghost looks like and he knows Izzy's still here. Most of all he knows they both can identify him."

Brant jumps up. "Let that bitch come for her and see what he will find."

I turn to all the men – the men I call brothers. "I know Frank violated my girl and it kills me to say this, but before any of us do anything to him, we need him to find out wat the Russians are up to and if our girls are still being targeted. I don't want wat happened to her to leave this room. It stays with us, but at least we know Dom's dead."

The room erupts with everyone talking over each other, but my eyes are locked on Luc. Beau moves to stand next to me. "I don't think it should be him reaching out."

"Snow and Alex are supposed to be DJing this weekend. We need to put out some feelers and try to get as much information as we can before they do," Dallas says to the group.

Maddox tenses next to him. "I...I can reach out to my family. We don't need Frank." He pauses, looking over to Chad and Ethan, his two main men. "Let's connect and dig. At least we know who we're looking for and what they want."

"I can help out, just let me know what you need," Dallas offers.

Luc has been pacing back and forth for ten minutes not saying anything. He finally stops, gripping the chair in front of him, leaning over. Taking a deep breath, he says, "I have some other connections, not linked to Frank, that I can get in contact with."

"I'm gonna talk to the Feds and see if they have any more information on this Miguel guy. He's contracted, so he shouldn't be a threat unless someone still wants payment," I explain.

When Quick and I leave an hour later heading back to our women, we both feel better about having a plan and security in place for all our girls.

"Do you think you and Iz will be up to watching Bella all night?" Quick asks as we walk toward the girls' new place.

"I'm sure we can. Iz seems her happiest when Bella's with her. Why, wat's up?" I reply.

"I need to have some alone time with Firecracker. She's been busting her ass, and I want to take her to the clubhouse to let off some steam," he rambles.

I chuckle, "I gotcha, brother. Go have *craic* tonight."

As we walk into the apartment, we hear laughter. My heart lifts hearing my girl laugh. When Bella sees Quick, she squeals, "Qwak is back Mamma!" Within seconds she's jumping into his arms giving him a nosey-nosey, pressing her nose to his. I've noticed the two of them doing that a lot lately. *Me boys doting* hard for the two lasses.

My eyes roam the room noticing Ruby in the kitchen cooking something and Izzy's relaxing on the couch with her foot elevated. When our eyes meet, she smiles big and it actually reaches her eyes. It's not some fake ass half-smile. She looks really happy.

I smile. "Doll, *howaya*?" I rasp out while plopping down next to her.

"Hiya, good looking." Her voice is low and breathy.

Christ, she's beautiful. I want her so bad. My dick stirs to life, making me shift positions. Izzy's eyes roam down my body landing on my crotch.

"Doll, ya need to stop. I only have so much control," I state.

She giggles next to me, reaching for my hand.

"Legs, I talked to Redman, he's cool with watching Bella tonight, but I wanted to make sure you're okay with it too," Quick says as he hands me a Guinness, before sitting down across from us. Bella jumps into his lap. "Qwak, I want to go with you and Mama," she pouts, pulling on his hat.

Izzy laughs next to me, watching them together. Quick replies, "Baby girl, I want to take your mama out on a date."

Bella starts with her million questions. "What's a date? Why can't I come?" Quick's face looks panicked with all the questions, but the girls come to the rescue saving him.

"Bella Bug, we can play dress up with Uncle Redman tonight," Izzy says laughing as I snap my head toward her mouthing, 'dress up?'

"Bella, Mama and Quick are going to go out and do adult things tonight. If it's okay with Auntie Izzy and Uncle Redman."

Bella's sitting on Quick's lap gawking at me with a very serious look. We sit and wait for the princess to answer. I stare back with a smile, wondering what she's thinking to have her looking so serious. I know I'm in trouble when she gets a huge grin on her face. "Uncle Red, will you play with us?"

Quick looks over with a shit-eating grin. "Yeah, Uncle Red."

I laugh. "Whatever me little princess wants. I'm here for your entertainment." Bella squeals in excitement, jumping off Quick's lap and running into her new room, telling us all the things she's going to do to me.

I look over at Izzy. "Doll, ya owe me big time."

Ruby falls into Quick's lap, kissing him, and says, "Are you two sure about this?"

Izzy replies immediately with a smile, "You've been running around doing all my shit. I want you to go have some fun."

I nod my head in agreement.

Ruby squeals just like her daughter, jumping up and rushing off to her room to get ready. Quick drawls after drinking from his beer and laughing, "Thanks Legs. I owe you one."

"You're welcome. I just want her happy here. I know it's been hard on her with all this bullshit," Izzy explains.

Quick snaps his head back. "Iz, don't speak like that. In a way it's good - I mean, it got her here a fuck of a lot faster. She's here to stay. Just need to deal with some shit, but we got our girl."

It's a fucked up situation, but he's right. She probably would have taken her sweet ass time moving here if it wasn't for what happened to Izzy. Having them here has been a godsend. Bella hanging out with Izzy has helped, so much. I just need to get my Izzy back. My outspoken, lively, wild girl. I wanted her submissive in the bedroom but not in life.

"Uncle Red, here I come," Bella yells from her room.

CHAPTER TWENTY THREE | IZZY

"Is she asleep?" Gus asks when I finally hobble back to my room.

I stop in the doorway to take a break as I take in the God-like man lying half naked in my bed. My body heats up looking at his enormous chest with his back propped up against the headboard. He's freshly showered, I'm sure to clean off all the makeup we put on him. I see there are no more clips in his hair too. I giggle, thinking of Bella having so much fun with him.

"Ya alright?" Gus asks sitting up worried.

I shake my head and say, "No I'm good. Just looking at you."

"Oh, yeah? Do ya like whatcha see?" he smirks, leaning back.

"Mmm-hmm," I mumble, making my way over to my bed. For the last week, I've finally been able to walk without crutches or any help. I should get my cast off next week. My ribs are the only injury that still needs to heal.

When I woke up today, after having the talk with Gus, I felt like a new person. I took a bath, saved my one leg, did my hair and put on my matching bra and panties. Loose comfy clothes are all I've been able to wear, and it takes me forever to get dressed since I'm still sore, but I felt so much better.

"Wat ya want to watch tonight?" he asks, flipping through the channels.

I stand up from the bed, pulling off my dress.

"Mother of Christ, Isabella." Gus groans behind me.

I look over my shoulder with a seductive smile. "What? See something you like?" I tease, turning back around and giving my ass a wiggle.

A second later I'm being lifted off the ground by two massive arms as we fall onto the bed. I squeal like Bella was tonight, calling out his name, "Gus."

Gus rolls us, carefully positioning me on top of him. "Fuck yeah, I like wat I see," he says, grinning wide.

I let out a sharp breath.

"Does this position hurt ya?" Gus questions me, sounding concerned.

"No, you just take my breath away. You're so handsome," I answer honestly.

Gus' eyes twinkle. "Doll, I almost had a heart attack seeing ya."

I laugh. "Just making sure you still want me."

Gus rolls us again, laying me on my back with half his body laying on me. Just like the night he made me come. My breath hitches thinking about what he did to me.

"Doll, it doesn't matter wat ya wear..." He drags his pointer finger down my chest, circling each breast, tracing the bra. "I want y –o –u no matter wat *cos*..." He spreads his hand out over my chest, slowly dragging the tips of his fingers down my stomach. I bite my lip with a moan. "You are mine..." he says, stopping his hand at the edge of my lace panties, using his pointer finger, sliding it from side to side along the edge. "But..." he exclaims, making me jump. "Wat ya've got on - definitely does it for me." He leans down, placing kisses across my stomach, up my chest and to his favorite spot on my neck.

I'm lost in his words, focusing on how he feels next to me. How I'm feeling my body react to his touch with tingles and goosebumps spreading across my body. "Isabella, you're so beautiful. Never feel like I don't want ya, *cos* Doll, you're all I want." Gus' husky voice is filled with desire. I tilt my head toward him, taking his mouth as I turn my body into his, cupping his face with one hand.

"Aengus," I murmur into the kiss.

"Isabella..." he groans, moving his hands around my waist,

slipping them into my panties and gripping the globes of my ass. He pulls me tight against him, and I instantly feel his erection at my core.

I break the kiss tilting my head back, "Yes, Aengus."

Gus sucks and kisses along my neck. "Say it again," he grunts, moving me to my back and placing himself between my legs.

I cup his face in both hands. "What?" I answer, panting, out of breath.

"*Me* name, Doll," Gus rasps looking down at me, shifting his body up against mine and grinding his cock against my center.

"Aengus." I wrap my good leg around his waist. "Aengus."

"Christ, I'm going to lose *me shite*," he grunts, sliding his hand between us, and as soon as his hand slips into my panties, I start to flash back to Miguel, hearing him whisper in my ear.

No. No. No... Don't freak out. It's Gus. It's Gus.

Gus' eyes are closed, he's breathing hard. He slips a finger between my wet folds, and says, "Sweet Jaysus. You're so ready."

I take a bunch of short breaths as tears slide down my face. When Gus leans down and whispers, "Mine," while kissing my ear, it's Miguel's voice that I hear, I scream and start pushing at Gus.

Gus instantly flies off of me with panic in his eyes. "Isabella, I'm sorry. Are ya alright?"

I curl into a ball crying. *Get out of my head. Leave me alone.*

"Isabella, come back to me," Gus murmurs softly, next to me on the bed, but he doesn't touch me. He just lays on his side waiting for me to look at him or say something.

I can't face him yet so I yell in frustration, "Miguel's in my fucking head. I can't get him out. I'm sorry," I cry, curling myself tighter into the fetal position, the same position I laid in the whole time I was in the cage.

"Don't be sorry. I'm here for *you* an I'm not going anywhere," Gus states sternly.

I tilt my head up with tears streaming down my face and say, "I want you so fucking bad. I'm so sorry. I heard him in my head when you put your hand down my panties," I try to explain, ending in a sob.

"Please, let me hold ya. I need to hold ya, Isabella," Gus pleads with a look of sorrow on his face.

I nod my head, and within seconds he engulfs me into his massive arms, holding me tight against his even bigger body. Instantly I feel safe - my protector.

"I'm so fucked in the head," I sob into his chest. "It was the fingers...and feeling trapped. I—"

Gus cuts me off. "Doll, it's okay. It's my fault. We shouldn't have gone that far. Ya need time," Gus says apologetically.

I end up falling asleep in his arms only to wake up screaming from a nightmare. Gus holds me tight until I fall asleep again.

It's been a week since I freaked out on Gus. I've been throwing myself into my music. I've been working on a few songs, and once I got into Luc's personal studio at his house, I let loose. Using all my anger to fuel me, making a completely new song.

I'm known for my EDM - Electronic Digital Music remixes, taking old songs and putting new age electric sounds to it. But this new song I'm mixing is from a whole different genre. I'm putting it all out there, letting everything I'm feeling guide the music. It's intense. It's raw. It's me. I have a ways to go, but I have a really good feeling about it. It's completely different than anything I've ever done before.

Within a week I've laid out the baseline, it's heavy. I don't know what the girls will think, but I feel like I'm releasing all this pent-up anger and bullshit I've been holding on to for all these years. I guess listening to Prodigy those first few days stuck with me. Bringing out a whole new side of me, and not being able to get rid of Miguel's voice in my head just pisses me off.

My days pretty much consist of Gus taking me to Luc's penthouse studio to work on music. Gus leaves to do club or security stuff I guess, to be honest, I don't really ask. No one bothers me while I'm there, thank God. I've been mostly by myself, only seeing whoever comes by my apartment or when I'm on my way to the studio. Ruby and Quick have been in and out a lot lately, dealing with their own shit. All I know is, I need to sort out my own head right now, and music is the key to dealing with it.

I got my cast off yesterday, and I didn't have a panic attack going to or from the hospital. Well, at least not one that was noticeable to everyone. Gus kept asking me if I was okay. There was talk about everyone going to White Wolfe last night, and if I wanted to go, but I said no.

Since telling Gus everything, I haven't seen either of the other girls, just Ruby. I've texted with both of them, but it was mostly business or small talk. I'm scared they're mad, but Gus assures me they're just giving me time. Both Alex and Ginger have been picking up my slack in DJing around here.

I feel bad that Gus doesn't get to go hang out with his boys because I don't want to go. I've told him to go without me and have fun, but he got upset, telling me to quit being an idiot or in his words an, *eeijt*.

I went back to the studio that night and ended up working until midnight. Mia and Luc were at Club Spin checking on the other DJs, so Gus just hung out, patiently waiting, not saying a word until I was done. We got into bed, and he pulled me to him like he does every night, but it was different not having my cast on.

We've been staying at Gus' place to give Quick and Ruby some time alone. They've been dealing with some stuff since the night they went out. I feel like a horrible friend for not pestering her to find out what's wrong. I've asked, but she says they're just dealing with the move and stuff. I know my girl, she would tell me if she needed me. Truthfully, I think she doesn't want to bother me with it, and I'm so fucked up in the head I'm letting her.

Gus shifts in his sleep, gripping me tighter. Some nights when I'm awake I watch him sleeping. He always has some kind of grip on me, never letting me go. Just in case I have a nightmare or need him. He takes my breath away. My body is always humming when he's around. My lady parts are screaming at me daily waking up to him. Telling me I need to get laid, but my subconscious isn't having it.

"Ya gonna tell me wat's wrong?" Gus asks while opening one eye. I'm laying on his chest with my head to the side just staring at him. I let out a deep breath and make circles around his nipple with my pointer finger.

"I…" I stop, taking another deep breath. "Honestly… I'm enraged. I'm sad. I'm scared. I…um…I'm fucking lost," I answer honestly.

Gus slides from under me, moving to sit up against his headboard and says, "Come here," motioning for me to sit up. I start to crawl up his giant body. I guess I was too slow because he cups his hands under my arms, pulling me up onto his lap to straddle him as I place my hands on his naked chest.

"Look at me," he says, placing his finger under my chin and lifting my face, wanting to see my eyes. "Look at me, talk to me."

I feel like I'm about to explode, like I want to hit something. I'm so angry. I ball my hands into a fist. "If ya need to get it out, hit me. Do whatever ya need to get yourself out of this funk," Gus says with pleading eyes.

"I don't know how to explain it. I'm so mad about what happened to me. I'm sad because I want to go back to DJing without feeling scared. But, I'm afraid to leave the building, thinking someone will try and take me again. Then I go back to being angry, wanting to hurt someone. And…" I look down at my hands in frustration.

Gus lifts my chin back up and keeps his hand there to hold it in place and says, "And...um..."

I lock eyes with him and say, "And I want to be with you so fucking bad, but I'm scared you touching me will trigger something."

Gus leans forward, wrapping his arms around me, bringing our chests together and smiles. "Well, I hate to break it to ya, but I feel the same way. I know it's not the same as wat you're going through, but I want all the same things for *you* too. I want *me* ol' Izzy back. Honestly, seeing ya get so fired up right now has me feeling pretty good."

I throw my head back laughing, "What?"

Gus leans in, kissing my collarbone, and explains, "I finally see the fire in your eyes again. I've been watching ya on video DJing in Luc's studio. It makes me happy to see ya releasing whatever you're feeling. I see *me* girl coming back."

I wrap my arms around his neck and confess, "I'm trying. I've got these songs in my head. It's just so hard to explain. I feel like I'm floating through life."

Gus smiles. "Maybe you're just finding your own footing in life. It's made ya really look at yerself. Ya need to let it all out."

"Well I feel lost and extremely angry."

"Wat do ya need from me?" Gus asks, and without thinking I blurt out, "I need you. I *want* you."

Gus smiles. "Doll, hate to tell ya this but ya've had me for a really long time. All ya have to do is take me. Take wat ya need from me. I'm here for ya." He runs his hands up and down my back before grabbing both butt cheeks, pulling me against his erection.

Biting my lip, I debate inside my head what to do. He doesn't like it when I make the moves or demand things. He'll say no and deny me.

"Wat's going on in that crown of yours?" He chuckles, leaning back against the headboard.

"I honestly don't know what to think about us. I don't know what I can and can't do with you. You've denied me for so long and I just…" I trail off, not knowing how to explain it.

"Quit thinking. Just do wat ya feel is right," Gus eggs me on, massaging my ass, thrusting me against him.

"Don't you need to be in control? You've always told me to wait," I dare him.

"Doll, right now it's about wat ya need. If ya need to take control of the situation and us right now, then go for it. Ya need to get it through that thick crown of yours that you and I are a 'we' now," he says, finishing with a soft kiss on my nose.

"I didn't know. We never had our talk. You told me that I needed to understand who you are. I thought you needed to lay it out for us."

Gus interrupts me, "Isabella, you're over thinking this. All ya need to think about is wat *you* need right now and how to make this work so ya will feel safe. I'm not going anywhere. I want —"

I don't let him finish, I crash my lips brutally hard against his thrusting my tongue into his mouth, but panic and pull back. "I'm sorry. Did I hurt you?"

Gus leans back against the headboard laughing. "Doll, don't be sorry. I liked it. I want this - take me."

The last two words go on repeat in my head. I feel my body temperature rise, and my mind focuses on one thing. *I want him. He wants me. Take him.*

I rip my nightshirt off over my head, exposing my breasts. Gus' eyes darken with desire. I cup his cheeks with my hands and slowly devour his luscious mouth again.

Gus growls, wrapping his arms around my small waist and pulling me snug against him. I'm all over the place with my hands pulling his hair, scratching down his chest. I feel crazed. I bite his lower lip, tasting blood, and when I pull away, he has the same hunger in his eyes.

He wants me.

I rock my hips against his cock, feeling it pulse against me. Gus leans his head back, closing his eyes. I move down his body, kissing the crevice of his neck. Sucking and nipping all the way down his chest to his nipples as I feel his body tense and his breathing increase.

Thinking I need full control to get past my fear, I explain, "I need you not to touch me, don't say anything and keep your eyes closed." I hold my breath and wait for him to deny me, but when he nods his head, I become frantic with need. The need to touch him. The need to lick and consume all of him.

I grab his hands, placing them to his sides as I move lower to his stomach. I look up, watching his face when I pull his boxers down, releasing his - *holyfuckingshititshuge* - cock from his pants. I slide his boxers all the way down his legs and just stare at his beautiful cock. I don't think pussies or cocks are very beautiful, but fuck me - he's like the Holy Grail - long, thick and mother fucking heaven. A giggle escapes me as I lower my head inches away from his cock.

"Isabella..." Gus warns me. I know it's killing him not to be able to see or be in control. I need to make the most of this while I can.

"Hmmm..." I hum as I suck the thick tip of his cock into my overly wet mouth. My mouth waters just at the sight of his body flexing. I feel my wetness pooling between my legs. It's been so long since I've had sex. His cock's so big I have to slide it in and out of my mouth a few times to get it wet enough to take it deep into my throat.

I moan against his cock, circling my tongue playfully around the tip before sucking it all down until he bottoms out.

Gus' whole body tenses up, his jaw is clenched so tight his veins are popping up in his neck. I slide up and down slowly until he starts pumping his hips, meeting my mouth thrust for thrust. I slip off my shorts and grab his cock with both hands.

I need him inside of me.

I need him to consume me.

I need him to take away all the bad shit.

Dominic hurting me. Miguel forcing me. Everything bad in my life, I need him to erase it.

I need him to mark me for life.

I pump his cock a few more times before sliding up his body again. I straddle him, placing his cock between my legs so I can rub up against it, letting it slide between my folds, hitting my clit. I lean forward, kissing his neck where his favorite spot to kiss me is. He groans.

"Are you ready for this?" I ask him.

"Isabella…" he swallows hard. "Yes. Take me."

I lean in, pressing my chest to his as I raise up, wrapping an arm around his neck. I reach between us, gliding his tip to my entrance then returning my hand to his shoulder. My body is so in tune with his. I need him. "Look at me," I say, and as he opens his eyes I lower myself down, impaling myself on his cock. It's pure ecstasy. My body shakes as I cry out in pleasure, "Holyfuckingshit."

Gus moans, "Yes, Isabella."

Our bodies are pressed together so tight and my nipples are hard. If his chest was glass, my nipples could cut it. I begin to thrust up and I can feel every inch of his cock slowly pulling out. Fuck he feels so goddamn good that it has me talking gibberish, because the shit coming out of my mouth is not English.

I need more, slamming back down, we both cry out our approval. I let my body adjust to his thick cock, but only for a second because I need to start moving. I grip Gus' flexed biceps as he clenches the bedding on either side of him. He never breaks eye contact, and that's when I see it. He cares for me so much it's taking everything in him to not be in control so I'll be okay.

I grab his neck, pulling his head to my chest as I lean back. "Touch me, suck me," I order.

Gus grabs my tits aggressively, like a starved man. He devours one of my breasts while kneading the other. I'm just as hungry, wanting more, I move forward and back, then up and down. Gus wraps his arms around my waist, grunting into my neck, "Isabella, *gra mo chroi*."

"Yes, Aengus. Ah, fuck yes," I rasp out, picking up speed, riding him harder and faster. I grip his shoulders, digging my nails into his skin. The tension in my core starts to build as I chase my climax. Gus tightens his grip on my ass cheeks with each thrust, moving me faster against his swelling cock. We're both so close.

"Aengus. ah...ah." I tilt my head forward, passionately kissing his mouth as I ride him harder. "Deeper. Harder. Fuck me please," I beg between kisses, sounding like a crazed woman.

Gus pulls back to look me in the eyes. "Are ya sure? he asks, breathlessly.

"Yes, Aengus. Please take control, take all of me," I beg again, letting him know how I feel.

Gus switches into a feral animal and with a deep husky roar, he flips me onto my back, grabbing my knees and spreading them wide. I look him in the eyes, seeing his control take over, I say, "Fuck me. I'm yours." Gus groans, leaning over me, covering my body. As he slides his dick back in his eyes roll back in ecstasy. "Aengus..."

"Yes, *gra mo chroi*," Gus whispers against my neck, sending tingles across my body as he starts biting and sucking my neck, increasing his thrusts and going deeper.

Fuck. Yes.

Gus bites down hard like a vampire biting his prey. Pounding his hips harder and harder as he sucks my neck into his mouth. He has me pinned to the bed with his upper body holding me in place, thrusting faster and faster. I pull my knees up so he can go deeper, causing his pelvis to hit my clit just perfect. I start to pant, "Yes, oh. Fuck yes. Aengus. I'm...ah... I'm..."

Oh, God, I'm going to come.

Gus, still sucking my neck, bites down hard, marking me as his own. Sending a jolt of pleasurable pain through my body. I cry out, "Yes."

My orgasm is at the brink of explosion and I can barely form a sentence. "Oh, fuck. Oh, right there. Yeah. I'm..." Gus continues to hammer in and out of me with quick hard thrusts making his pelvic bone rub vigorously against my clit. I moan, "I'm gonna...

"Sweet Iz. Oh, God." His cock swells just as my walls suction around his dick as a life-altering orgasm crashes over me.

I scream his name, "Yeesss... ah... Aaeennguus..."

Gus leans back gripping my hips, frantically pounding into me. The slapping of our bodies together intensifies. Every muscle in his upper body is taut, covered in sweat, with his skin as red as his hair.

"Christ," he bellows out, throwing his head back, letting his release spill into me.

He slows his thrusting but never pulls out. Leaning over me, he kisses me slow and deep, stealing my breath. I reach up, pulling him down on top of me, wrapping my legs around his waist.

"G'lawd, I need more," Gus says, breathlessly.

"I'm all yours."

Gus pumps a few more times before pulling out. He goes into the bathroom and returns with a warm cloth. As he cleans both of us, his cock starts to rise and I giggle.

"Wat? I told ya I needed more," Gus chuckles, crawling up the bed. "Ya just opened the floodgates. I'll be ridin' ya all day and night."

I lick my lips seeing his cock almost fully erect again. I smile. "Thank the gods."

Gus kisses me as he slips his cock back into me with one thrust. "I need ya just as much as ya need me. Just let me know if anything triggers ya. I want to make ya feel good."

I nod, wrapping my arms around his thick neck, pulling him down for a kiss. "What did you say to me or call me earlier?"

Gus pumps his hips a few times. I can feel his erection building to full girth inside me as he leans back to look me in the eye, and says, "Ya mean *gra mo chroi?* It means love of my heart."

I'm so overcome with emotion that tears begin to fall, sliding down my face. I smile, whispering, "Ditto."

"You're my everything. We're one now," he says softly as he slowly moves inside me.

"Always and forever," I breathe against him.

Gus nibbles along my throat and neck, whispering next to my ear, "Oorah!" Making me giggle. He slowly rocks up against me with his body covering every inch of me. I relax, giving myself to him, letting every bit of him engulf my senses.

"Isabella…" he breathes, inches away from my ear. "I'ma, make love to ya slow an easy now." Lowering his head, he kisses me right beneath my earlobe.

I whisper back, "Yes, my Aengus."

CHAPTER TWENTY FOUR | GUS

"What's got you in such a good mood, Redman?" Mac asks, sitting next to me at the clubhouse bar.

I take a long swig of my Guinness before I can answer him when Quick announces from behind me, "Redman's finally getting shagged," slapping me on the back as he takes the seat on the other side of me.

"About damn time, brother. You and Legs have been dancing around that shit for years," Mac says, raising his glass to cheers me. I chuckle, saluting him back.

"Who's been dancing around what?" Shy asks, walking up and taking a seat as Maze delivers our drinks.

"Redman finally claimed Legs," Mac announces.

"Finally, goddamn. You've been pussyfooting around that shit for too long. Good for you, brother," Shy says, lifting his beer to his mouth and taking a drink.

"Shots!" Maze announces, walking up with a bottle of Jameson Whiskey - my favorite.

I chuckle. "Christ, the lot of ya are acting like I just won the lottery or something."

"Brother, you've been dancing around Izzy for years. In our eyes, brother, you did just win and to me something even better than a million dollars - you won your *one*."

I raise my glass of whiskey and say, "Fuckin' aye, *Sláinte,*"

"Cheers!" Maze says, along with all my brothers.

"What the fuck did we miss?" Dallas asks, walking up with Brant and a few other brothers from the club.

"G'lawd," I breathe out, lowering my head.

As usual Quick spouts off first, hence his nickname, "Redman's finally hitting it, no wait... he got his shag on." Everyone starts to laugh at his joke, he continues, "No, this one is the best, he had a grand ride. Redman, tell us how you Irishmen say getting fucked."

I laugh, "Fuck off, ya fuckin' arsehole," making everyone laugh.

Leaning over the bar, Quick says, "Seriously, brother. Which one is it?"

Finishing my Guinness, I place it on the bar. I motion for Maze to refill my shot glass with whiskey. Once she's filled it, I turn toward Quick. "When talking about sex or fuckin', ya say - shag her, take her riding, or I'd throw it in - not hitting it." I slam my whiskey back. "Now are we having a meeting or talking about shagging all day?"

The clubhouse lights up with laughter. I shake my head at my brothers. All they think about is pussy and fucking. I look over at Maze who's smiling at me with the Jameson bottle ready to pour me another glass.

"Fuck it," I say, sitting back down.

Thirty minutes later we're still sitting around the bar, but now the clubhouse is full of members, along with Brant, Maddox and his boys.

"I thought we were supposed to have a meeting today?" Brant asks.

"Yah, I thought so too," I answer him.

"Are we waiting on anyone?" Brant questions.

"Alright fuckers, let's hit the club office and get some business done so we can get back to having fun. Get a drink, and let's lock it down," Shy yells from behind me.

"Perfect timing," Brant says, grabbing his new drink.

Everyone grabs their drinks and heads to the club office. Since we've been remodeling the clubhouse, and no one is allowed in the club room except members, we decided to knock a wall out in the office to make it bigger and put a few more tables in. We've been working with Beau's security team and Maddox's team so much we needed to have another room to hold secure meetings without anyone hanging around or club girls hearing us.

We ended up making two conference-like rooms, one for our club meetings and one for all other business. Member meetings are once or twice a month. We have a meeting with Beau, Luc and Maddox just as much, if not more, depending on the shit going on.

Everyone files into the room with Shy at the head of the table. He starts, "Okay, so first things first. Where are we with the Russian intel? My birthday bash is Saturday night at the White Wolfe, and our girls are DJing Friday night. I want to know what the plan is for security?"

Maddox speaks first, "I sent word and spoke to a few of my family connections. They said once Kirill was released, he went back to Russia to meet with his father, and no one's heard from him since. It's been almost two months since Izzy was taken, they've gone radio silent, and he hasn't returned to the States."

"So we haven't heard shit then," Shy replies.

Maddox shrugs. "They think they're laying low because Kirill was arrested and his father isn't too happy with him."

"Redman, do you think Legs will be ready to leave the building this weekend?" Shy asks, concerned.

"I dunno. I'm hoping so," I reply honestly. "I'ma try to get her to come at least one night."

Shy's face lights up. "Well I hope you get her to come Saturday because I'll be making a huge announcement and I guarantee she won't want to miss it," he says, smiling ear to ear.

Most of the men start chattering around the table. Shy lifts his hand to silence everyone. "This doesn't fucking leave this room, or you will pay the price, but I'm asking Snow to marry me at my birthday bash."

The men erupt in congratulations with men hitting the table in agreement. Shy raises his hand again. "Thank you, brothers. It will be nice to celebrate something good for a change. These last few years have been rough on all of us. Our club is almost done and will be up and running soon. Our alliance with Madd Dog and BB Security has blossomed. We have lots of good things coming our way. We just need to figure out and end this Dominic shit."

Everyone again hits the table in agreement. I know Izzy won't want to miss out Saturday, but I'm a little hesitant and worried it will throw her back into the scared Izzy when I'm finally getting my sassy girl back.

I'm lost in thoughts of the last few days that Izzy and I have been holed up in my apartment. Sex with her is everything I've dreamt it would be and more. I'm keeping myself in control, not pushing her too fast. She's so submissive and was definitely worth the wait.

"Redman, you here, brother?" Mac says from across from me.

"Wat? Yah, wats up?" I say, shaking my head, trying to clear my thoughts of Izzy naked.

"You look like you zoned out. Are ya doing okay?" Mac asks with a smirk like he knows I was thinking of riding Izzy.

"Nah, I'm good," I say.

Ethan and Dallas start talking about all the stuff they found on the men that were arrested. Miguel and his brother are like Ghost. If they don't want to be found, they won't be. Supposedly, an aunt came to claim their other brother's body. I think they left to handle that, but who knows.

The Feds have no leads on their cases either. They're working to put Bossman away, but Maddox thinks he'll get off. If that happens, we'll have a big threat on our hands because he's got some powerful people in his pocket.

Chad, the head of Maddox's security team, tells us about all the men they will have Friday night at the club. They'll have some sleepers, or undercover guys, there as well. My mind wanders off again, wondering if Izzy will come out Friday.

"Redman, you working this weekend or you still taking time off?" Chad asks me, pulling me from my thoughts of Izzy again.

"I'm taking this month off, but if Izzy goes, obviously I'll be her point man. No one will be guarding her again," I say with determination. "She's mine to protect."

Chad nods his head, "Okay, well, we should be set with Beau's guys and our team in place, the girls will be secure. Plus, Club Spin has doubled their security, so we shouldn't have any problems."

Everyone chats for a bit more about miscellaneous shit, but within an hour we have adjourned and the men start to trickle out.

I'm getting ready to head back to the bar when Shy tells me to meet him in the club room. I glance back, noticing the officers are following me. I don't bother picking up my phone, I just head across the hall to the member room and stand against the wall. Since I'm a prospect, I don't sit at this table. I always stand in the back.

Shy, our president, Mac our vice president, Worm our secretary, Quick our road captain, and Tiny our sergeant at arms, all file into the room. When Shy closes the door, shutting out the rest of our members and prospects, I get kind of concerned. Usually, more members are in here.

"Redman, take a seat please," Shy says, pulling out his own chair.

I don't say anything. Instead, I pull out a chair and mimic him sitting down.

Once everyone is seated, Shy says, "Redman, you're in this meeting because Quick wants you in here so you know what's going on."

I look over at Quick, he's lost his happy demeanor and is all business - completely serious. Lethal to be exact. My body tenses, ready for whatever they need me to do.

"Redman, I know you and Quick have become close but what we discuss in here is never to be repeated again to anyone." He pauses looking to Worm and Tiny. "That goes for you two also, what we are about to discuss is never to leave this room."

Now everyone in the room is alert, leaning their forearms on the table, ready to do whatever's asked. They're my brothers now, and no one says a word until Quick clears his throat.

"With all of this shit with Dominic and Izzy, I haven't brought my problems to the table. But, over the last month that Ruby and I have been together, some shit has happened. It might come to bite me or both of us in the ass."

No one says anything, just listens intently.

Quick continues, "Ruby's soon-to-be ex-husband has been harassing her. She was so overwhelmed with Izzy and trying to get her life set up here, that she just kept putting him off. I told her I would handle it, but she kept telling me no that she'd deal with him." He pauses, leaning forward on the table. "Well, one night I had her phone and her ex called. I answered. Let's just say our conversation didn't go very well. It was so bad that after talking to Shy, I made a phone call to a trustworthy associate down in LA to have it handled. I knew he was home because he was pissed off at Ruby, saying he wanted to see Bella," Quick says, looking at me.

"Jaysus Christ, Quick," I say pissed off. "Why *dinna* ya talk me?"

"Have it handled?" Tiny questions but Quick never turns from looking at me.

Quick answers me, "As I said, you were dealing with so much, Ruby too. She's my woman, and no motherfucker is going to threaten my girl like that. So, I had it and dealt with," Quick says, leaning back in his chair.

"So wat happened? Did ya kill the cunt bastard?" I ask, concerned he's about to tell us he killed Ruby's ex-husband.

"No, we just sent him a message and maybe put him in the hospital," Quick says with a smirk.

Worm chimes in, "So what's the problem, brother?"

"Well, that only pissed the cocksucker off more and now he's hired a private investigator to look into me," Quick says, leaning back over the table on his forearms looking nervous.

"How Quick and I met could become a problem if he goes digging too much. Some of our skeletons could resurface, making our lives a living hell. Quick relocated his life here," Shy says in a monotone voice.

"Wat do ya need me to do? I'll do whatever ya need me to do, brother," I say, pledging myself to them.

"Thank you, brother, but right now, nothing's come of it except he sent some pictures of himself in the hospital to Ruby the other night."

"Fuckin' prick. How did she handle it? Is that why ya been fighting?" I ask, knowing they've been fighting a lot. That's one of the reasons Izzy and I have been staying at my place, to give them some alone time.

"She was pretty devastated at first. The motherfucker sent some pretty bad photos. He threatened me, saying he knew it was me that had him jumped, and he was going to press charges. But I sent him copies of his text messages and threats he'd sent Ruby. So, right now we're at a standoff. Ruby and I are going to LA, like we planned, to get the rest of her stuff to drive back, and he wants to see Bella," Quick explains.

"Wat do ya need from me? You look nervous?" I ask again, feeling like he is leaving something out.

Tiny pipes up again asking, "You worried about your past?"

Quick, Shy, and Mac both snap their heads up at Tiny's observation. That's when I know something bad happened.

"Are ya afraid if the cunt finds out, he'll tell Ruby and she'll leave?" I question, hoping I'm wrong, but the look on his face is telling me I'm right.

"No, if the fucker finds out about his past that means we'll be going to war with the Black Crows," Shy explains, looking just as concerned.

"Motherfucker," Worm and Tiny both grunt out in frustration.

"Wat? Who are the Black Crows?" I ask, clueless. I don't know a lot of other clubs.

Everyone in the room shakes their heads. "Mean motherfuckers. Wolfe's worst enemy, they called a truce a little over four years ago, but if they find out he's alive," Shy explains, pointing at Quick. "Then the war will find its way to us again."

Everyone looks to Quick. "Wat the fuck ya do brother?" I ask the question I know everyone is thinking.

"He saved my life," Shy says through gritted teeth.

I'm so lost. I put my elbows on the table and slice my fingers through my hair trying to put the pieces together.

"Okay, so again, wat do ya need me to do? Why can't the other club members know and the five of us can?" I ask.

"Most the members who've been a Wolfeman longer than three years knows about it. We've kept Quick's identity a secret. Pretty much no one asks what your real name is anymore. We don't want to alarm anyone yet. We just wanted you all to know this since you're officers, and Gus, he wanted you to know just in case..." Shy doesn't finish the sentence.

"So, if something happens, I can deal with Ruby," I finish for him.

"No, I wanted you to know because you're one of my best friends and I want you to know what's going on. You're always with us and if something pops off, you'll be ready," Quick explains, looking exhausted.

"Okay, just let us know what you need us to do. We got you and will do anything you need. Brothers for life," Worm says, and we all hit the table in agreement.

"Thank you, guys. I wish I could've just taken care of the cunt of an ex, but that's Bella's dad," Quick says, sounding conflicted.

"We just need to keep our eyes and ears open, if the motherfucker keeps pushing, we'll figure a plan out. Wolfe's on this as well. He's got a bunch of connections, so if the Crows know about you, he'll hear first. I'm sending a few men with you, for protection, while you're down there. I know Whiz and his boys will also protect you, but you need to have some of your own," Shy tells Quick.

"When ya heading down?" I ask, hoping it's not for a while.

"Next week, after Shy's birthday. The fucker will be there for a few more weeks before he has to leave again. She's hoping to finalize the divorce and get all her stuff."

"Let me see where Izzy's at mentally and if she'll want to go. She should be good in a few more days. We'll see after this weekend," I explain.

Everyone gets up, patting Quick on the back, giving him our support. I know there is more to this story, when he's ready, he'll tell me.

CHAPTER TWENTY FIVE | IZZY

I'm so consumed in my song that I don't even hear the studio door open. I have my headphones on trying to place this beat. It's not until I feel someone staring at me that I turn around just as Alex is reaching out to tap my shoulder. I scream, jumping back in my chair, clutching my chest.

"Holyfuckingshit!" I screech out in shock.

"Oh, my God. I'm so sorry, Iz," Alex apologies, holding her own chest.

Ginger runs in. "What's wrong?"

"Iz had her headphones on and didn't hear me come in. When I went to tap her shoulder, she turned around, and I scared the shit out of her," Alex says with a chuckle.

I'm still trying to calm my racing heart but start laughing too. "You scared the shit out of me," I laugh.

"I'm sorry," Alex apologizes again.

I stand up, asking, "Whatcha girls doing?" while giving both the girls a big hug.

They both have big smiles on their faces so I know they're up to something. I fold my arms. "You two are definitely up to something. I can tell," I say, giving them a look to fess up.

"What? We can't come to hang out with our girl and hear this song everyone's talking about, that we haven't gotten to hear yet?" Ginger says, putting her hands on her hips, acting like she's mad but wearing a huge smile.

Seeing them and having them here, knowing they're not mad at me, has me smiling big. Ginger knows me too well. "We wanted to come hear your song and talk to you."

Alexandria just grabs me, giving me another big hug. "I can't believe you would ever think we would be mad at you."

Tears pool up in my eyes, and once I blink, they continue to fall. "I'm so sorry. I just... um... I just didn't know what to say. I'm so lost," I mumble as I cry in my friend's arms. Ginger comes over, hugging us, and smashing me between them.

"Girl, out of anyone, you should know better, we wouldn't leave you. You've been both of our rocks through our shit. We gotta stick together." Ginger's voice is shaky with emotion.

"We love you and are here for you Iz. Don't shut us out," Alex says.

"I don't know what I would do without you girls," I say with a sob.

Ginger squeezes and shakes us making all of us laugh. We break apart, wiping our eyes. I sit back down and they follow, pulling up chairs around me. "So do you want to let us hear your song, do you want to talk, or we can all sit here quietly. It's your choice, but we're not leaving you in here alone anymore. We gave you enough time," Ginger says, folding her arms, looking determined as ever.

I smile. "Well, what do you know or have your men told you?"

Alex and Ginger both look at each other and then back to me. I instantly know, they know everything, and say, "Good, I'm glad you know everything I've told Gus. I'm just really happy you're both here. I'm going stir crazy," I confess with a smile.

"You're right, we know what you've told Gus, but we're here if you need to talk or vent about it some more. Whatever you need. And... if you're going stir crazy, come out tonight. We're both DJing at Club Spin. It will get you out of the house. If you can't do that, then tomorrow at White Wolfe for Shy's birthday bash," Ginger says, bouncing in her chair. "I think you need to go both nights. We miss you."

Alexandria nods her head in agreement. I start to battle in my head if I can do it or not, I've only left the building a handful of times, and it was stressful. Gus told me about both nights, and I told him I would try, but seeing my girls and feeling their energy has me jumping.

"Okay, I'll go both nights."

The girls squeal with excitement and both lean in to hug me. "Good, because my dad got a limo to take us." Alex beams with excitement.

I start to panic, thinking of all of us in the car together. What-ifs start popping in my head.

"Iz, breathe. It will be okay. We'll have all the men in the car, plus someone following us. No one will hurt any of us. We'll be fine," Ginger says, pulling me from my panic attack.

"Now tell us about this song. My parents have told me it's one of a kind, and you're going to kill it," Alex says, distracting me.

I take a deep breath. "Thank you, you two." Exhaling slowly. "Okay, the song." I turn back toward the mixing board as I wipe my eyes.

I start to tell them about these songs I have stuck in my head. Parts that I'm focusing on and what I'm going to do with them. When I let them hear my vocals both girls freak out. I recorded my own voice saying three different verses. 'Say it,' 'Do it,' and 'Fuck you, motherfucker.' After I recorded them, I tweaked it with voice enhancements.

When I finally played what I had so far, they were flipping out with excitement. Both of them started to give me some ideas where I was stuck, and for the next few hours, we made my vision come to life.

Life was like it used to be with us girls just vibing off each other. Music is the one thing that has saved all three of us. Both of them have major talents, and even though we have a different sound that we mix, we mesh so well together and always have.

When we left, I felt like my old self again. I was excited to go out and get past what happened to me. We drop off Alex on her floor before going down one more to where both Ginger and Gus' apartments are located.

Stopping at Gus' door, she pulls me into another hug. "Iz, I love you, girl. No matter what, if you need anything please just tell me. I'm so excited you're coming out. I think it will be the best thing for you." Ginger's voice is filled with happiness which makes my heart swell. I have amazing friends.

"Gin, I do want to say one thing, and please let me say it. I… um…I'm just so blessed to have you as a friend, and I'm so sorry for what happened to you because of me."

"Izzy stop. Stop blaming yourself. It was their fault. You did nothing wrong. Please. Stop blaming yourself," Ginger says. Forcefully grabbing my arms, she gives me a couple of shakes. "Nothing you did made Dom be who he was. It was all him. Please. You will upset me more if you keep blaming yourself. I love you girl." She pulls me in for a tighter hug, holding me and letting me know she means what she said.

We pull away just as Gus' door opens with him standing there wearing nothing but basketball shorts and a huge smile. "Wat's goin' on? You girls good?"

Ginger and I look him over and bust up laughing as we embrace each other to say our goodbyes.

"Are ya alright?" Gus asks, moving me in front of him as we walk into the VIP booth at Club Spin.

I smile. "Yes. I'm actually doing okay," I answer him honestly, because *I am* doing okay now. It took everything I had not to cancel earlier, but once everyone came over to have some pre-party drinks, I relaxed.

Luc rented us a limo, and I actually felt safe being in the limo with everyone and knowing that we had two other cars escorting us. Really there were so many people it was kind of an ordeal getting all of us together, which took my mind off everything else. Gus has had me hooked to his side the whole time. Plus having a handful of shots kind of helped calm the nerves.

I did, however, have a slight panic attack when we arrived at the club, but everyone got out, and security formed a wall around all of us. Gus tucked me into his side, with the men surrounding us women. They hurried us through the throng of people.

The crowd went crazy when we walked in for Maddox, Alex, and Ginger who will be performing tonight. Now walking into a club is a high of its own, but my favorite part of DJing is the adrenaline of performing and seeing the crowd go crazy. Even tonight, tucked into Gus' arms, I still heard my fans, and I'm not even DJing tonight. It makes my heart swell with happiness to hear my fans calling out my name.

Now that we're in the VIP area and no one can come up here, I feel much better. The VIP area is higher than the main floor giving us the view of the whole dance floor and stage. This area is always reserved for Spin It employees and performers. I still feel like people are watching me, but I tell myself I'm a DJ, so there will always be fans watching me.

"Ya sure, Doll?" Gus breathes into my neck placing a kiss in his favorite spot, sending goosebumps down my body.

"Gus..." I giggle. "As long as you're by my side I'm fine. Promise," I say, calmly looking him in the eyes so he knows I'm serious.

I play with his collar, acting like I'm fixing his shirt, but really I just want to feel his hard chest under my fingertips.

"Doll, behave," Gus says, wrapping both arms around my waist and pulling me flush with his enormous body. We fit perfectly together, even with my three-inch heels on, he's still taller than me.

I lean back, facing him, and smile. "You... Redman, are one hot motherfucker," I say seductively.

Gus leans down kissing me, and when he deepens the kiss, I wrap my arms around his neck.

"Goddamn, get a fucking room," Brant bellows as he walks up to us.

We break our kiss, but Gus doesn't let go of his hold on me. "B, I've been waiting fuckin' donkey's year for this, so fuck off, yeah?" Gus says with a laugh and then turns back to me lowering his face and nuzzling it into my neck, making me giggle.

"Fuck me," Brant says, walking away from us and heading toward Mac.

"I could really get used to this attention," I breathe into his earlobe, raking my fingers down the back of his head through his wet hair.

"Doll, ya have no idea how bad I've wanted this," Gus murmurs into my ear, engulfing me into his massive arms when he hugs me.

"Redman, fuck, let her breathe, brother," Quick yells, walking up with Ruby, each of them holding a drink for us.

This time we pull away from each other to face our friends, grabbing our drinks from them. Gus doesn't let go for long. He tucks me back into his side, holding me with one arm while holding his drink in the other. I feel like we're fucking high school kids that can't keep their hands off each other.

Everything seems so different now, even being here at the club with Gus as my boyfriend and not my bodyguard. It just feels so surreal, like I need to pinch myself to wake up from this dream. I've wanted this for so long, but we've both fought it. I can honestly say being here with him has me all giddy, and no man has ever made me feel like this.

Yes, I've had men, and we've had fun at clubs, but, never have I ever wanted to be hooked to a man's hip as I do right now with Gus. It isn't even about feeling scared. I truly want to be next to him, touching him. I've seen it with the other girls but always thought they were crazy. Well, now I know.

I look over to see Maddox and Alexandria snuggled together in the booth talking to Chad, Mac, Dallas, and Brant. And, when I look over to the stage, I see Ginger DJing with Shy right behind her with a couple of club members. Everyone's dressed up in slacks and a nice shirt. Club Spin has a dress code, so no MC leather cuts unless it's a private party or event.

"What are you looking at?" Ruby asks from beside me, attached to Quick.

I laugh, replying, "It's just different now - you know being here with Gus, and even you. It just doesn't seem real."

Ruby tilts her glass up. "Cheers biatch!"

"Cheers biatch, I love you!" I salute her back, taking a drink of my vodka martini.

Gus squeezes me, nodding his head toward Quick as we head over and sit down in the booth. Everyone has been really cool and not asking how I'm doing, well besides Gus. I look around watching all the people dance. Ginger's killing it on stage. She's got the crowd bouncing as she plays "Mr. Saxobeat" by Alexandra Stan. She's really come a long way from when I first met her. Her music has always been good, but her stage performance has become so much more, as well as her interaction with the crowd.

"Whatcha lookin' at?" Quick asks, sitting next to me.

I don't take my eyes off Ginger when I answer, "Gin, she's blossomed so much with Shy by her side."

I take a sip of my drink, feeling Gus' hand slide up my leg, gripping my inner thigh. My body instantly reacts to his touch. My God, sex these last few days has been the best I've ever had. I know he's holding back, letting me heal physically and mentally, but he's more in tune with my body than any man has ever been. I glance over at him, he's talking to Brant and Maddox, sitting across from us.

Quick leans forward, looking over to the stage where Ginger

and Shy are, and says, "Well, I can honestly say I agree with you. Seeing her DJ all those years without him by her side *and now* that he's by her side - she's killing it. I think they bring out the best in each other, but all I know is since they've been together, he's one happy motherfucker to be around now." Quick laughs, leaning back and snuggling into Ruby, who has been totally quiet tonight.

I realize that I'm sitting between Gus and Quick and that Ruby is on the other side. I know something's wrong with Ruby, I just haven't taken the time to question her. Until today, I've been self-absorbed with my own shit.

I lean forward to look at my best friend. "Rube, why the fuck are you over there and not sitting next to me? You two switch," I demand, laughing.

I'm turned facing them as they switch. Gus never lets go of my thigh, keeping me close, always touching me.

"There! I felt like you were way the fuck over there," I say, picking my glass up to cheers her again.

"Sorry, I just love this club and all the music. Goddamn, Snow's killing it tonight." Ruby's dancing in her seat next to me while watching Ginger on stage.

"I guess I've never really sat here and just chilled. I'm usually bouncing around dancing or mingling." I pause to look around the booth when Alexandria catches my eye.

"What?" she yells from across the table making everyone look at me.

I smile and shrug. "I'm just looking at how much we've changed."

Alexandria smiles, lifting her shot glass. "Cheer biatches!" Everyone at the booth raises their glass, and us girls repeat her, but the boys yell, "Nut up, fuckers!" We all laugh taking a drink.

Ginger starts to mix in her next song, and I get excited, hearing her 'Mercer' mix she just made. I look over to Alex, and she hears it too. We smile at each other and simultaneously punch an arm up in the air and yell, "Be a boss!" and automatically start bobbing our head to the song "Boss" by Mercer. The whole table starts to recite the lyrics as we all move to the beat.

I watch everyone laughing, which makes me happy. It's like every cell in my body is overfilled with joy. I love seeing all my peeps with smiles, having a good time and dancing. Gus slides his hand up my thigh cupping me between my legs as he leans back against the booth, moving his upper body to the song. I instantly get wet seeing him relax and let loose. Gus isn't a big dancer, but I've caught him grooving to the beats before. But then again, he's usually always working so he couldn't dance.

Ginger mixes into the next song, "Your Love" by Mercer, making all of us girls dance in our seats.

Alex yells across the booth to us, "Let's dance right here." She motions right in front of the table and Ruby, the firecracker she is - jumps up instantly, moving in a circle bouncing from foot to foot.

Alex is next out of the booth and I turn to Gus leaning in giving him a kiss before hopping out of the booth to join the girls. It feels good to be dancing and laughing with my girls. I feel alive. I move my arms above my head, swaying my hips when the third song mixes in, "Satisfy" feat. Ron Carrol by Mercer.

I turn to face Gus who's captivated watching me dance in front of him. He looks different - happy or maybe relaxed. I bite my lip, blowing him a kiss, as I bounce around and then sway side to side. I point to him, enticing him while I sing. Instantly his face changes from enchanted to feral.

He sets his drink down as he stands up, reaching for my hand. He pulls me to him, and says in a deep husky voice, "Come on."

I think he's upset until he places a quick kiss on my lips. "Where are we going?" He doesn't answer me, pulling me with determination through the VIP area. I grip his hand stopping him. "Gus, where are we going? I don't want to leave the VIP area," I say panicked, seeing all the people on the dance floor. I look to Ginger, holding her headset, mixing in the next song by Calvin

Harris, "One Kiss, with Dua Lipa." He doesn't answer me, so I ask again, "Gus where—"

He turns abruptly kissing me. I moan into his mouth, wrapping my small hands around his muscular waist, feeling his rock hard erection.

Breaking the kiss, he leans into me, placing his lips inches away from my ear, and he drawls sexily, "One kiss, is all it takes. I'm riding ya hard in the jacks, real quick. *yeah*?" His heavy breathing against my skin has me turning into a bitch-in-heat, becoming instantly wet.

I nod my head with a devilish smirk, and that's all it takes as he grabs my hand leading us out of the VIP area.

Best night ever! I must be dreaming.

CHAPTER TWENTY SIX | GUS

For years, I've been standing on the side watching her, wanting her, craving her. Finally, she's mine. My life is all about control, but Izzy pushes me beyond that. Christ, watching her dance in front of the booth had me fuckin' losing my mind. I can't handle it. I need to be in her, consume her, and make sure every cocksucker here knows she's taken.

Now that she's mine, I didn't know I would feel this different. Being here at the club with her, as her man standing next to her and not as her bodyguard standing behind her feels so fuckin' right. I can't keep my hands off of her, wanting her within arm's reach all the time. I'm not used to having all these emotions control me.

Izzy giggles behind me as I pull her toward the private bathroom for performers. When I see Hunter working security, I grin, giving him a nod and the look, letting him know not to let anyone in. He nods back with a smirk, as we enter the bathroom together. I swing the door open, letting Izzy enter first.

"Red...man..." Izzy giggles. "You're a naughty little boy." Obviously, the few drinks she's had tonight have given her the giggles.

Bolting the door, I turn around to find Izzy bent over, swaying that beautiful ass of hers while checking under the stalls. I try to tell myself to be easy, to go slow with her but every muscle in my body tells me I need to dominate her. I growl, "Legs..."

Izzy pops back up giggling, and I'm instantly behind her twirling her around in my arms. I begin to back her toward the lounge area where there's a couple of chairs and a mirror. I continue until she's flush against the soft plush wall opposite the mirror.

When I see her eyes glaze over, I know she wants this just as much as I do. With my hands on her hips pinning her to the wall, I crush my lips against hers with a groan. I slide my tongue in and out of her mouth, fucking her with my tongue. I feel like I'm a crazed man needing to claim her.

Groaning, I pull back breathless, and say, "I've wanted to do this for far too long. Fuck… seein' ya dancing… I…I couldn't wait. I need to be inside ya." I push her long hair back behind her shoulders, giving me full access to her divine neck.

Dazed, she simply says, "Yes." As I lick down her neck, biting the crevice of her perfect neck, she moans, "Redman…" placing her hands on my shoulders for support.

She's beautiful with her face flushed, wanting and ready for me. I demand, "Keep your eyes open." I run my hands down her hips, tugging her black shiny skinny pants slowly down her legs. I remove her fuck-me stiletto heel so I can slip one leg out. Placing her heel back on, I begin to slowly kiss my way back up her leg. "Christ, these legs are fuckin' grand. It's why you're named Legs and they're my legs now," I say, my voice sounding deep and husky. It's always been her legs and neck that get me all crazed. My fetishes are screaming to come out and play, but I need to control my urges until she is ready.

Izzy moans with her lips parted, breathlessly saying, "Yes."

I'm kissing and gliding my hands up her inner thighs, as I move up her body. I make sure I stop before touching her center, knowing it's one of her triggers.

As I undo my trousers, I grab her waist, pulling her flush against my body. Looking into her eyes I say, "Doll, keep your eyes on me. If I do anything to trigger ya, just say stop. I need ya so fuckin' bad. This riding's gonna be hard and fast, yeah? I just need to be inside ya. Like a goddamn junkie needing my next fix."

I bite her neck, sucking her flesh into my mouth, wishing I could wrap my hand around it and claim her as mine.

She throws her head back against the wall with a hiss, "Yes, Redman..." I suck harder, biting her neck, knowing it will leave a mark. *Mine...*

I growl, "Legs, say it again." Grabbing her ass cheeks, I lift her up, pinning her to the wall as I slip my swollen cock in her soaked entrance. I love hearing her moan my club name.

Izzy's labored breathing has her mouth ajar. Goddamn, she looks like a little sex kitten in my arms, those red lips and her hair all disheveled. I slam my dick into her, immediately pulling out and slamming back into her, bottoming out.

"Fuck, yes," Izzy cries out.

"This fuckin' pussy's mine," I growl, sounding possessed as I lock eyes with my little sex kitten. I start to pump in and out of her, looking down to watch my cock slide in and out coated with her arousal. "Jaysus Christ, Legs, watch your cunt take all of my cock. G'lawd... I'm going to come." I look back up to find her transfixed with her eyes glazed over staring passionately at me. I grip her ass tighter, slamming my cock into her. I move faster, picking up speed. We're both lost in pure pleasure, moaning and panting with each thrust.

"Red...man," she rasps out.

"Legs," I grunt.

"Redman, fuck me," she demands, digging her fingers into my hair and tugging it, snapping my head back. I roar a deep roar, hearing her order me to fuck her has the animal in me wanting to break loose. I grip her tighter, hammering her against the wall.

"Sweet Jaysus, this cunt of yours. Fuck!" I yell, hearing our bodies slapping against each other loudly. My balls tense up, and I'm so close to coming. "Isabella...ah fuck," I grit out, my legs and ass muscles starting to burn with each thrust.

"Red...I'm...uh...ah..." Izzy throws her head back. I lower

my mouth to her neck, biting and sucking. I'm addicted to her throat. I can't wait until I can do so much more to this neck.

"Fuck..." I grunt. "Legs come, baby," I say breathlessly.

"Faster Aengus... Fuck. I'm...I'm..." Izzy screams as her climax splits her into a million pieces.

My thrusts become erratic with her tits and head bouncing.

Fuck I'm close. Goddamn, her pussy is so - it's so fucking tight.

I feel her pussy spasm, squeezing and milking my cock. "Oh, fuck. Yeah. Fuck, Doll. Yes..." I come so hard, filling her full with each thrust.

Izzy starts to giggle underneath me, bringing me back from my lust induced state. I pump a couple more times before pulling out of her. I release her legs, letting her stand. *Holy shit*, I'm out of breath, and my legs are screaming, but fuck that was good. I cup her face, bringing my lips down to kiss her. I deepen the kiss, becoming drunk on her taste, with Izzy melting into me with a moan.

Breaking the kiss, I confess, "I can't get enough of ya now, Doll. I feel like we have so much to make up for."

Izzy laughs. "I have to say I like this side of you. You can have me as much as you want. It's so much better having you *in me* rather than *around me*," she teases.

I grab her chin, holding it up as I stare down into her eyes. "I was thinking the same thing. I don't ever want to let ya go or stop touching ya. I want everyone to know who ya belong to." I kiss her, sucking her lower lip. "Now let me clean ya up so we can get back to our friends." I make sure she's okay to stand without my help before I go get us a paper towel. When I return I wipe her clean and squat down to help her put her foot back into her pants.

"Thank you," Izzy whispers softly, holding my shoulders. "I've known for so long you were amazing and now you're actually mine," she says, sounding choked up.

I chuckle, slipping her foot back into her red stiletto. I look up and say, "Perfect fit. Must mean you're my princess and I'm your beast."

Izzy grabs my face with both hands. "I sure fucking hope so because I've waited a long time for you." Laughing, we meet each other halfway and kiss.

"Let's head back out before I take ya again." I chuckle, smacking her ass as she walks to the sink to freshen up.

It's the end of the night, and I'm sitting in the booth watching my girl dance with the other girls. Maddox and Alex are DJing right now doing the closing set. Me, Shy, Quick, Brant, Worm, and Tiny are sitting around the booth drinking whiskey while the girls dance in front of us. Maze showed up a little bit ago with Tiny and Worm. As soon as she got here, she joined Ginger, Ruby, and Izzy dancing.

Mac, Dallas, and Chad are dancing with six bitches. I look over watching them grind on each other. The night couldn't have gone better. *Thank fuck.* I was so worried something would trigger Izzy.

After we fucked in the bathroom, the beast stayed dormant. As long as I can see her, I'm good. My hand twitches to touch her but I know she's mine and isn't going anywhere. I'll have my way with her again tonight. My sexy little kitten is teasing me shaking her ass, dancing all fucking sexy and shit. My dick has been hard most of the night. The girls are pretty plastered, and I can honestly say I'm pretty *scuttered* myself.

"Redman, she seems to be doing good," Shy says, leaning in closer so only I can hear him.

Never taking my eyes off of her I nod my head. "Thank fuckin' Christ."

"Have you had the talk with her yet? I've meant to ask you, but with everything going on, I'd forgotten."

One night when I was shitfaced drunk at the clubhouse, I told Quick and Shy about why I hadn't claimed her yet. I went into all my shit. They both told me I was fucking stupid for waiting this long. It was around the same time that all the shit with Dominic started happening, and I knew my boys were right. I needed to pull my head out of my arse and take what was mine.

"Nah, not yet. Was gonna when she came back from LA but that went to *shite*. She knows we need to have a talk, but I told her no matter wat she's mine, regardless of having the talk. Nothing will change that," I explain.

"Good to hear brother, good to hear. I'm just glad you pulled your head out of your ass and claimed her finally. She's been flaunting it in front of you for far too long," Shy says, laughing next to me, giving me a slap on the shoulder. He leans back in. "Oh, I forgot to ask you, but do you think Legs is up for DJing a little bit tomorrow for my birthday?"

I laugh, looking at my watch, "Ya mean tonight?" I lift my drink. "Happy birthday, brother." Everyone raises their drinks to cheers, yelling out happy birthday. The girls bounce over saying happy birthday and pull him up to dance. They surround him, and I can't help but laugh at the poor wanker as each girl takes a turn dancing with him.

All the girls get distracted laughing at Maddox and Alex messing with each other on stage. Letting Shy make his escape, when he comes to sit back down with us, we start to razz him.

All of a sudden, Izzy stops dancing. She's frozen in place staring out at the dance floor. I fly up from my seat pulling her behind me. I look out over the crowd for anyone that might have set her off. Then we hear it, whistles, the rest of the men spring into action looking around for who's whistling.

We spot a group of young ravers in the middle of the dance floor whistling along with the song, and everyone relaxes except

Izzy. I can feel how tense she is from behind me. Turning, I pull her into my arms. Guiding us back to the booth, setting her in my lap, I push her hair out of her face and ask if she's alright. Ginger, Shy, Ruby, and Quick crowd around to make sure she's okay.

In a soft voice, Izzy says, "I thought I saw him." I see Shy bolt up grabbing a few men. Izzy continues, "I heard the whistle and thought I saw him. But, after I blinked, he was gone. I can't live my life in fear of whistles." I close my eyes. Thank God Shy heard her and went to check to make sure she didn't really see him. Izzy takes a deep breath. "I'm safe with all of you by my side," she says, turning to face me with a smile that steals my heart. "Well, mostly I have you by my side now, so I'll be fine." Leaning down, she places a soft kiss on my lips.

"Doll, ya keep talkin' and touchin' me like that I might need to take ya to the loo to throw it in ya again before we leave," I say teasing, hoping to relax her. I'm anything but relaxed, but I can't let her know.

Izzy's eyes heat with desire and a smile, saying, "Anytime, Redman."

Growling, I pull her closer, giving her another deep kiss.

"Goddamn, you two are worse than any of these fuckers," Brant exclaims, sitting next to us.

We break our kiss laughing. Izzy shifts, turning in my lap so she can see the stage and dance floor.

I grip her hips, pulling her closer to me. Let's pray Shy doesn't find anything.

Mine...

CHAPTER TWENTY SEVEN | IZZY

"Are ya goin' to do it?" Gus asks from the bathroom. I roll over in bed stretching, feeling all my muscles ache from our couple rounds of sex last night. A smile spreads across my lips thinking of the mind-blowing hot sex we had after coming home. Everyone ended up heading to the clubhouse, except Ruby, Quick, Gus, and I. Ruby had a babysitter for Bella, so we decided to come back to the apartments. Gus and I ended up moving to his place knowing we wanted some *privacy*. And boy, did we need it.

"Are ya listening to me, Doll?" Gus says, walking out of the bathroom freshly showered, wearing only boxers with a towel around his neck. Goddamn, I love his hair. He's got red hair like Kevin McKidd from *Grey's Anatomy*, but a *fuck me* body like Chris Hemsworth. My mouth salivates watching him towel his hair dry. I raise up on my elbows, exposing my breasts, with a smile.

"Sorry, I was just thinking of all the amazing sex we had last night," I say seductively, biting my lower lip.

"Doll, you're bein' bold," he says, dropping his towel and crawling on the bed. "I need to do some club business today and get ready for the party tonight." He continues to climb up my body. "Otherwise" —grabbing my breasts and lapping each one— "I would have no problem staying here bonking ya all day."

I moan, my elbows collapsing, as he takes one of my breasts into his mouth.

I run my hands through his glorious hair, lost in his touch. I forget about everything but us and the way he makes me feel, as another throaty moan escapes me. I hear the sheets being pushed aside, and boxers being discarded. Minutes later I feel his hard warm body cover mine.

My body lights up like a fucking Christmas tree, wanting more, needing more, I beg, "Aengus, please..."

Gus shifts, releasing my breast, as he slowly moves up my body to nuzzle his face in my neck. "I guess I could throw it in real quick," he murmurs, inches away from my ear, grazing and sucking my lobe.

"Yes. God, yes," I entice him, locking my hands behind his neck, pulling him closer. I lick his neck down to his massive trap muscle. Sucking his flesh into my mouth, I bite...hard.

Gus growls loud, shifting up on his forearms, he locks eyes with me. What I see is a wild animal hungry for his prey. His face is tight, with his jaw clenched he looks enraged. My breath catches in my throat. I'm about to apologize to him for biting him so hard when he smashes his mouth against mine demanding entrance.

Gus reaches between us placing himself at my entrance, slamming himself deep inside me, never breaking the kiss. Both of us let out a deep throaty moan, feeling the carnal electricity ignite between us like it always has. I push for more, entwining my fingers through his hair and tugging hard. Gus' head snaps back, breaking the kiss, he roars, "Fuck yes," thrusting himself deeper and bottoming out.

"Harder," I grit.

Gus stops his movement and looks down at me with mixed emotions. "Doll, I don't want to hurt ya or trigger anything bad," he says, sounding concerned. His eyes are wild wanting more...I know he wants to be let loose.

I think about all the sex we've been having and how gentle he's been - sticking with missionary style positions with me, except last night in the bathroom when he took me against the wall. It was fucking amazing. Holding his stare, I reply, "Gus, I want you. I love everything we've done so far, but you know what I like. Fingering and choking aren't on the table right now, but I trust you.

I've wanted you for so long. I think we can figure out other ways to satisfy my...or I mean *our* cravings."

Gus silently searches my eyes for something - what...I have no idea. So, I pull his head down, placing a soft kiss on his lips and breathe, "I want you to fuck me harder." Then, I tug his hair hard again.

Gus closes his eyes and groans a deep...long... loud...groan. I begin to think he's going to deny me when he pulls out of me. He shifts himself up onto his knees, and leans back on his shins, between my legs. I can see his chest muscles strain as he grips my ankle flipping me over. I yelp with excitement, "Aengus..."

Grabbing my waist, he pulls me up onto his lap with my back to his front. In a rough voice, he says, "We'll try this for now." Taking a long deep breath, nuzzling his face in my hair, he kisses my shoulder saying, "I gotta leave soon, but this should tame both our cravings for now."

Gus' hands slide from my waist to my breasts. Cupping them, he softly squeezes my erect nipples between his fingers, like a tender suckle. Placing my hands over his, I encourage him to grip them tighter. He complies, tightening his hold as he twists and pinches my nipples sending shots of pleasure and pain straight to my core.

I moan, "Yes," leaning my head back against him as I circle my ass over his twitching cock beneath me, causing his breathing to become labored.

"Put your hands on the bed," he commands in a deep, resonant voice.

Moaning, he moves with me, positioning us on our knees. When I place my hands on the bed, he inhales deeply through his nose before lifting off my back.

My body is wound so tight that I start to pant, anticipating the release of the animal I see inside him. I know he's domineering, I see it in his eyes. He wants to dominate me completely, but he's been holding back because of what happened to me. Which is understandable, but I want him, no I need him to come out and play.

Gus swipes my hair over one shoulder exposing my neck, shoulders, and back. I can hear him take deep heavy breaths through his nose, I try and do the same to slow my breathing, but it's not working, the anticipation is killing me. Slowly, he begins to rake his fingertips down my sides. Gripping my hip with one hand, he palms his dick with the other, slapping it against my ass before sliding it up through my slick folds coating it with my desire.

He curses, "Christ, your cunt's fuckin' perfect" —moving his hand from my hip over my ass cheek, massaging it— "always ready for me."

"Hurry...I want you," I clip, needing him deep inside me.

Gus places his cock at my entrance, pushing the tip in just a bit before withdrawing, teasing me. "Remember. Patience..." he says while continuing to bob his cock in and out of my pussy, never fully entering me. "Ya want me cock?" he says, sounding amused.

"Yes, please," I beg.

With both hands, he palms the globes of my ass, gripping them hard and spreading them open. "Tell me how fuckin' bad ya want *me cock* and wat ya want me to do to this cunt of yours." His voice is deep and commanding as his cock continues to slip it in and out of me.

My pussy throbs with each word that leaves his mouth. I comply, "Fuck me. I want your cock so deep inside me. Please Red, fuck me harder."

Gus growls, gripping my ass harder, digging his nails into my flesh. "Christ, I like when ya call me Red."

"Fuck. Me. Red. Please," I beg, hoping to push him further.

He roars, slamming his full length into me. I cry out, "Oh, yes, Red," tightening my grip on the bed. He begins to hammer into me vigorously, going deeper than he's ever gone.

"G'lawd, your cunt's fuckin' tight," he growls low in his throat.

I gasp, "Ah, yeah. Harder."

Gus chuckles behind me....*smack*. I throw my head back in ecstasy as he smacks my ass three more times between thrusts.

Gus grunts, "Christ, your pussy's dripping down *me balls*. Ya like that, dontcha?"

My body electrifies, sending waves of tingles across my body as the pain turns pleasurable, making me want more. I moan, "Yes..."

Gus continues to slam into me while running his fingers up and down my torso, ending with a hard smack. My pussy starts to throb, clenching around his girth.

"Aengus... ah...yes," I pant.

Leaning over me slightly, gripping my shoulder with one hand, he starts to jackhammer into me fast. "Jaysus, my balls... I'm close, Doll," he grunts, breathless.

My knuckles turn white as I grip the bed. I'm panting hard, moaning every time my ass slams against him. I'm close too, thrusting back against him, slamming our bodies together.

"That's it...touch yerself," Gus grunts harder with each pump. "Come for me."

Gus' thrusts are more powerful as his cock swells. My arms give out, I collapse, falling forward and face planting into the bed. Gus groans, gripping my hips and holding my ass up in the air. I can feel his balls hit my clit in this position. I slide both my hands between my legs, feeling his cock powering in and out of my pussy before circling around my throbbing nub. My orgasm explodes, shattering me. I scream out my release into the bed.

My other hand cups his balls, softly fondling them, sending him over the edge. Gus erupts with a loud guttural roar, digging his fingers into my hips as he jacks me harder, filling me full of cum. "Fuck me." He keeps thrusting into me as animalistic noises escape him.

I feel another orgasm building, so I increase my finger motion around my clit. I place my other hand against my pussy, spreading my fingers, gripping his cock between two fingers. I massage his hard cock and my pussy lips as he keeps thrusting inside of me. I moan loud into the bed, pushing my hips back, demanding more as my walls contract around him.

"Sweet Jaysus," he exhales, breathless, grabbing around my waist and pulling me up against his body.

I release his cock but continue to flick my clit. Gus slows his thrusts, keeping himself seated inside me.

"Fuck ya... come again," Gus breathes into my ear, nipping it with his teeth. "This cunt's mine. I want ya to touch it." Gus' voice is thick and raw with emotion.

"Ah..." I rotate my ass over his thrusting pelvis, feeling him hardening with each thrust. I tilt my head back letting out a long deep moan. I'm so fucking close. I'm so lost in euphoria and the promise of another orgasm I don't listen to what he's saying. I just hear him murmuring something.

I need more so I start to move up and down on his dick. Gus curses in his native tongue as he thrusts up into me harder and faster, making me bounce on his lap with each thrust. I start panting, "Yes," over and over again as I work my clit faster. Gus reaches up and pinches my nipples so hard I come instantly, going limp against his chest as my orgasm consumes me.

Chasing his own orgasm, he reaches up over my chest, gripping my collarbone, securing me to him. He rasps, "Christ this neck of yours. The things I want..." before biting my neck and sucking it hard as he pounds up into me.

"Aengus..." I purr as a third orgasm hits me. Gus grunts, releasing my neck as his own release comes, filling me up.

"Jaysus, Doll," he says, collapsing forward as we both fall flat against the bed. My body is still twitching and my limbs are heavy from the mind-blowing orgasms. I feel high and can't move my body.

"Sweet Mother of Christ," Gus mumbles behind me, catching his breath. "G'lawd, the things I want to do to ya, but fuck, I gotta go."

I lay limp in my orgasmic high when his phone rings. Gus groans, rolling over, grabbing his phone from the side table. "What's the story?" he answers hoarsely, clearing his throat. "Okay. I'm on my way." Shutting his phone, wrapping his arms back around my waist, he pulls me back against him. "I gotta go, Doll," he says softly.

I moan, letting him know I heard him but still can't move or speak.

Gus chuckles. "So are ya gonna DJ tonight? Shy needs to know."

I nod my head, still not able to form any kind of words. Gus laughs, rolling his enormous body over mine so we're facing each other. "Doll, are ya sure? I need ya to look at me and tell me ya, okay?"

I open my eyes with a smile, "Ye— " but stop to clear my throat. "Yes, Red. I'm going to DJ."

He smiles, kissing me. "Fuckin' gran."

CHAPTER TWENTY EIGHT | IZZY

God, it feels good DJing again. It's packed here tonight at the White Wolfe Lounge. Everyone's here for Shy's birthday bash. When he asked me to DJ, I freaked out at first. But, I realized I was being stupid and that I needed to get over my fear. Shy filled me in on his plans for the night, and I freaked out, totally excited for my girl. She's going to flip out when he asks her in front of everyone.

Looking out over the crowd, I spot Gus laughing with his friends at the bar. He seems happier and more relaxed since we got together. My heart skips a beat thinking about how much happier I am with him. Gus glances over, making eye contact, giving me a nod making sure I'm okay. I smile and pucker my lips to kiss him, which makes him smile and wink back at me.

My God, he's hot as fuck and all mine.

"You've got it bad," Ruby says from behind me. "I'm so happy for you."

I turn to face my best friend with a huge shit-eating grin on my face. "Hell yeah, I've got it bad. He's finally mine," I answer, ecstatic.

She laughs but doesn't say anything.

Sensing something is wrong, I ask, "Are you okay?" I know her and Quick have been dealing with something, but I haven't had a chance to talk to her about it yet.

"Yeah, I'm just tired of dealing with Brody," Ruby says, sounding exhausted.

"Are you and Quick okay?" I ask, hoping they are.

My best friend smiles, but I can see in her eyes something is wrong. "He's too good to me. I feel bad—"

I interrupt her, "Why?"

"I- I have all this baggage, and I feel like he feels he should deal with everything. I've told him I could handle Brody, but..." She trails off.

"But...what?" I push her to spill what's going on.

Ruby bites her lip nervously. "Brody has been threatening me and—"

I flip out, cutting her off. "He's been threatening you... how?" I say, pissed off, adding, "And why haven't you told me?" I put my hands on my hips, emphasizing I'm upset with her. We have always protected each other. I've always handled people being mean to her, and she's guided me through this life. It wasn't until she got married and I moved to New York that we started to drift apart from each other.

"Iz, I just didn't want to bother you too with my drama. You've been dealing with your own shit," she tries to explain, but I'm not letting her off the hook.

"Rube, you better start talking, and I want to know everything," I say, folding my arms over my chest.

She begins telling me about all the text messages and voicemails that Brody's been leaving her, which makes my blood boil. He's always been a fucking prick who likes to manipulate Ruby, but this is a whole new level. I tell her to hold on while I mix in another song and try to calm down. When I turn around, I ask, "What does Quick think of all of this?"

She doesn't look happy and says, "He talked to Brody one night, and it didn't go well. Quick told me not to worry about it. Well, I guess he called some friends who live in LA and had them rough him up. Quick didn't tell me, but Brody sent me pictures of himself from the hospital."

"Are you fucking serious? Holy shit," I gasp, placing my hand over my mouth, making a mental note to hug Quick later. But I know she doesn't want to hear that so I hide my appreciation and act shocked.

"Yeah, so that's what we've been kind of fighting about. I was mad at first, but he explained, no one threatens him or his ol' lady." I want to say something about him calling her his ol' lady, but I keep my mouth shut and let her finish. "That he'll always take care of me and that I shouldn't have to put up with that kind of bullshit," she says, sounding conflicted.

"So... are you two okay?" I ask. Before she can reply, I add with a smile, "Because...It's kind of badass how he's protecting you *and* calling you his ol' lady." I fold my arms over my chest again, finishing with, "Because, if I could, I would kick Brody's ass too."

Ruby chuckles, then she becomes serious, sounding nervous. "I'm just scared. I don't want anything to happen to Quick now that Brody is on a rampage. We leave in a few days to head back home to get the rest of our stuff, meet with the divorce lawyer, and so Bella can see her dad. I just don't want any more trouble."

"It will all work out, but you need to let Quick protect you, because if it isn't me, I'm glad it's Quick. Brody is a piece of shit," I say, giving her a hug.

"Thank you. He makes me unbelievably happy. It would be even better if we didn't have to deal with Brody all the time. I wish he would just go back on tour," she says as I release her from my arms.

I hear someone calling my name. I turn around to look at the crowd and see Shy moving toward me, "Legs!" he shouts again.

I nod my head in recognition, and he gives me the thumbs up, so I lower the music. Shy reaches into the DJ area and grabs the mic from me.

"Hello? Test. Test. Quiet, everyone. Can you all hear me back there?" he asks toward the back of the lounge. When we hear Mac yell back, "Yes," Shy continues, "I want to thank everyone for coming out tonight for my birthday." The crowd yells back making Shy laugh. "Yeah. Yeah. Yeah. Let me finish." The crowd becomes quiet again. I see Ginger moving toward Shy, carrying his cake lit with candles. Her dad and uncle are parting the crowd for her.

She starts singing, "Happy birthday to you," and everyone falls in sync with her singing happy birthday to Shy. Once the song's over, Shy blows out the candles. Her auntie Storm grabs the cake from her as Shy leans in to kiss her, pulling her into his side.

"Now most of you know, but for those of you that don't, I've loved this girl since she was sixteen years old." Shy pauses a second for people to whistle and cheer. When they settle down he continues, "And well... I think it's about fucking time I did this *and* since y'all are here."

Ginger looks at Shy curiously while everyone starts cheering. Shy turns to Ginger, bending down on one knee. Ginger gasps, lifting both hands to cover her mouth in surprise. "Angel, will you make me the happiest man alive and marry me?" Shy pops open the ring box, and with tears in her eyes, she nods her head yes. The room erupts with hoots and hollering. Shy stands up, putting the ring on her finger, sealing it with a kiss.

Wolfe, Ginger's father, grabs the mic. "Let's give them a few minutes, shall we?"

As I start the song, "Marry Me" by Train that Shy picked out. The crowd spreads out, giving them some room, as the couple stands there kissing. When they break, Ginger has makeup under her eyes from crying. Shy helps clean it off as they both laugh.

I'm so captivated by them I don't even notice Ruby leaving the room. I sense him behind me, even before his two big hands slide around my waist, pulling me back against his chest. I'm so happy for my friends a few tears escape my eyes. Gus leans down and kisses my temple when I sink into him. We both just stand there watching our friends slow dance, laughing.

Gus breaks the silence murmuring inches from my ear, "Do ya know how happy I am? How right this feels?" He grips me tighter.

I turn in his arms, placing my hands on his chest. "I hope it's as happy as you make me," I say softly in return. Gus pulls me tighter against him, enveloping me into his massive chest.

"Doll, things are gonna be changing for us... a lot of good things to come," Gus says with a promising voice as he lightly kisses me.

"Quit fuckin' kissing and join the party," Dallas yells from the dance floor.

"I can't wait. Now let's go celebrate with our friends." I pull his head down for a deeper kiss before heading out to join everyone.

"After you, Doll," Gus laughs, swatting my ass.

When I get to the dance floor and see Ginger surrounded by my girls, I cry out, "Ohmygodohmygodohmygod!" bouncing up to them. Our tribe starts squealing like little school girls as we jump up and down holding each other — Eva, Alexandria, Maze, Ruby, Ginger, and I all hug. "I'm so happy for you girl! I love you!" I choke out as tears roll down my face.

"Love you too," Ginger says, beaming.

"You bitches know what time it is - time to drink!" Maze yells, pulling us toward the bar.

Thirty minutes later we're all tipsy, hanging out in the lounge area that's roped off for us. There are like ten of us girls now with Ginger's family and friends from West Virginia here. All the men are surrounding the bar. Everyone is laughing and having a great time. I love to watch Gus with his friends, bikers, and security crew.

I was relieved when no one brought up what happened or asked me how I was doing. In the last year we've all had some major shit happen to us, but tonight we've put our own drama aside and just relaxed, basking in the celebration. We all need to move forward from the shit that has been plaguing us. Hopefully, tonight's celebration will be one of many to come.

This is good!

It's like Gus said, good things are coming. God knows we deserve it.

I get up from the oversized plush chair I'm sitting in to refresh my drink. I move toward the table with the vodka but am pulled back against my burly man. I laugh. "Red, what're you doing?" I say, turning in his arms to face him.

Gus chuckles. "I wanna touch ya." His eyes glaze lustfully, and I can see he's a bit intoxicated. He has to be feeling good from all those whiskey shots I saw them taking.

Gus tilts his head down slightly, giving me a quick kiss, pressing his steel length against me. I giggle, caressing my hands over his muscular biceps.

"Well, I like you touching me," I sass back, feeling frisky myself. The girls have been doing shots too and add in the vodka tonics I'm drinking, I'm feeling pretty good.

"Dance with me, Doll," Gus murmurs against my ear, kissing me just under my lobe.

I'm shocked he wants to dance, so I pull back to look him in the eyes, and question, "Really?" I smirk.

"Uh huh," Gus answers, pulling me toward the dance floor. "Tennessee Whiskey" by Chris Stapleton, blares across the lounge.

Gus grips my hand and twirls me around before lifting it to his chest, securing it with his. I giggle, loving how affectionate he is in public with me. He slips his other hand around my waist and pulls me close. We both inhale a long deep breath.

Swaying to the music, Gus slowly slides his hand from my waist to the middle of my back. I can't believe he dances - and he's good. I thought he was perfect before, but seeing this soft romantic side of him has me falling even more in love with him.

Humming along with the music, he lowers his head, nuzzling his face into my neck. He rasps, "I can't wait to taste ya...hmmm. Christ, you're sweet as wine and smooth as my favorite whiskey." Making goosebumps erupt across my body.

I'm lost in his words as he makes up his own lyrics to the song.

Gus' long legs move us around as he holds me tight against him. I moan each time his cock rubs against me. My center is throbbing with need, soaking my panties.

He kisses my neck a couple of times, and we both groan. "Christ, Isabella, I can't get enough of ya. I always want more," Gus says inches from my lobe.

"In Case You Didn't Know" by Brett Young mixes in. I love this song, making up my own lyrics I sing to him, "Mmmm… here goes nothing. Aengus, in case you didn't know I couldn't love you any more than I already do." I tilt my head back to look up at him and giggle. "*But* damn… I had no idea you could dance."

Gus chuckles, making his chest vibrate.

Moving our hands from his chest, he lifts my head, kissing me softly, and says, "Doll, there's a lot of things ya don't know about me…but you'll find out soon."

I can't wait.

CHAPTER TWENTY NINE | IZZY

Waking up in Gus' arms is probably the best thing ever. Well, besides sex *and* dancing with him.

By the end of the night, the girls were so drunk the men had to take us home. I was exhausted from being out late two nights, and I passed the fuck out.

Lifting my head, I see Gus' still sleeping heavily. I wiggle out of his grasp and head to the bathroom.

I need coffee.

We stayed at his place again last night. I have a feeling I'll be over here more than my place.

I throw on one of Gus' t-shirts and make my way to the kitchen so I can start some coffee and for once make my man some breakfast.

I'm starved.

Gus is always taking care of me, I need to start returning the favor. He's always up before me, getting me coffee, food, or whatever I need. He says he loves doing things for me. Since I've been home, we've been pretty much inseparable. He plans everything, keeping us busy doing shit all day. I guess it's a good thing, since I don't do much anyway except work on songs and DJ. I have money, so I do what I love... music. It's never a dull moment with my Irish beast.

I pull out my phone and put in my wireless earbuds. The music starts as I move around the kitchen making eggs, bacon, and potatoes. I know my man loves to eat and always has food. Lost in my own thoughts, dancing to the tunes, I don't notice when Gus enters the kitchen.

I've been bouncing around the kitchen cooking. When one of my jams comes on, "We Speak No Americano" by Yolanda Be Cook & DCup comes on, I start to bounce side to side on the balls of my feet as I nod my head back and forth to the beat. I hum along, swinging the spatula in the air, in between mixing the food. When the food is done, I grab the skillet and swirl around. I scream, almost dropping the food, not expecting to see Gus leaning against the wall smiling at me.

Setting the skillet down on the island, I pull my earbuds out clenching at my chest. My heart feels like it's going to burst through my skin, it's beating so hard.

"Red, you scared the shit out of me," I blurt out, laughing.

Gus' gorgeous ass is still leaning against the wall with his arms crossed, laughing. I'm frozen in place as I totally eye fuck his very naked, very large chest, and lick me please - sculpted abs.

Lordy-lordy, he needs to give me some of that yum-yum. I lick my lips just salivating at the thought.

Gus moves like lightning from the wall, taking two long strides, pulling me to him for a quick kiss, making us both moan. "Isabella, you keep looking at me like that, and all this food you made will either be burnt or cold by the time I'm done with ya."

My stomach growls as I swallow hard. Gus throws his head back with a full belly laugh.

"Jaysus Christ you're adorable."

Snapping out of my lust induced stupor, I swat him on the arm, giggling, "Let me go before we burn the bacon." Grabbing the spatula, I point it to the bar stool on the other side of the island, "Now go sit and let me feed you."

"Hmmm, ya've no idea how bad I want to spank ya right now with that fuckin' spatula," Gus says - sucking his lower lip into his mouth, biting down, making me totally wet between my legs.

Putting his breakfast on the plate in front of him I laugh, saying, "Nope, not yet, *but*... maybe later after we eat and talk, because right now we have an island between us and lots of food to eat. *So...*let's get this talk over with." Turning away from him, feeling kind of nervous, I move around the kitchen.

Gus grabs a piece of bacon, taking a bite, he asks, "Okay, where do ya want to start?"

I stop and look at him, replying, "What do you mean where to start? We have more to talk about than just us?"

Gus chuckles. "No, but there's a lot to talk about. For instance, how it's been between us lately - do ya like it or not? Do ya like staying with me every night - how do ya like the sex - wat are your hard limits - safe word..."

I just stand there with my mouth hanging open.

Gus laughs. "See, we have a lot to talk about, but let's start with some easy yes or no questions. Tell me - do ya like sleeping with me every night?"

I immediately reply, "Yes."

Gus grabs his fork and takes a bite of eggs. "Would ya want some nights without me?"

I fire back, "No. I want and need you next to me."

Gus smiles, inhaling a piece of his bacon, he points to my food and commands, "Eat. Ya need to eat while we talk." Looking at him, I do as he asks, grabbing a piece of bacon while waiting for his next question. Something flickers in his eyes, and his jaw twitches. "Now - do ya like me doing that?"

Not understanding his question, I reply, "Do what?" while shoving eggs in my mouth.

Gus is looking at me like I'm a piece of bacon. "I like taking care of ya and sometimes it might seem like I'm bossing ya around, but lately ya don't seem to notice, obviously." He points to me eating.

I shrug. "I notice, but it's usually something I need to do for myself, so I do it," I answer him honestly.

He laughs. "Some would say it's called submissive. Before, the only time ya ever fought with me was when ya didn't get your way. Now that we're together, ya haven't been fighting me."

It's my turn to laugh. "Well that's because I've wanted you and you were playing hard to get."

Gus chews, his mouth full of food, and swallows. "No, ya've had a boyfriend, but let's not go back there, let's keep moving forward. We're together now and that's all the matters." He grabs his water taking a long drink. Putting his glass down, wiping his mouth, he asks, "Isabella, I know sexually we need to go slow because of wat happened to ya, but can ya tell me all your hard limits?" His voice is deep and raw.

I take a drink, placing my glass down too, I wipe my mouth. When I look up, I see his emerald eyes darken with desire and full of emotions. I gulp. "Well, um… right now, hair pulling, choking, fingering, blindfolds, and restraints. They're not *hard limits,* but I need some time. We'll need to be cautious and go slow when trying them again. I usually love that stuff, the kinkier the better. I'm game for almost anything once. Obviously, I like pain, but not the abusive kind."

Gus' face hardens, saying through gritted teeth, "I would *never* hurt ya. *Everything* I do to ya will be about your pleasure and my control."

"I know, and I trust you. I always have," I rasp.

"Isabella, I do have some fetishes, like your neck. Christ that neck of yours, I know it will come in time, once you've moved past the healing process. But, fuck me, your neck has my cock hard as a rock."

I grab my neck, knowing he loves leaving marks on me. I close my eyes, envisioning him choking me, and my nipples harden instantly.

"Isabella, ya need to stop. You're making me dick hard holdin' your neck like that."

I open my eyes to see Gus' are hooded, and he's adjusting himself on the stool. I smile.

"Now, wat I do need is to be in control of every aspect of my life. I told ya a while ago, ya'd need to understand and get used to me. Wat I was talking about is how I like to plan and control everything, including ya. Like I said before, I've been doing it to ya for a while now, and ya don't even notice. I'll never change anything about ya.

"Obviously, ya have your own ideas and can make your own decisions, but I'd like to be involved in your decision making. You seem to enjoy it." He chuckles the last part.

I wring my hands together. "I do like it. I love it actually. I just want someone to care about me and love me back. People seem to abuse my love by harming me or doing what's best for them and not me."

Gus puts his silverware down, giving me his full attention. "Okay, now wat do ya want or need from me? Since ya know I would never abuse my control or dominance of ya."

I bite my lip and take a deep breath looking up to the ceiling, taking a minute to think. When I lower my head and make eye contact, I smile. "I need a protector, someone to love me unconditionally and someone who will put up with my kinky, spoiled ass. Oh, and most of all, I want and need... you. All of you."

Gus' eyes blaze with heat, pure lustful desire sparking. He gets up like he's going to pounce on me, rounding the island he smashes his mouth to mine. We moan for more, and instantly I reach up, raking my fingers through his already disheveled hair. Gus breaks the kiss, holding my face in his hands and says, "Well ya might not know this, but from the day I laid eyes on ya, and ya opened that sassy as fuck mouth, I knew that very second ya were made for me. It just took me a while to make sure ya were ready for me, because once I let ya in and we became one, it was going to be final for me. I love ya, Isabella. You're *me one*. We can work out all the other *shite* later. Ya know wat I need from the relationship, and I know wat ya need, that's all that matters now."

Tears run down my face. "I love you too, my Aengus," I say in a throaty voice.

Lifting me up, he ravenously kisses me. I wrap my legs around his waist as he carries me back to bed.

I guess our food is going to get cold after all.

CHAPTER THIRTY | GUS

"The Feds said that since Kirill was released a few weeks ago, he's gone underground. They know he went back to Russia but hasn't been seen since. They asked if we've seen Dominic, I told them no," Luc explains to the lot of us here meeting at the clubhouse. It's Shy and Mac from my club, Wolfe and Cash from our original chapter, Brant and Beau from our security team, along with Maddox and myself.

"They contacted Izzy too, and she told them she hasn't seen or heard from anyone. They don't believe she's in any more danger, but said to be alert," I tell them.

"Well, my cousin said that the word going around is Valdik's pissed that Dominic is missing. I didn't tell anyone about what I know either. I didn't want anyone looking our direction for answers. Maybe Kirill offed Dominic without his pop's approval?" Maddox added, getting all our attention.

"Well, if that's the case he'll want Izzy gone since she knows the truth," I throw out there, getting upset thinking Izzy isn't out of trouble yet.

Brant chimes in next saying, "Yeah, but so did a lot of people. Didn't Izzy say that Miguel guy and other men were in the room too? What's he going to do, kill them all?"

"I don't know, but we all just need to stay alert and keep the girls close," Luc says.

Shy speaks up, "Well that leads us to our next topic. I'll be gone, along with a few others. We're flying down to Los Angeles to do some club business and meet up with Quick. A couple of us will ride back with Quick, Ruby, and Bella, making sure they get home safe."

I sit forward since this is news to me and ask, "When was this decided? Quick *dinna* mention it to me. Who's going and who's staying?"

Wolfe answers, speaking for the first time, "Most my men will be going. We got business to deal with in California, plus Shy and a few of his guys."

I look to Shy. "Am I going?"

Shy shakes his head. "Sorry, brother, but you're needed here with the women. You, Mac, Tiny, Dallas, and the other prospects will hold down the place while we're gone. Mac's in charge while I'm gone. He needs to deal with some shit at the lounge that might include you."

Frustration sets in that I'm letting my club down. Shy must see it on my face because he adds, "Redman, I need you here, brother, protecting my fiancée. I need you to watch over our girls. Until this is over, that is where I need you, brother."

I want to ask if this abrupt trip has anything to do with our little meeting the other night, but I hold my tongue and nod my head, but I'm not happy. I'm torn between my club and keeping my girl safe. Luckily, they made the decision for me because, really, I wouldn't be able to leave Izzy while all this shit's still unknown. I left Dallas at our building in case any of the girls needed anything while we were here. Quick's usually always there, but he left for Los Angeles with Ruby and Bella a few days after Shy's birthday.

The meeting's over and everyone grabs their phone as they exit the conference room. I pick my phone up, seeing I have a couple missed calls and voice messages from Izzy and Dallas. A slight panic erupts in my stomach as I hit voicemail.

Hi Red, I received a text message from my old landlady telling me I was supposed to turn in my spare keys and that there was a problem with returning the deposit. She was asking me to swing by right now if I could since she was there. Dallas said he could take me. A couple of Luc's guys are here too, so there are four of us heading over. Call when you get out of the meeting. Love you.

The second message is from Dallas.

Redman, your girl needs to go over to her old place. I was in the security room with a few of the guys. Hunter and Elijah are staying here since Mia and Ginger are still here. I think Chad and Roc are around here somewhere, but I'm taking Trey and Nick with me. I just wanted you to know, so hit me up when you're out of the meeting.

As soon as I hit the end button, I immediately call Dallas. My heart drops when I have a bad feeling wash over me. Sensing something's wrong, Shy and Mac head my direction as I make my way toward the door, I yell, "FUCK."

No answer. *Fuck!*

"Something's wrong," I rush out, explaining what the messages said. Luc and Beau are calling their men, and everyone else's on my tail out the door. We all spread out, half going to the building, and half going to her old place.

Still no answer.

Jaysus, Mother of Christ, not again!

CHAPTER THIRTY ONE | IZZY

"Did you leave him a message too?" I ask Dallas as we enter my old building. Trey dropped Dallas, Nick, and I off at the door before going to find a parking spot.

"Yeah, he'll be fine. We have plenty of people with us," Dallas reassures me, even though I'm fine. I feel safe with them, and it's getting easier to be in a car now.

I ask the front desk if my landlady is still around. They tell me she was showing the place earlier and I can head up, that she should still be there since they haven't seen her leave. I hope she's not showing it when we get there, but we take off up the elevator anyway.

When we approach the door, I knock. When I hear someone talking, I look over at Dallas and say, "I think she's showing the place to someone."

I knock again, calling out my landlady's name but still nothing. Dallas pulls his gun from his holster, I look at him like he's lost his goddamn mind, and hiss, "Dallas, you'll scare the lady to death, put that away."

Dallas ignores me, moving me to the side as he looks over his shoulder giving Nick a look. Nick, who is quite a bit taller than both of us, moves both of us out of the way, pulling his gun out and taking the lead. Good-god, he's big, I can barely see the door now. Dallas bends over, pulling a very small gun from his boot and handing it to me.

I'm shocked, asking, "What the fuck am I supposed to do with this?"

"Just amuse me and put it in your jacket pocket just in case. I'm not taking any chances with you," Dallas demands.

I huff, irritated, but take it, putting it in my jacket pocket. I remember Ginger and Gus teaching me to shoot when we visited her in West Virginia. I was pretty good, but I hate guns. They wanted me to carry a gun after that, but I said no. I had Gus to protect me and felt I didn't need one. Dallas puts his hand on my arm, telling me to hold on a minute, as Nick tries the door and it opens.

I grumble to myself, "This is ridiculous. She's a hella old lady."

Nick enters the place with us following a few steps behind. When all of us are in the entryway, I shut the door and yell out again for my landlady. I snap my mouth shut when both men turn around, giving me murderous eyes, and in a split second, it happens. It happens so fast I don't even have time to scream.

A very large man turns the corner firing off five shots, putting a bullet in Nick's head, dropping him instantly. Nick's body shielded us for a split second as Dallas shoves me behind him, covering me as we fall to the ground. Dallas grunts but doesn't move. The enormous man, who looks familiar towers over us, kicking Dallas' gun away, holding his gun aimed at Dallas.

I scream, "No," putting my hand up, trying to cover Dallas, but he's pinning me under him.

Then I hear it… a series of whistles. The large man whistles back. I look around frantically - the whistling sounds closer.

No. No. No…

And then.

The voice.

The voice that haunts my dreams rings out from somewhere, "*Conejito*, I've missed you. You didn't think I would leave you behind, did you?"

I start to cry, holding Dallas against my chest as I try to stop the bleeding, but I don't know where he's hit, I only see blood. The big man, who I now recognize from the mug shots, is Julio Sanchez. Miguel's brother takes a step even closer, and I beg, "Please. Miguel, please don't kill him."

Dallas tries to move but falls back against me. I remember the gun he gave me in my pocket. When Dallas tries to move again, I feel something hard press into my leg. He has another gun behind his back.

Dallas looks up at me, and I cry, "Dallas stay with me. Please, stay with me." Dallas closes his eyes.

"*Conejito*, get up. I want to see you up close," Miguel says in a deep sinister voice, making my skin crawl. I look around but still don't see him.

Another series of whistles fly between Julio and Miguel, but this time they sound different. As Julio moves toward Dallas, grabbing him by his cut, lifting him off me, he tosses Dallas a few feet away. Dallas moans as he rolls over, but his eyes are still closed.

Then I see him. Miguel turns the corner from my kitchen area into the entryway and saunters over to me. When he bends down to grab my hand, I shuffle back. He moves fast, gripping my biceps, pulling me into his arms and twisting me so my back is to his front. His hold around me is too strong. He whispers against my ear, "Oh, how I've missed you. Have you missed me?" I try to wiggle out of his hold, but he hugs me tight, lifting me as he moves me to the living area against another wall, pinning me against it.

Miguel flips me around again, looking me in the eyes - the soulless black eyes that make me scream in terror at night. The scarred face of the man I've tried hard to forget. I close my eyes and start to freak out, shaking my head, repeating no over and over in my head.

Miguel pins me with his body, gripping my face he tries to kiss me, but I scream. He chuckles, "I was hoping your big Irishman would be here so I could kill him too. You know how I don't like other men touching what is mine."

I spit out, "I was never yours. Someone paid you to take me - to sell me off. I was *never* yours."

Miguel laughs an evil laugh. "Oh, but you are. Kirill may have hired me, but when I found out his father didn't sanction it, all bets were off. I was planning on taking you myself after the auction. If it wasn't for your friend over there and your Irishman, I would have pulled it off."

Miguel's brother kicks Dallas, making him groan.

"And when one of them killed our brother, I knew two things. One, I needed revenge for my brother's death and two, I needed my *Conejito* back," Miguel says with murderous eyes.

Why! Oh, God he's going to kill Dallas and Gus.

I slump against the wall, and mutter, "Why me?"

Miguel caresses my face with the back of his fingers. "*Conejito*, you're like an angel. I've never had something as beautiful and responsive as you. When Kirill killed your Russian boyfriend, well that was your breaking point. I had you where I wanted you, and I look forward to seeing you break again when I kill your friend there and then your Irishman." Miguel leans in to kiss me again, but I move my head and begin trying to fight him off, hitting his chest and yelling at him to let me go. I become enraged at the thought of him killing Dallas and Gus. Flashbacks of Dominic being killed have me kicking and screaming. I'm making such a fuss, Miguel loses his patience.

"Enough," Miguel roars, furiously slamming me against the wall, bouncing my head off it. I'm dazed, but I don't stop fighting. "Enough," he says again, backhanding me, sending me flying. I put my arms out to brace myself. Pain shoots through my wrists collapsing my arms, hitting my head hard against the ground. I groan as stars flash before my eyes.

Lying on the ground trying to clear my head, I hear him whistle. I crack open my eyes as Miguel turns, walking toward Dallas and his brother. Slipping my hand into my jacket pocket, I grip the gun.

"You will pay the price for our brother's death you fucking *puta*. And I *will* find her man and kill him too," Miguel spits.

Dallas opens his eyes, I raise my gun and pull the trigger. The door smashes open, I curl into a ball taking cover as gunshots erupt around me.

"Isabella!" Gus roars. *He came for me...my protector.*

I open my eyes to a room full of men swarming around. Gus drops down to his knees feeling around on my body. "Are ya shot? Where are ya hurt?" Gus asks in a panic, seeing blood all over me. I'm about to say it's not mine when I remember Dallas.

I become hysterical. "Dallas. Dallas needs our help." Gus pulls me on to his lap as I try to get to Dallas. I see Shy, and Mac leaning over him, and I scream, "No. No. Dallas, stay with me. Dallas..."

Gus holds me tighter. "We've got him. Ya need to calm down. Breathe. Are ya sure you're not hit?"

I can't breathe. Dallas. Oh, God, he's going to die because of me. Fuck! I need to breathe - my head.

"Iz, breathe. Iz..."

Everything starts to fade away as more men rush through the door.

Dallas...

"Ms. Rogers, can you hear me?"

"Isabella, can you open your eyes?"

"Why isn't she responding?" I recognize Gus' voice, and I let out a groan.

"Ms. Rogers, you're in an ambulance, can you open your eyes for us?"

I crack an eye open trying to remember what happened. I jolt up but am restrained. I panic, "Dallas. Where's Dallas?"

As the men hold me down, trying to calm me, Gus answers, "Doll, he's in the other ambulance. Ya need to calm down."

"Ms. Rogers, please lay back so I can finish looking you over. You will be with your friend as soon as we arrive at the hospital, but we need you to stay calm," the EMT pleads with me.

I look between the two men, but all I can think about is what if Dallas is dead? I start to cry, "Is he dead? Aengus, please tell me he's not dead. Please. I need Dallas to be alive."

Gus says grimly, "He was shot three times and lost a lot of blood, but he was alive when the ambulance left."

"Ms. Rogers, do you remember what happened? Are you hurting anywhere?" the EMT asks again, but I just stare at Gus.

"Yes, I remember everything. My face, head, and wrist hurt. Otherwise, I'm fine," I answer the EMT, never taking my eyes off Gus.

The ambulance comes to a halt and the doors open. "Ms. Rogers, we're going to do a full check up on you just in case."

"Dallas…" I plead to Gus to go find out.

Gus nods but stays with me as they cart me into the ER.

I've been in this bed for a few hours. I have a concussion, sprained wrist and will have a nice black eye from Miguel hitting me. Dallas has been in surgery, and we still don't know anything.

Gus is the only person they've let in my room, but I guess everyone's here in the waiting room.

"Ms. Rogers?" I crack an eye open, seeing the same federal agents from before stroll into my room.

Gus stands up, moving closer to my bed, gripping my hand. When I don't answer, they continue.

"Izzy, It's Agent—"

"Marquez," I finish saying her last name.

"Yes, I hope you're doing okay. We don't want to take up too much of your time, but we need to get a statement from you," Agent Marquez says in a soft voice.

Agent Thompson clips, sounding irritated, "The whole story Ms. Rogers, if you could please."

"Wat's that supposed to mean?" Gus fires back at them.

I close my eyes, knowing damn well what it means. I've held back information from them.

I squeeze his hand. "It means I need to tell them everything," I say softly, looking up at my protector. "I need to tell them about what happened to me before and this time," I finish, looking over at Agent Marquez. You might want to take a seat. This's going to take some time," I smile at the agents, tugging Gus to sit on the bed next to me.

For the next thirty minutes, I tell the agents everything... What Miguel did to me, what Kirill said about Dominic, how Dominic died, what Miguel told me at the very end about Kirill, all the way down to me pulling the trigger.

When I'm done, I lean my head back and take a deep breath.

Fuck, I can finally breathe. It's over.

Agent Marquez speaks first. "Wow, that explains the pieces we've been trying to put together. All the information you've given us will be extremely helpful to close out this case. Thank you. We'll look at this a little more and let you know if we find out anything more about Kirill. From what we know, and what you just told us, it looks like you and your friends should be out of danger. If you need anything give me a call."

Once the agents leave, Gus turns toward me. "I'm so proud of ya."

I smile.

"Ms. Rogers," Gus groans, turning to see who's coming through my door. When I see it's the doctor, I sit up. "Ms. Rogers, you're free to go, but please, if your head begins to hurt or you get dizzy, call or go see your regular doctor. Concussions are not something to take lightly."

I'm moving to get off the bed and ask, "Do you know how my friend is doing? Is he out of surgery?"

As the doctor heads for the door he says, "I'll go check, meet me at the nurse's station."

When I stand up my head starts to hurt, but I don't say anything, I just want out of here.

At the nurse's station, I sign my discharge papers, when I turn around, I see the doctor walking with a woman in surgical gear.

"Are you relatives of Alec Carsen?" the pretty woman asked.

"Yes, he's my family. I was with him when he was shot," I lie, hoping she'll tell me what's wrong. I start to tear up.

"I'm Dr. Hart. I was the one who operated on Mr. Carsen. He—"

I blurt out interrupting her, "You're a doctor?" I blink a couple of times in shock.

This woman is beautiful and young.

She smiles, clasping her hands together in front of her. "Last I checked yes, I'm a real doctor. Now back to Mr. Carsen. I was able to remove the bullets, but he lost a lot of blood. He should be fine, as long as there are no complications. He's in post-op right now, the nurse will let you know when you can go in to see him."

She smiles, turning toward the nurse's station.

I'm still in shock that this woman is a doctor. Gus squeezes my hand pulling me from my stupor. "Thank you, Dr. Hart."

"Sorry, yes. Thank you so much," I say with an apologetic smile as Gus tugs me to follow him.

"Well, at least Dallas will be happy to know his doctor is hot as fuck," Gus chuckles, pulling me to the waiting room where all our friends are waiting.

I glance over my shoulder to see the beautiful doctor watching us walk away, so I smile once more giving her a friendly wave.

CHAPTER THIRTY TWO | IZZY

"How much you want to bet she isn't even thirty?" Dallas says when I walk into the room.

"Twenty bucks that she's at least thirty," Mac replies.

When Dallas sees me walk in, he smiles big and calls out my new nickname, "Hey Killer."

It took him a bit to finally become coherent. He's been calling me that for the past three days. He told everyone I killed Miguel in one shot before the door was busted in. I guess Dallas pulled his gun and shot Julio.

"Hey, Alec!" I fire back, using his real name and his smile drops. I've been harassing him about his real name since then too.

"Why you gotta be like that - it isn't funny," Dallas says, looking like his feelings are hurt.

"Aw, come on. Alec's a cool name," I tease him.

The door flies open and in comes the hot doctor. "How's Mr. Carsen doing today?" she asks, cheerfully looking over his medical information.

Dallas' smile reappears. "Doc, I'm in pain." He tries to sound like he's in pain but fails horribly.

She looks up and sees his face light up, knowing he's completely bullshitting her like he's been doing for the past few days. Poor lady's been putting up with all these big, brawny men. Once Gus and I told everyone about Dr. Hart, the hottie, every single man has come to visit him to see for themselves.

She laughs. "Mr. Carsen, I'm sure you'll be fine."

Mac gets up letting the doctor move next to Dallas and asks her, "Hey Doc, personal question. How old are you?"

"Another question huh?" she says, looking sideways at Mac standing there with a big ass grin. She looks at me, and I shrug, so she turns back to Dallas, folding her arms over her chest and adds, "Who has money on what today?"

I laugh. I like this lady. When Dallas was really himself and could see his doctor was fucking hot, they started betting. The first day Mac bet she was in a relationship but lost. Yesterday, Mac bet she liked women and lost again. I smile and say, "Today... one says you're under thirty and the other one says you're over."

She smiles at me. "What do you think, Ms. Rogers?"

The first night I was here and found out she was his doctor, I googled her, so I know she's over thirty.

Oops... so I'm cheating.

Oh well, and I answer, "I say over thirty."

Dr. Hart chuckles. "We have a winner, folks." Mac fist pumps the air. "Fucking finally."

I laugh. But Dallas, he just stares at the young doctor, and says smoothly, "Well, I like older women."

Dr. Hart moves to leave the room. "Have a good day Mr. Carsen. The nurse will be in shortly to check on you."

Mac and I bust out laughing - poor Dallas. The doctor just totally dismissed his ass, which is new to him because he usually gets any woman he wants. The boy next door just got denied!

"Where's Redman? Y'all are fucked up," Dallas groans as he tries to get out of bed, wincing and grabbing his stomach.

I plop myself down into a chair next to Dallas. "He's down the hall talking on the phone to Quick," I answer them in a cheerful voice.

The first twenty-four hours, I wouldn't leave, Gus threw a fit, but I wasn't leaving Dallas. When Dallas came to the first time, I cried like a baby. The second time, when he was more coherent of his surroundings, I yelled at him that I would kill him myself if he ever threw himself in front of me again. Each time Dallas would just chuckle.

The agents came and took his statement yesterday. They told us again that everything should go back to normal for us and if they saw or heard anything about Kirill, they would inform us immediately.

The first night when I stayed here, I didn't sleep much. I kept telling myself Miguel was dead and that I was safe. The few nights at Gus' I've been okay, only waking up a couple of times. I know I can and will get through this.

Ruby called after it happened to say she was on her way back, but I told her I was fine and that she needed to deal with her shit. Gus hadn't left my side except when I made him go home that first night. I just needed to be here when Dallas woke up, and I explained that to Gus and the club members that were all still lingering around.

It also gave me time to get my own shit together. I know it upset Gus that he couldn't control what happens to me, but I explained to him that he couldn't be with me every second of every day. He needs to go back to work with Beau, and now he has club business on top of that. He can't control everything. He didn't like that little fit I threw, but he left with Shy that night and came back okay.

"Mac, I seriously need my laptop. I need to be doing something while I'm laid up in this place. The doctor said I have another week," Dallas complains.

"You're lucky she's letting you go at two weeks. You're lucky to be alive, so deal with it and rest," I rasp out.

Dallas glares at me just as the door flies open with my bear of a man sauntering in looking all gorgeous and badass. My body comes alive just looking at him. I want him so fucking bad, but he hasn't touched me since before Miguel tried to take me again.

I don't know if he's working through shit in his own head or if he thinks I need time, but whatever it is, it fucking sucks. I want him, and I need him to want me. Lying in his arms every night and not getting his cock is torture in itself.

I smile, shifting in my chair as my pussy starts to throb just thinking about sex.

Gus smiles back moving toward me, and he glances to Dallas giving him a nod. "Ya good, brother?"

Before Dallas can answer his eyes are back on me and in two long strides he's bending down giving me a quick kiss.

"Yeah, I'm fucking grand. Don't mind me laying here just go fuck and get it over with. Fuck," Dallas grumbles next to us, and Mac laughs.

Before I can think better of it, I snap back, "Don't get your panties in a bunch. We're not having sex either, so fuck off."

Everyone's eyes snap to me, two are in shock, and one pair is furious. I can feel his stare before I look up at his scarlet red face. His face is redder than his hair... that is red.

Holy Shit!

"I...um. I mean," I start to stutter, but he stops me.

"Ya best stop while you're ahead, Doll," Gus fumes.

Mac pipes up as he starts for the door, "I'm going to get something to drink."

Dallas yells, "The fuck you are. You ain't leaving me in here alone. If I can't leave, then you can't leave."

Gus grabs my hand, hauling me up and out of the room. At first, I think we're going to leave, but he opens a door down the hall, but it has supplies in it. Then we try another door and another. Just when I'm about ready to stop this madness and ask what the fuck he's looking for, he pulls me into an empty room with a table and bed.

Shutting the door, he locks it. *Fuck.*

"What are you doing? If you want to yell at me, we can do it outside or at home. I'm—" I'm cut off when Gus shoves me up against the door, smashing his mouth to mine as he towers over me.

I reach up to touch him, but he grips my hands lifting them above my head.

Gus breaks the kiss, looking down at me, seething, and rants, "I'm so goddamn furious with ya that I can't see straight. I don't know if I should fuck ya senseless or punish ya. Ya've mouthed off to me twice now in front of *me boys*. I've been giving ya time to deal with yer shite, but again ya need someone to control ya. So…" Gus steps back leaving me wanting more… needing more. My arms are still above my head as I stand there, mouth parted and praying like hell he fucks me senseless.

I can see he's warring with himself as his face changes from furious to hungry with desire. I'm about ready to lower my arms when he finally speaks, "Go sit on the bed, place your hands on your knees and for fuck's sake don't speak unless ya can't handle it, then say stop."

My eyes go wide with my brows hitting my hairline. He's never ordered me to do anything like this, making me wet instantly. His voice is strained but controlled. My heart races and without hesitation, I walk over to the bed and do as I'm told.

When he turns to me, he closes his eyes and takes a deep breath. Gus is a very tall man, so when he stands in front of me, he really towers over me so I have to crank my neck far back to look up at him. Gus reaches with both hands cupping my face, moving one hand up, pulling my hair from its loose bun on top of my head. As my hair cascades down my back, fire blazes in his eyes.

He caresses me, swiping loose strands of hair away from my face. "I'm torn between punishing ya and fuckin' ya. I think ya want me to punish ya."

I swallow hard with excitement.

I've never heard him speak like this to me. My nipples harden instantly and when he notices he slides a hand down my face pausing at my neck, like he wants to grab it. I can see his neck muscles twitch, but he continues down, gliding over my aroused breast. He chuckles. "Uh-huh. I see. Keep your eyes on my face at all times." Gus steps back grabbing his belt, undoing his pants, freeing his rock-hard erection from his trousers. I can see it in my peripheral, but I don't look away from his face.

"Christ, Isabella," Gus groans, biting his lip as he palms his cock.

My body starts to tingle all over. I grip my knees wanting so badly to watch him touch himself.

"Ya remember that time at the hotel, and I told ya I was goin' to shag meself off. Shake or nod ya head," Gus orders. I nod my head.

"Fuckin' gran," he grunts.

"I want to shag ya real fuckin' bad, but now ya have to wait. I'm going to come watching ya." His voice becomes labored, I can see his arm moving, stroking his cock in my peripheral.

"Actually, I need some assistance from ya." Gus moves closer. "I want ya to suck me cock. Lube it up for me but keep your eyes on me and hands on ya knees. No fuckin' touching," he orders.

I open my mouth, salivating at the idea of his enormous cock gliding in and out of my mouth.

"Doll, ya like this dontcha?" Gus groans as he places his cock to my lips. "*D'ye* look away from me."

I keep my eyes locked with his that are hooded and barely open.

When he slips his cock into my mouth, he intakes a deep breath. "Sweet Jaysus."

I keep my mouth open as he slowly pumps in and out as I coat his cock with my saliva.

"Mother of Christ, I *dinna* think it would be this fuckin' hard…" He starts to pant, pumping deeper. "But fuck ya mouth is like fuckin' heaven." Gus' eyes are barely open, and when I moan, vibrating around his cock, he pulls out. "Fuck this. I'll punish ya later."

Fuck yes. There truly is a God.

Within seconds I'm yanked up, turned facing a wall, my

leggings are yanked to my knees, and Gus is fully seated inside me. "Jaysus Christ, you're soaked." Gus' breathing picks up and is heavy against my neck. "Keep your hands on the wall and don't say a word."

I do as he says and he starts thrusting erratically into me.

"For fuck's sake, I'm gonna come fast like a fuckin' wee boy."

He assaults me in the best fucking way ever, pounding into me, gripping my hip with one hand and my shoulder with the other.

Yes. I needed this. I needed him. I'm so close.

I start screaming in my head as soft moans escape me, my pussy tightening around his cock.

"Hold on. Ya come when I come, not until then," he commands, breathless behind me.

"Touch yerself…don't come…Wait…"

I moan, biting my lip, moving my hand down the wall to circle my erect bud. I'm at the brink of screaming out my release.

I can't hold on… shit.

"Now…Come…Now…" Gus grunts his release as my walls contract around his pulsing cock.

I moan but don't say a word as my orgasm ripples through me leaving me gloriously spent.

Gus pulls out of me. Bending down he grips my leggings, sliding them back up before he turns me around to face him. He leans me up against the wall, making sure I can hold myself up before he puts himself back together.

Still catching his breath, he barks out, "We're headed home. Fuck this hospital shit. I need more of this sweet cunt of mine."

I smile.

Gus kisses me hard, slicing my lips with his tongue, demanding entrance. "Legs, ya can speak now, but we're going to say goodbye and head home. No more mouthing off, ya still have a couple of punishments I need to deliver. Maybe even a spanking."

My eyes gleam with anticipation.

"Christ, let's go before I ride ya again," Gus grunts, grabbing my hand and leading me back to our friend's hospital room to say goodbye.

"I'm going to ask her out," Dallas tells me while I'm waiting for him to be released from the hospital.

I ignore him like I have every day this past week. The first week was all fun and games, but this last week, when everyone went on with their lives, Dallas became obsessed with this woman.

When I finally brought him his laptop, he went to town researching her and yes invading her privacy. Well, that was until he couldn't find much on her. That's when the obsession began.

The questions never ended between him and Mac. She has been a saint through these past two weeks because I would have told him to fuck off.

"Goodbye Izzy," one of the nurses says to me, walking past us.

I wave with a smile. "Goodbye Cheryl." I've been here every day along with Ginger. Shy took off with most of the members leaving Mac and Gus behind. Ginger and I have been having a field day teasing Dallas.

"Mr. Carsen and Ms. Rogers, I'm sad to see you leave, but I'm glad you're well enough to go," Dr. Hart says with a smile as she walks up behind the counter. "I'm going to miss your daily questions."

I laugh.

"Whatcha got for me today? You only get one more," she teases Dallas, and right then it hits me.

"Today's a two-part question. The first part is, do you think he will ask you out and the second part is will you say yes if he does? *Annd,* today Doc, the stakes just went up from twenty to fifty," I laugh, seeing Dallas turn two shades of pink, looking at me with murderous eyes.

Ginger walks up laughing.

Dr. Hart folds her arms, looking between all of us and then to the three nurses who have now crowded around to hear today's question. It seems this floor has become very interested in these questions, and some have even put money down on a few of them.

"Can we put money on this too?" one of the nurses says, laughing.

Dr. Hart laughs. "No, it's rigged," she pauses, looking at all our faces except Dallas' and adds, "You put him on the spot, so you know he's going to ask me now. When he does ask, you'll think I'm going to say no, but I could say yes to win my money back. Sooo..." She puts her hands on her hips. "Y'all need a new question for the day. I've got rounds."

She laughs, handing one of the nurses the clipboard with all of Dallas' papers. She's about to walk away when Dallas throws on his Wolfeman cut that Ginger just handed him and walks over, towering over her. "You're right. Fuck it. All bets are off. My only question to you is, will you go out with me?"

Dr. Hart slowly looks him up and down, stopping at the name on his cut before locking eyes with him. "Nah, I don't date my patients. It's against my rules," she says with a smile as she starts to walk away. Stopping halfway, she turns and says, "But, I have seen you naked already, so..." Pausing like she's thinking about it, a devilish smile spreads across her face. I watch, thinking she's going to say yes, when she answers, "Yeah, no. I don't date my patients."

She walks away, leaving all of us women shocked with our mouths hanging open. While Dallas stares, looking star struck.

Turning to him, I start to worry he's upset, but he laughs,

"Goddamn that woman gets me harder than I've ever been. Fuck yes!" he yells after the beautiful doctor. "Challenge on, Doc!

Ginger and I bust up laughing. Only Dallas could switch a shitty situation into something positive. This's going to be interesting.

EPILOGUE | IZZY
EIGHT MONTHS LATER

"Congratulations to you both!" Luc says, shaking Gus' hand and giving me a hug, adding, "You're getting there."

Oh, shit!

"Congrats for wat?" Gus asks, looking over at me as Luc hugs me.

Luc looks at me then to Gus before saying, "Izzy's song hit Top 50 internationally today."

Shit. Shit. Shit!

Gus turns me to face him. "Did ya know about this?"

Fuck!

"I...Um...I..." I pause. "Yes, I knew about it this morning, but today is about you. I didn't want it to be about me. This whole week it's been about me," I ramble nervously.

Ever since my song, "Say It" dropped last week, it's been all about me and how my songs been climbing the charts. But today's supposed to be about him.

"Isabella," Gus growls next to me.

I turn my body completely toward him, placing my hands on my hips. "Don't you Isabella me. It's your day. We can celebrate my day tomorrow. Like Luc said, it's climbing, we'll have many more days to celebrate my song but today's about you," I huff, hoping he'll let it go but knowing him. He won't.

Luc laughs, "Uh, I'll be at the bar," leaving the two of us glaring at each other.

Gus takes a step toward me, closing the gap between us. He grips the back of my neck as he leans down, placing a soft kiss on my lips. I immediately soften against him, moving my hands from my hips to around his waist. I love how just one touch from him has me turning to Jell-O.

A few months ago, this action would have thrown me into a full-blown panic attack, but now it's like my security blanket. Just his hand on my neck tells me I'm safe and his. We've come a long way in these last eight months since Miguel's death. It took a while, but his neck fetish and need for control have become my desires, loving the way he touches me.

I let out a breath when he says, "Iz, telling me and celebrating are two different things. Ya know I want to know about this. Don't keep shite from me," Gus says in a low rumble, sounding more irritated than mad. His hand still secure behind my neck, holding my gaze.

I smile.

"Okay," I say sweetly, hoping he'll drop it.

Gus laughs. "You're lucky you're cute, but you're still getting a punishment tonight."

I reply softly, "Okay," but inside I'm jumping for joy because his punishments mean I'll get it rough tonight.

Gus leans into my side, whispering into my ear, "I'm starting to think ya like these punishments. I think I need to change it up and maybe, I don't know - deny you an orgasm? Order you *not* to come."

I swallow hard as his words vibrate down my body, sending goosebumps trailing in their wake.

When he pulls back, still holding my neck securely, I tilt my head back looking up at him but don't say anything. I can't really say anything because he's right - I do love how he punishes me with pleasurable pain.

Gus locks eyes with mine. "Christ, I'm fucking hard just thinking about wat I want to do to ya later."

I smile, letting out a soft moan, moving my hips up against his hardening erection.

Gus closes his eyes, taking in a deep breath through his

nostrils. Exhaling, he leans close to my ear whispering, "Be ready. Tonight, we're going to push your limits even further."

I tilt my head to him with a moan, still not saying anything. He loves my obedience when he's in dominance mode. He likes when I speak with my body language which is always speaking to him. Always.

"Izzy!" my name is yelled from across the bar. Gus pulls back slightly, touching foreheads and says, "Behave tonight." Softly kissing me, he releases me when my club name, Legs, is yelled across the room. When I look up, I notice Ginger and all the club women at the bar.

I lean up on to my tippy toes giving Gus another kiss. "The girls are calling, gotta go. Love ya Red."

Gus laughs, swatting my ass as I walk away. "Behave. Love ya too, Doll."

When I reach Ginger, she starts to laugh. "Luc told us to rescue you. That he may have gotten you into trouble."

I giggle. "Well, if you call getting spanked tonight - trouble, then yes, he did."

All the ladies start laughing. The place is packed full of members, associates, friends, and family. Tonight is Gus and two other members patch party, so all the other chapters are here celebrating. It's been a rough few months for the club, so everyone is ready to blow off some steam.

"Congratulations!" all the girls yell as they circle around me. I laugh, looking for Maze behind the bar, needing a drink.

"Shh... It's Gus' night. We can celebrate tomorrow," I chuckle but feel on top of the world right now. My song moving up the charts is the best feeling ever.

These past few months have been a lot of hard work, with my healing and overcoming my fears. Not just with what happened with Miguel but also dealing with my own insecurities. This song has unleashed so much inside of me, and having Gus by my side helping me decipher what is what has only solidified our relationship.

"Bullshit, it's both of your nights. This just means we have more to celebrate, right ladies?" Ginger cheers next to me.

Maze walks up with a bunch of shots and a huge grin on her face. "Let's do this biatches!"

We all grab a shot, lift them to each other and chant our usual, "Cheers biatches!" before swallowing our shots.

I look over to see him laughing with all the guys, but his eyes are fixed on me. I can see the fire blazing behind those emerald irises.

My man. My beautiful Redman. God, he wants me. I'm one lucky bitch!

I think we both have come out of our shells. Gus talks more and is more involved with every detail in my life. It's like we complete each other in every way. He organizes everything in our lives, grounding us, which is good because I fly by the seat of my pants dreaming big for both of us. I've always wanted someone to love me for me and be taken care of. He goes above and beyond.

I smile giving him a wink.

Gus smirks back, raising an eyebrow, knowing I'm thinking dirty shit.

The ladies keep chattering around me, as Gus and I eye-fuck each other across the room.

Felicia, who everyone calls Lish and is Hawks ol' lady, catches me staring at Gus and says, "Legs, you need to quit eye-fucking your man and give him a show on that pole. None of this leaving early to fuck, bullshit! We came here to party. I want to see those legs on that pole."

She hardly ever comes because she's usually running her strip club in West Virginia, but everyone came out to celebrate tonight. The club has been dealing with a lot of shit, so it's nice to have everyone here.

I tilt my head to the side giving Felicia a side smile before turning back to look at my man. I lift my vodka soda drink to my lips and say in a devilish voice, "Oh, Lish, you have no idea. I definitely have something up my sleeve for Redman tonight."

"Well alright, let's get this party started," Felicia laughs.

Yes… let's get this party started.

THE END

Keep reading for a preview of Quick, book one in the Wolfeman MC series.

QUICK

WITHDRAWALS

Ruby Malone.

My little firecracker.

Jesus Christ. I can't stop thinking about her.

I grip the bridge of my nose, applying pressure before rubbing my eyes. It's only been two fucking days.

Two.

Fucking.

Days.

A groan escapes me as I grab my beer, downing half of it in one swig. I try to focus my eyes looking around the bar. Thank the gods above no one is around to see me sulking, well except Maze, the bartender who has been moving around stocking the bar.

"Fucking pussy," I murmur to myself. Yeah, I've been hit with the motherfucking voodoo pussy. I'm ruined for any other women. I huff, taking another long swig, almost finishing the beer. Who am I kidding? I can't even jack myself off, I'm so fucked in the head. And it's only been two motherfucking days since she left - *two!*

I shake my head pissed off with myself. I need to get past this and get it together. She's still married. She can't just pick up and leave.

Fuck!

My heart constricts just thinking of never seeing her again. And again, it's only been two days since she left to go back home with Izzy.

"What the fuck? You havin' a fight with yourself?" a voice booms from behind me.

I look over my shoulder to see Shy, club president and my best friend, making his way over to the bar. I just shrug before finishing my beer, then slamming it down on the bar.

"That bad huh?" Shy chuckles as he takes a stool next to me. As soon as he's seated, Maze walks over.

"He's been sulking for over an hour. I couldn't take the negativity, so I've been leaving him to his own accord." Maze says, placing two fresh beers along with two shots in front of us. "Maybe you'll have better luck," she chuckles, making her way back to the other end of the bar.

"Brother, what the fuck?" Shy questions, but it's more of a statement by the look on his face.

"Don't even give me shit. You had it just as bad when Ginger was away. Fuck, maybe even worse, so don't fuck with me," I say, looking straight ahead as I fidget with the bottle label.

"You like her that much huh? I thought she would be out of your system by now? It's been what—"

I cut him off before he can finish. "Two motherfucking days. Brother, I'm trying, but... *fuck!*" I yell in frustration.

"Do you think she's the one?" Shy blurts out, shocking me.

"Jesus Christ," I breathe out. I turn my head to face him and say, sounding defeated, "I think she *is* the one."

"Are you sure?" Shy teases and I can tell he's goading me.

This time I turn my whole body to face him as I place my forearm on the bar and lean forward so only Shy can hear me. "I told her my real name. So yeah, she is 'the one.'" When I'm finished talking, I lean back waiting for his response.

Nothing.

Shy can mask his face like no one I've ever seen. You can never tell what he's thinking. I'm about ready to say something when he says, "Huh."

I about lose my shit. "What do you mean, *huh*? You know how big that is for me and how *no one* can know it. I've been freaking out about it. I've never told anyone - let alone a woman, my real name." I stare at him with wild eyes.

Feeling like I'm going to crack, I grab my beer and take another long swig.

"Brother, believe me, I know how big of a deal it is about your name. I'm just shocked. She's a good girl, and I wouldn't be worried about her knowing your name. But, I have to ask why did you tell her?" Shy asks in a calm, soothing voice.

I'm anything but calm and soothed when I answer him. "I don't fucking know. She wanted to fuck, and I wanted to talk about *us*. What fucking guy does that?" I groan.

I don't want to see the look on his face, so I drop my head to the bar. "I sound like a fucking pussy. I don't know what's wrong with me. I've never felt like this. Fuck!" I yell, lifting my head up off the bar.

I look over to see Shy smiling as he takes a long pull from his beer.

"It's like what you've been telling me all these years about how you knew when you heard Snow's voice for the first time. You hadn't even seen her face, but you knew. Well, I saw that wild fucking hair flying around and that goddamn marshmallow jacket of hers, and it hit me." I punch my chest. "At first I thought I just needed to fuck her, but then she opened her sassy little fucking mouth and those fucking eyes," I finish, turning to face the bar again as Shy stares at me, assessing me, thinking like he always does before he talks.

I hear a chuckle beside me. "Brother, tell me what we're trying to figure out here? What's the problem? What's got you all fucked up? I've never seen you this down or troubled. Do you want her or don't you? I don't see where the problem is here?"

"I want her. It's like she tapped into the old me and the new me, mixing them all together and it's really fucking me up," I answer him truthfully.

"Jake," Shy says my birth name. I snap my head around, making sure no one is in earshot.

Shy turns to face me, and says, "Jake, you can say your name. No one here's going to come after you. It's been over five years. No one knows where you are. Everyone thinks you're dead, and even if they did, look at you!" —he points to me before pointing to himself— "Fuck, look at us! We are completely different people. We look completely different. Yes, you are still Jake Reeves, and I am still Micah Jenkins, but we're so much more now. It's not bad that the girl you love knows your name. Shit, Snow calls me by my given name all the time. She should know the old you and the new you because it makes you-you."

My brain is on overdrive, and all this information is giving me sensory overload, it's all too much. I sit there in shock, face to face with my best friend, my brother, shit, my savior, and most of all, he's the president of the club I've sworn my life to. Only two things keep circling around in my brain - one, he just said my full name out loud and two, he said the girl I love. Fuck yes, I'm in shock.

"Look, we've talked about you seeing people from our past. You were going to see your good friend in LA, but we had to rush back. We can speak your name if we want to, but now everyone knows you as Quick. It isn't that we *can't* say your name anymore, it's just we don't. Same as me, I don't go by Micah anymore." He pauses, assessing me before he continues. "All I'm saying is you are and will always be protected. We can handle any threat that comes after us. Don't use that as an excuse, or stress out about it. I think you're tripping about how much you care for her and are using any excuse to freak out."

I'm still frozen, not saying a word. The last five years have been about keeping me hidden, not letting anyone know my real name.

He continues, "My only question now is why are you sitting here? You can compare my situation with Snow to this. I gloated because I *couldn't* go get my girl. Brother, you *can!*" Shy crosses his arms over his chest. "*So again*, what's the problem we're trying to figure out here? Because, it seems to me you have all the answers, but you're just sitting here feeling sorry for yourself. You need to go get your girl."

I'm shocked. He just handed me my ass on a silver platter, putting me in my place.

I cough, clearing my throat before I speak, "I thought we agreed to keep my true identity hidden from the Crows?"

Shy shrugs his shoulders. "I'm not saying go announce to the world you're alive or your real name, but telling your girl or anyone important to you, shouldn't be stressing you out so much. If the Crows find out your identity, or where you're at, believe me, we'll handle it. Just like we did all those years ago." He reaches an arm out, gripping my shoulder. "Brother, we're in this together. Don't let the past and future dictate your life, just live. I want to see you happy, like really happy, and Ruby seems to do that for you."

Keeping his hand on my shoulder, he reaches for his shot with his free hand. As I grip my shot, I reach out, clasping his shoulder, and I say our little motto, "Nut-up, brother."

Shy laughs. "Exactly, Nut-the-fuck-up, *brother*." We both hammer our shot back, slamming them down, grabbing the second one, slamming it back as well.

"Thank you," I choke out.

"Anytime. I owe you my life. Do you know how many times you've talked me off the ledge?"

"Are you fuckers going to kiss it out or what? Fucking get a room if you are," Dallas says with Mac laughing next to him as they walk up to the bar signaling Maze to bring us drinks.

"You jealous, Dallas, my boy?" Shy teases, releasing my shoulder, turning to face the bar.

My mind starts swirling around with what I should do or what I need to do to get my little firecracker back. The three of them start talking club business, but I grab my phone and start to text Izzy. It's time to start a fire.

When I hear them talking about Ruby's aunt, I stop texting and listen to Dallas. "Her aunt owns and runs one of the biggest escort services I've seen. Plus, her club is well known but needs some help with a new renovation. One of her biggest clients is none other than the Sons of Saints," he says, looking over at me.

"Sons of Saints?" I question, making sure I heard him correctly. Dallas is our information, IT and all-around go-to guy. He's a fucking brainiac - smartest dude I know and completely lethal in combat. He's a silent but deadly, motherfucker. He looks like the boy next door with this pretty face and baseball cap.

Shy looks over to me with a brow raised. "Seems like there's more than one reason for you to head down to Los Angeles. It's time to be reborn, brother. It isn't coincidental this just popped up, or that Whiz is president down there, it's all meant to be."

I just stare at the men I've come to think of as family while having flashbacks of my life so long ago. Whiz was like a father to me, took me in and watched out for me after my folks died. Now he's down in LA and president of the SoCal chapter of the Sons of Saints.

Jesus Christ. Here we go.

"Well, it looks like I need to make some calls," I say, grabbing for my phone.

"I think it would be a good move, but we need to get all the intel and bring it to the table. We all need to be on board and vote on it," Shy says before emptying his second beer and slamming it down.

Anxiety stirs in my belly. I'm going to be resurrected, and I don't know if that's good or bad, probably a little of both. I slam the rest of my beer before standing up.

"I want Chain and Jammer with you at all times once you leave here," Shy orders.

I turn back toward him. "You want me to take the two new prospects with me? I'd rather ghost in and ghost out."

"You're not leaving here without someone with you no matter what intel we find out," Shy demands.

I huff but don't say anything. Instead, I flip open my phone and dial a number I know by heart, but haven't dialed in six years.

"Guess who, motherfucker?" I chuckle into the phone as I make my way to my room at the clubhouse.

...to be continued.

ABOUT THE AUTHOR

Crazy, outgoing, adventurous, full of energy and talks faster than an auctioneer with a heart as big as the ocean... that is Angera. A born and raised California native, Angera is currently living and working in the Bay Area. Mom of a smart and sassy little girl, an English bulldog, and two Siamese Cats. She spends her days running a successful law firm but in her spare time enjoys writing, reading, dancing, playing softball, spending time with family, and making friends wherever she goes. She started writing after the birth of her daughter in 2012 and hasn't been able to turn the voices off yet. The Spin It series is inspired by the several years Angera spent married into the world of underground music and her undeniable love of dirty and gritty romance novels.

FOLLOW AND CONNECT
Email ~ authorangeraallen@gmail.com
Website ~ www.authorangeraallen.com
Facebook ~ www.facebook.com/authorangeraallen
Instagram ~ www.instagram.com/angeraallen
Twitter ~ www.twitter.com/angeraallen
Amazon ~ https://amzn.to/2A6dX8L
Bookbub ~ www.bookbub.com/profile/angera-allen?
list=author_books
Goodreads ~
https://www.goodreads.com/author/show/16200622.Angera_Allen

Available ~ Amazon – iBooks – Nook – Kobo

ALSO BY ANGERA ALLEN

STANDALONE

Firecracker – Click Here

SPIN IT SERIES

Alexandria – Book One – Click Here

Ginger – Book Two – Click Here

Izzy – Book Three – Click Here

COMING SOON

Quick – Book One – The Wolfeman MC Series

Dallas – Book Two – The Wolfeman MC Series

BB Securities – Book One (Brant's Story)

ACKNOWLEDGMENTS

Holy Shit - what a ride! Izzy's finally fuckin' done! This book has been one of the hardest books for me to write. First, to reference back and forth from the first two books of Spin It and Firecracker. Second the Irish and Russian slang. FML. Third, reading dark shit and writing is not the same. UGH... I was pulling my hair out - literally. And last, having it be written during the same time frame as Quick, which is the first installment of my new MC series. So, yeah, I'm just glad it's done.

First and foremost, to my baby girl: Thank you for understanding Momma has to work on her computer all the time now. It killed me sometimes to hear you say, "Momma not again. Pay attention to me." But, your daily smiles, hugs and I love yous are priceless. The love and support you give to me is the strength I need to keep going. I love you, my little sunshine. Lastly, to my mom for loving me unconditionally. I hope and pray I will be as good of a mother to my baby girl that you have been to me. You are, and will always be, my best friend.

To my die-hard BETA readers: Jennifer G., Kim H., Jennifer R., Kari J., Marlena S., Heather H., Tanya W. and Michelle K. All of you ladies have been with me each step of the way, giving me honest advice and unwavering support, even when I didn't want it. Thank you for always dropping what you are doing to read the newest chapters, and respond with your advice. I love each and every one of you.

Tanya F… guurl! Thank you for all your help with my Irish slang. I can't wait to come to meet you in person. I bet you're saying to yourself, "Thank Christ this cunt is done with this book." LOL. Seriously, thank you for putting up with my American ass all these years! Our messages are priceless. Love ya girl!

Angie D, Jennifer R, and Michelle K: Thank you for keeping my Angels group going strong with all the planning, building, scheduling of takeovers and daily devotion to the group. I love you girls and thank you for all you do.

Jennifer G, Kim H, and Michelle K. Thank you too for pushing me each step of the way. I just want you ladies to know how much it means to me. For all the phone calls and text messages helping me work through something in my head. Dropping everything to answer my calls to calm me down. For fixing my mixed up words and just knowing what I'm trying to say. You ladies are very important to me, and I hope you know it. I love your opinion, the ideas, and advice you give me. I really love how you get so excited, push for an idea or even get mad at me with each character. I promise so much more to come. Jen, I promise a baby is coming! Teehee

Heather Coker & Jennifer Ramsey: Thank you, ladies, for designing and making my swag. I love them! Both of you have been by my side through all my books, and I am so grateful to have each of you in my life.

To all my friends who helped in making this book by giving me advice, doing "research" or stating the facts: Amy W., Jen C., Michelle K., Northrups, Worm, Baby J, LO and all the men and women from the MC next door. Thank you so much for all your advice. I love you all.

CT Cover Creations – Clarise Tan, thank you for being patient with me. Girl, you are A-Maze-Ing, and I look forward to many more cover designs from you. This is by far one of my favorite. She is so damn beautiful! Thank you!

To my editor, Ellie McLove: All I can say is THANK FUCK for you! Seriously, you rock! TACOs all day long!

My bloggers: There are too many to name now but know I love each and every one of you. Thank you for loving my books and for helping me promote them.

HEA PR and more: First, thank you to Kathy Coopmans for referring them to me. Kathy, I cherish your friendship so much. You are my go-to Mama Bear for everything. I love ya girl! Ladies of HEA PR and more, thank you for taking me on this year. Well, and years to come! LOL For helping me keep it together for my book covers and releases. I would be so fucked if it wasn't for you! Thank you, and I look forward to working with you again soon.

To my Angels, we are 500 strong! Thank you for all your love, support, and helping me build my dream. I love my group, and it just keeps getting bigger… let's keep it going!

To my Angera's Street Crew! I look forward to bouncing my ideas off you and having y'all there to help me make decision. God knows I need help. Thank you!

To all my friends and family that have pushed me and supported me through this very LONG YEAR, I just want you all to know I love you and thank God every day for you. Without your love and support, I wouldn't have been able to finish this book. I know I am going to forget people, and I'm sorry for that, but just know I'm so thankful for everyone that had a part in making this dream a reality.

Last, but definitely not least, to my fans. I know it has been a CRAZY year, but I hope it was worth the wait. Thank you for all the emails, messages, and most of all reviews. They all mean so much to me. I can't wait for you to meet my Wolfeman….

I love each and every one of you.

With love, Angera

57747188R00157

Made in the USA
Columbia, SC
13 May 2019